Hope Springs Series

Road to New Beginnings

ASHLEY FARLEY

ALSO BY ASHLEY FARLEY

Palmetto Island

Muddy Bottom

Change of Tides

Lowcountry on My Mind

Sail Away

Hope Springs Series

Dream Big, Stella!

Show Me the Way

Mistletoe and Wedding Bells

Matters of the Heart

Road to New Beginnings

Stand Alone

On My Terms

Tangled in Ivy

Lies that Bind

Life on Loan

Only One Life

Home for Wounded Hearts

Nell and Lady

Sweet Tea Tuesdays

Saving Ben

1

STELLA

Standing at my front door, I stare across the street at Hope Springs Farm, the historic inn and surrounding buildings my grandfather built in the early 1920s. I feel as though I've lived in Hope Springs my whole life, when I've been here only a short sixteen months. During that time, I renovated the inn, fell in love and got married, made friends with women I admire and respect, and established relationships with the family my mother kept from me for reasons I won't go into here. I moved from New York to the mountains of Virginia, looking for a fresh start. I found that and so much more.

Shrieks of laughter break my reverie, and I return to the doorway of the family room where my husband is waltzing around with a life-size teddy bear—a shower gift from Jazz, my half sister, soon-to-be-adopted daughter. Jazz insisted she pick out a special present for the baby, just from her. After setting eyes on the bear at the toy store, she refused to consider any other options. I smile at Jazz across the room, and she gives me a sassy I-told-you-so head bob in return.

Presley is like a child on Christmas morning as she tears through her shower gifts. I'm encouraged to see twinkles of excitement have temporarily replaced the sadness that has taken up residence in her gray eyes of late. She hides it well, but I can tell Presley's troubled by the rumors circulating social media about the affair between her country music star husband and this year's American Idol winner. I admire Presley's courage. Being a single parent is not what she bargained for when she married Everett. But she's fortunate to have a network of family and friends to support her.

Presley receives a car seat from her grandmother, a stroller from her mother and aunt, and a Pack 'n Play from Jack and me. Cecily, head chef at the inn, gives the baby its first feeding set—complete with a bamboo plate, cereal bowl, and toddler-size eating utensils. And Ollie, manager of our wellness center and director of mountain excursions, contributes a hiking backpack which doubles as a diaper bag.

The number of gadgets and gismos needed to care for a newborn baby overwhelms me. Come next March, I'll be needing double of everything.

Parker, the inn's bartender-in-chief who I hired for the afternoon to serve and clean up, passes flutes of champagne and sparkling cider for the games portion of the baby shower. Laughter fills the house, and the ladies appear to enjoy themselves. It's nearly six o'clock in the evening when most of the guests finally leave.

Jack enlists Parker to help take Presley's gifts to the inn so I can have some time alone with my friends.

Jazz skips across the room with our golden retriever bounding behind her. "Can Angel and I come too?"

Jack smooths back her flyaway hair. "Of course, kiddo. We can use an extra set of hands and paws."

Jazz plants her fists on hips. "Ha ha. Funny. Not funny."

I laugh. She's eight years old going on sixteen.

Once they're gone, my friends help me transport the dirty

glasses and food platters to the kitchen. Cecily changes the background jazz to country music and turns up the volume. She pops the cork on a bottle of champagne and fills two flutes, setting one down on the marble counter in front of Ollie.

Ollie pushes the flute away. "I can't. I have an early flight in the morning."

Cecily slides it back. "Come on, Ollie. I hate drinking alone. And since Presley and Stella are pregnant, you're it."

"All right," Ollie says reluctantly and accepts the glass. "I guess a little won't hurt."

I turn down the volume on the stereo. "I have news, which I believe calls for a celebration."

My friends are suddenly all ears. "Do tell," Cecily says.

"When I went for my checkup on Thursday, my doctor heard two heartbeats. I'm having twins!"

Presley clasps her hands together. Ollie lets out a squeal. And Cecily offers me a high five. "That is fabulous news, girl-friend. Congrats."

"We haven't told Jazz yet, so please"—I hold my finger to my lips—"keep it between us for now."

Presley furrows her brow. "Are you worried about how Jazz will react? I would think she'd be thrilled."

Moving to the sink, I rinse glasses and place them in the dishwasher. "Jazz hasn't been herself since school started two weeks ago. She insists nothing is bothering her, but I can tell something is off."

Ollie joins me at the sink, filling the second basin with sudsy water to wash the platters. "So, you're thinking it has something to do with the baby coming?"

I shrug. "Maybe. Or maybe we were premature in assuming she was coping with her mother's death."

"It could be anything." Cecily smooths her honey hair into a ponytail, securing it with an elastic band. "Maybe some bratty kid is giving her a hard time at school."

"I've thought about that," I admit. "But second grade seems a little young for bullying."

"Not necessarily," Cecily says. "Kids grow up too fast these days."

"I won't argue with that," I say.

Silence falls over the room as often happens when the subject of Jazz's mother's death comes up. Naomi had more enemies than friends. While no one wanted to see her die in a tragic car accident, Jazz is way better off living with me.

Presley sets the teakettle on the stove to boil. "So, Cecily . . . What's going on between you and Parker? You seem like you're really into each other."

"We're just friends. Friends *without* benefits, in case you're wondering." Cecily picks up a dish towel and begins drying the platters. "I'm not denying we have crazy chemistry. But I value our friendship. If we sleep together and it doesn't work out, we could end up hating each other. Besides, I'm not ready for another relationship. I don't even know if I'm completely over Lyle yet."

Presley retrieves two mugs from the cabinet beside the stove. "Could've fooled me. I watched you and Parker today. I never saw you flirt with Lyle like that."

Cecily stops drying and glares at Presley. "What are you suggesting? That I didn't love Lyle?"

Presley pours steaming water over tea bags. "Love comes in many forms, Cecily. Some relationships are meant to be. Others aren't. Sometimes love is strong enough to go the distance. Other times it's not."

"And how would you categorize your relationship with Everett?" Cecily asks in a sarcastic tone.

Presley spins around to face Cecily. "I have faith in Everett. I wouldn't have married him if I didn't believe in him."

"Chill, Presley! I didn't mean to make you mad."

Presley softens. "No need to apologize. You're the only one with the guts to ask what everyone else is thinking." She turns her back on us. "Truth is, I wish I knew what was going on with Everett."

"You'll hear from him soon," Cecily says with a note of confidence.

I cross the kitchen to the french doors. Throwing them open, I inhale a deep breath, filling my lungs. "Ah, the first taste of autumn. Let's sit out by the fire pit."

We take our beverages outside to the lounge chairs on the terrace. Cecily sits to my left with Ollie and Presley opposite us.

"Have you finished packing for your trip yet?" I ask Ollie.

"All but my toiletries."

Cecily holds the champagne bottle out to Ollie's glass. When Ollie waves her away, Cecily chugs straight from the bottle. "How long will you be gone?"

"I'm not sure." A pained expression crosses Ollie's face. "The prosecutor says the trial could last a week. And I need to meet with my parents' attorney about their estate. If all goes as planned, I'll put the vineyard on the market while I'm in California."

Cecily's hand shoots up. "Back up a minute. Your brother admitted to starting the fire. Doesn't that make the case open and shut?"

Ollie looks away, staring across the lawn at the sun setting over the mountains. "Alexander now has an alibi for the night of the fire."

Cecily stiffens, the champagne bottle near her lips. She lowers the bottle. "But you have his confession on the surveillance tape."

"He claims he was under duress, that I was threatening him. He's hired a psychiatrist to testify he was mentally unstable at the time. That he was distraught over the death of our parents." Ollie's voice breaks, and she brings a fist to her mouth.

I give her a minute to compose herself before asking, "Who's the alibi?"

"His so-called girlfriend. Her name is Dana Reese, and she's an executive at a cyber security firm. Multiple witnesses saw them having dinner at Ad Hoc in Yountville early in the evening. Alexander claims they went back to her house after dinner, and he spent the night. Dana is corroborating his story."

Presley places a hand on Ollie's arm. "I know this is hard for you. But it'll all be over soon."

"I hope you're right," Ollie mumbles, her eyes filling with tears.

I shift my gaze to Presley. "Tell us about your trip to Raleigh on Wednesday."

Cecily chimes in, "Yes! Tell us. Are you excited about meeting your biological father?"

"Hardly. The man's a rapist." Presley squirms in her seat, as though uncomfortable under the weight of her baby. "I'm worried about Lucy's manner of approach. She's scheduled an appointment with him, as though we're clients seeking legal advice. No telling how he'll react when he finds out who we really are. The confrontation could cause Lucy another setback."

"Her new therapist has worked wonders," I remind Presley. "Lucy is much stronger than she was a month ago."

"That's true," Presley says, but I can tell my words of encouragement do little to ease her fears.

"I really should go," Ollie says. "I have a long trip ahead of me tomorrow."

We all stand at once. "This seems like a good time for us to make a pact, to stay in touch regardless of where our journeys lead us." I hold out my hand, and Cecily places hers on top.

"A friendship pact," she says. "A promise to always have one another's backs."

Ollie adds her hand to the pile. "To never keep secrets from one another."

Presley follows suit. "And to always tell one another the truth."

We drop our hands, and I pull my friends into a group hug. "I love you guys. More than you'll ever know."

"And we love you." Presley pulls away, swiping at her gray eyes.

We're migrating toward the driveway when Jack's truck pulls in and the occupants pile out.

Parker drapes an arm around Cecily's shoulders. "I'm hungry! Wanna grab a pizza?"

She flashes him a brilliant smile. "As long as you're driving. I've had too much champagne."

Jazz runs over to me, barreling into me as she hugs my waist. "Jack says we can order pizza, too. Can I go with him to pick it up?"

I glance over at Jack, who shrugs as though he doesn't care, but I can tell he's tired.

"He'll get back quicker if he goes alone."

"Aww." Jazz pushes me away.

"After you feed Angel, we can sit by the fire pit."

Her face lights up. "Can I have some hot chocolate?"

I laugh. "Not before dinner. But you can have some apple cider."

"All right," she says and disappears inside.

After seeing the others off, I return to the kitchen and warm two mugs of the apple cider I purchased at the farmer's market.

ASHLEY FARLEY

Jazz and I sit side-by-side at the fire pit with an exhausted Angel at our feet.

Jazz wraps both hands around her mug and blows on her cider. "When you have a baby shower, can I help open the gifts?"

"I would love that. Opal has offered to throw me a shower."

Jazz punches the air. "Yay, Opal! Do you think she'll let me help plan the party?"

"Absolutely. She's counting on it." Jazz and my eccentric maternal grandmother have forged a unique friendship. Jazz often goes to Opal's for sleepovers on weekend nights.

Jazz's expression becomes pensive. "Do you think the baby will look like me?"

"Maybe. You never know about genetics. He or she could have your amber eyes." I envy my sister the golden eyes she inherited from our father.

"But she won't have my skin color," Jazz says.

"No, because you got your skin color from your mom."

Jazz's lower lip quivers as though she might cry. "I wish I had your skin color."

"Why? I'm tan now from the summer sun. But in the winter, my skin is white and pasty." I grab Jazz's arm. "Your skin is beautiful year around." I nibble kisses up her forearm to her elbow. "And so tasty. Like creamy caramel."

"Stop!" Jazz giggles and jerks her arm away. "Will the baby be my sister?" She's certain the baby is a girl, although Jack and I have elected not to find out the gender.

"You're my sister, so technically you'll be the baby's aunt. But labels aren't important in this family. Once the adoption is final, you'll be my daughter. The change in legal status won't alter our relationship. Unless you want it to. I can be your sister or your mom or just Stella."

Jazz gnaws on her lip as she considers this.

"Since you'll be so close in age to the baby, it may make

8

sense for you to think of him or her as your brother or sister. But wait and see how you feel after it's born."

"Okay." Jazz sips her cider. "Can I quit gymnastics?"

This comes out of left field, taking me by surprise. "Not until you win at least one Olympic gold medal."

She kicks the fire pit. "I'm serious, Stella. I don't want to take gymnastics anymore."

"But you love gymnastics. And you're so good at it. Do you want to go back to ballet?"

"I wanna learn to play the guitar like Billy." Jazz leaps out of the chair. "Wait here." She disappears inside and returns a minute later with one of our father's guitars. Billy had so many, we let Jazz pick one to keep.

Lowering herself to her chair, she strums the chords of "Always You," the love song he wrote for my mother. Her little fingers glide across the strings with ease. She's a natural. But I'm not surprised. My little sister has many talents.

I wait until she's finished before asking, "How'd you learn that?"

"YouTube," she says, staring into the fire to avoid looking at me.

"You know the rules about using the computer without supervision."

She glances over at me. "But I wanted to surprise you."

"I'm plenty surprised." I take the guitar from her, studying the grains in the ebony wood. "I'll make a deal with you. If you stick it out with gymnastics, I'll arrange for you to have guitar lessons."

She folds her arms over her chest. "But I don't like gymnastics anymore."

My face tightens. "That's my deal. Take it or leave it."

"Ugh. Fine. I'll take the deal."

Jack's headlights appear in the driveway. Jazz jumps up and rushes over to greet him with Angel on her heels.

I strum the chords for "Sweet Home Alabama." I had taken guitar lessons as a child, and I remember enough to play a few songs. Maybe I'll take lessons with Jazz. I sense she could use some extra attention right now. Jazz doesn't want to quit gymnastics because she doesn't like it. I saw her tumbling across the yard this morning, practicing her moves. She has another reason for wanting to quit. One she's not comfortable telling me about. While we haven't known each other long, we've developed a close bond through the challenges we've faced. I can't stand to see my little sister in turmoil. Whatever the problem is, I aim to get to the bottom of it.

2

CECILY

Cecily's thoughts are on Parker as she traipses up the stairs to the second-floor garage apartment she rents from Stella. She doesn't see Lyle waiting on the landing until they are eye to eye. A dull headache has replaced her champagne buzz from earlier, and she's not in the mood for a confrontation. The landing is small, and the closeness to her ex-fiancé makes her uncomfortable.

"What're you doing here, Lyle?"

He gives her the once-over, taking in her borderline short flouncy dress and booties. "Waiting for you. I've been here for over an hour. Where have you been?"

"None of your business," she snaps.

The muscles in his face tighten. "You've been out with your boyfriend."

"I don't have a boyfriend, Lyle."

"Whatever. I need to talk to you. Can we go inside?" he asks, his hand on the doorknob.

"That's not a good idea. You'll have to say whatever you need to say out here."

He drops his hand to his side. "I miss you, Cecily. I've had a lot of time to think these past few weeks. We made a mistake in rushing our relationship. But our relationship wasn't a mistake. We're meant to be together. I feel it in my heart."

Cecily holds his gaze steady. "Rushing things enabled us to see how wrong we are for each other."

He jerks his head back as though she punched him in the jaw. "Was being with me that awful?"

"At times. The arguments we had about my job were nasty." Cecily's gut wrenches at the memories. "My career means everything to me. By not supporting me, you pushed me away."

Lyle hangs his head. "I admit I was wrong about that. If you'll give me another chance, I'll make things right."

"You say that now, but you'll soon go back to resenting the long hours. I want a family someday. In order for that to happen, I need a husband willing to take care of the children when I'm at work." Cecily thinks about Parker's secret ambition to become a novelist, about him admitting he wouldn't mind being a stay-at-home dad.

"I can be that person. Please, Cecily, just give me another chance," Lyle says, his tone bordering on begging.

Cecily looks away, staring out across the expansive lawn. "I care about you, Lyle. I want you to have a happy life. But I'm not the person who can give that to you. You need to find someone who wants the same things out of life as you."

"You are that person, Cecily." Lyle grabs her arm, pulling her so close she can smell the alcohol on his breath.

"You cheated on me, Lyle. I'm not sure I can ever forgive you for that. I certainly won't ever forget. What happened with Whitney anyway? Did the two of you break up?"

His face falls. "She took a job in New York."

Cecily draws herself to her full height. "So that's why you're here. It's over between us, Lyle. Accept it and move on."

Anger flashes in his hazel eyes as he takes hold of her arm.

"Why are you being so difficult? Does that deadbeat bartender have his hooks in you?"

Lyle's grip on her arm is tight. He spends a lot of time working out, and he has the muscles to prove it. He could easily wrestle her over the railing. Would she survive the fall from this high up?

"I told you, Parker and I are just friends." She reaches into her shoulder bag with her free hand and removes her keys. "I'm going inside now, Lyle. I have an early day tomorrow." Wrenching her arm free, she inserts her key in the lock and slips inside, closing the door behind her. There's no dead bolt, only the flimsy lock on the knob. Anyone could easily break in. She needs to talk to Jack about installing a dead bolt.

Cecily presses herself against the wall, holding her breath until she hears Lyle's footfalls descending the stairs. Crossing the living room to the window on the opposite wall, she watches Lyle's dark figure emerge from behind the garage. Instead of continuing down Stella's driveway, he cuts through the side yard to the main road.

Cecily remains at the window long after he's gone, replaying the conversation in her mind. Lyle was off somehow, not at all himself. He'd been drinking, but it was more than that. He had a crazy look in his eyes. A feeling of dread settles over her. Something tells her she hasn't seen the last of Lyle.

After spending a restless night tossing and turning, Cecily heads to work early the next morning. She's not surprised to find Fiona already at the computer in the office they share. Even though Cecily puts in at least sixteen hours six days a week, she's convinced that her young catering assistant works harder than she does.

Fiona jumps to her feet. "I finally finished revising the catering menu." She flaps a sheaf of papers at Cecily. "I think you'll approve. There's a wide range of dishes from simple to extravagant."

Fiona's enthusiasm lifts Cecily's spirits, bringing a smile to her lips. "Great job. I'll take a look." She sheds her fleece and slips her chef's coat on over her black tank top.

"Wait a minute." Fiona comes from behind the desk. "What did I just see on your arm?" She tugs the chef's coat off and examines Cecily's upper arm. "Are those bruises?"

"Where?" Cecily looks down at the angry purple bruises on her bare arm. "Oh, that's nothing. I ran into an open cabinet door." She pulls her coat back on over the bruises.

"Liar." Fiona looks at Cecily with big blue eyes. "Someone put those bruises there. Who was it? Parker?"

Cecily stares back at her as though she's lost her mind. "Of course not."

"I don't believe you. Come with me." Fiona drops the catering menu on the desk and takes Cecily by the hand, leading her out of the office, through the kitchen, and outside to the chef's garden. Planted with herbs and edible flowers, the garden has become Cecily's and Fiona's haven where they hide when they need to get away from the chaos in the kitchen.

"Start talking," Fiona says, pulling Cecily down to the bench beside her. "I want to hear everything."

Cecily lets out a huff of irritation. "There's not much to tell. Lyle was waiting for me when I got home last night. He asked me to give him another chance. I told him no. End of story."

Fiona cocks an eyebrow. "And the bruises?"

"He got a little angry and grabbed my arm too hard, but I handled it." Cecily gets up from the bench and follows the brick path around her garden.

"How'd you handle it?"

"I went inside and locked the door," Cecily says, bending down to pluck a weed.

Fiona is on her feet. "Okay, so you handled it this time. What about next time?"

Cecily straightens to face her. "Who says there will be a next time?"

"For your sake, I hope this was an isolated incidence. But I'd be willing to bet there will be a next time." Fiona drags Cecily back to the bench. "Do you remember me telling you my ex-boyfriend stalked me in college?"

"I remember. If you're implying Lyle is stalking me, you're mistaken."

"Just hear me out. I didn't tell you the entire story about what happened to me." Fiona combs her fingers through her sandy pixie cut. "I tried to break up with Tyler. I wasn't feeling it, and I didn't want to waste my last semester in college trapped in a dead-end relationship. He got rough with me, gave me bruises much like the ones you have. The next day, he brought me an enormous arrangement of flowers and begged me to forgive him."

Cecily leans toward Fiona. "What'd you do?"

"I forgave him. We were moving to different cities after graduation. I figured I could stay with him a little longer. But he was such a jerk to me, I couldn't take it. A month later, I broke up with him again. This time I did it in a crowded restaurant where he couldn't hurt me. I thought that would be the end. But it was only the beginning. He made my life a living hell. I filed a complaint with the police, but Tyler was too crafty to get caught. I finally gave up and finished the semester at home."

"I'm sorry this happened to you, Fi. But Lyle isn't like that. And he's not stalking me," Cecily says with more conviction than she feels.

"Not yet," Fiona says under her breath.

Cecily stands and pulls Fiona to her feet. "Come on. We have work to do. We're wasting time worrying about something that isn't even a problem."

They return to the kitchen and busy themselves with preparing the day's specials. But Lyle continues to plague Cecily's thoughts throughout the day. The anger she saw in his eyes last night unsettles her. Is it possible he's coming unglued?

Late afternoon, she's in her office when the bell captain appears with a massive arrangement of yellow and orange lilies. "These were just delivered for you, Miss Cecily," he says, placing the vase on her desk.

She smiles up at him. "Thank you, Elton."

No sooner has he left than Fiona appears in the doorway. "Are those from Parker?"

"I doubt it. These aren't his style." Parker brings her flowers all the time, stems of colorful roses and lilies and hydrangeas he cuts from his own garden or sneaks from the beds around the farm.

Fiona enters the office and approaches the desk. "Read the card."

Cecily removes the card from the plastic pick. The small envelope bears the logo of the most expensive florist in town. She slips the card out of the envelope and reads the message scrawled in Lyle's sloppy handwriting. *I miss you, Cecily. Let's try again.*

Fiona taps her foot on the floor. "Well? Who are they from?"

Cecily holds the card out to Fiona. "Lyle." She pushes away from her desk and leans back in her chair. "I obviously didn't make myself clear enough to him last night. What am I going to do?"

"There's no reasoning with guys like him. Don't acknowledge the flowers. Block his number from your phone. Be alert. Avoid putting yourself in vulnerable positions. And, for the time being, drive to work instead of walking."

A chill travels Cecily's spine. "Stop being melodramatic. You're scaring me."

"I'm not trying to scare you, Cecily. I'm making you aware of the potential for danger. You should assume Lyle is stalking you until he proves otherwise."

Cecily sweeps her hand at the arrangement. "Get the flowers out of my office. I don't care what you do with them. Give them to someone. Throw them away. But I don't want to see them again."

"I'm on it," Fiona says, wrapping her arms around the large glass vase.

A sick feeling settles in the pit of Cecily's stomach. Lyle won't be as easy to get rid of as the flowers.

3

OLLIE

Ollie exits the rental car lot at the San Francisco airport and gets onto the highway, heading toward downtown. She yearns to continue over the Golden Gate Bridge to Napa. Sadly, nothing is left on her family's estate but the charred remains of their home and winery.

She navigates the Toyota sedan through the congested traffic to the Ritz Carlton, where Stella booked her a suite at a considerably reduced rate. Turning her rental over to the valet, she enters the elegant lobby and stands in line at the front desk.

She's wrapping up the check-in process with the desk clerk when a familiar voice behind her says, "Welcome home, Ollie."

She turns and steps into her ex-husband's outstretched arms. The years fade away, along with the animosity over their difficult divorce. Sergio is once again the man who was like a big brother to her for most of her life. His strong arms comfort her, and for the first time in months, she feels safe.

When she sniffles, he holds her at arm's length. "Are you crying?"

She touches her fingertips to her face, surprised to find her cheeks wet with tears. "I'm feeling a little overwhelmed. The city. The traffic. The noises."

"Not to mention the purpose of your trip."

She offers him a soft smile. "That too."

Sergio hands her a red bandana. He always keeps a fresh one in his back pocket for crying females and bloody knees. "I don't know about you, but I could use a drink."

"A drink sounds good. But I need to see about my luggage first," Ollie says, glancing around for a bellman.

"I'll grab us a table in the lounge." He points across the lobby at the handsome room with rich gray-paneled walls and burgundy leather furniture.

Ollie locates a bellman, identifies her luggage to him, and stuffs a ten-dollar bill in his hand. She joins Sergio at a cozy table for two by the window, and a minute later, their server delivers two glasses of red wine.

Sergio holds his glass up to her. "I hope you don't mind me choosing the wine."

Ollie clicks his glass and sniffs the wine. "Ahh. The 2018 Merlot. An excellent year." She takes a sip, savoring the buttery wine. "The inventory will eventually be depleted, and Hendrix wines will be a thing of the past."

His husky voice is sincere. "It doesn't have to be that way, Ollie. You could always rebuild."

"I've thought about it a lot, actually. And I've decided I can't live with the ghosts." Ollie sits back in her chair, wineglass in hand. "How did today go?"

"Jury selection is complete. We have four whites, five blacks, two Hispanics, and an Asian. Seven women and five men."

"Will we be testifying tomorrow?" Ollie's been working with the district attorney's office for weeks to prepare her testimony.

"That's the plan. I'm up first, and then you." Sergio sips his wine and sets his glass down. "Ollie, I have no choice but to tell the truth about that night, about why I followed you home."

"You mean I was drunk out of my mind, and you wanted to make certain I got home safely."

He chuckles. "I'll be more diplomatic than that. But yes, I have to tell them you were drunk. The media are all over this case. The details of that night will inevitably get out."

Ollie watches a homeless woman passing by the window, pushing a cart loaded with her belongings stuffed in plastic bags. Life could be worse. "My reputation is the least of my concerns, Sergio. I'm worried about you. The district attorney thinks the defense will try to pin the murders on you."

Sergio hangs his head. "I'm aware. And I had a motive. The defense will ask us a lot of questions about our divorce. I sued your family and things got ugly. But I didn't kill your parents. You believe me, right?"

"Of course I believe you. You saved my life that night. I've heard the nine-one-one tape. You're the one who called for help."

Sergio lifts his gaze. "And then I bolted, which makes me look guilty."

"You're not though. You didn't start the fires. Alexander did. He killed our parents. We must keep the faith. The truth will come out."

"I pray you're right," Sergio says.

"I've had a lot of time to think these past few weeks. Our marriage was a mistake. And we hurt a lot of people." Ollie reaches for his hand. "You're the only family I have left now. Do you think it's possible for us to put all the unpleasantness behind us? Because I could really use my Big Bro right now."

"It's been a long time since you called me that." He brings her hand to his lips and kisses her knuckles. "I would very much like to put this all behind us. Besides, we stand a better chance of proving my innocence if we present a united front to the jury."

"I agree." She smiles across the table at him. "You shaved your beard."

Releasing her hand, he massages his ruddy cheeks. "For court. I'm hoping to make a good impression on the jury. I plan to grow it back once this is all over."

"When do I get to meet your fiancée?

"Tomorrow. I think you'll like May."

"I'm sure I will." Ollie finishes her wine. She's tempted to order another, but she craves fresh air more. She pushes back from the table. "I need to clear my head. I think I'll walk down to the waterfront. Maybe grab a sushi roll for dinner and call it an early night."

"Sounds like a good plan." He signals for the check. "May and I are staying at the Omni. It's only a few blocks from here. If you need anything, call me."

"Will do." Ollie stands. "I'd rather not go into the courthouse alone in the morning. Can we meet out front a few minutes before nine?"

He gets to his feet and kisses her cheek. "Sure thing."

Ollie feels slightly relieved and less alone as she heads up to her room to change into exercise clothes. She and Sergio had gone through some dark times during their troubled marriage and subsequent divorce. But never for a minute did she think him capable of murdering anyone, least of all her parents.

Sergio came to work for Hendrix Estates over twenty-five years ago. He was only twenty at the time, a hard-working kid from a poor family who eventually became their foreman. Ollie's father had thought of Sergio as a second son, and was thrilled when Ollie and Sergio started dating. He was certain Sergio was the only one who could tame Ollie. Turns out, it took more than a strong man to tame Ollie. It took losing her parents for her to finally grow up.

Ollie's panic rises as she waits for Sergio and May on the front steps of the courthouse the following morning. She's terrified of testifying. The defense attorney will be hard on her. What if she breaks down? What if she ugly cries in front of everyone in the courtroom? She's searching for an escape when she spots Sergio and his fiancée heading her way. Sergio had saved her life. He was protecting her that night. If she doesn't protect him now, he could be tried for murdering her parents.

Sergio introduces May, whose warm brown eyes and sincere tone of voice set Ollie at ease. Their conversation flows smoothly, as though they've known each other for a lifetime. Ollie is disappointed when the bailiff calls court to order at nine, and May disappears inside the courtroom.

Ollie and Sergio are instructed to wait in the hallway until they are called to testify. Once their testimony is over, they're allow to stay in the courtroom. Minutes tick slowly off the clock. An hour passes before the attorneys finish their opening remarks and call Sergio to the witness stand.

The judge breaks for lunch an hour later, but Ollie isn't allowed to converse with Sergio. She purchases a hot dog from a food truck and eats it sitting on the courthouse steps.

When court reconvenes, Ollie is called to testify. She holds her head high and chin up and marches inside. After she's sworn in, she makes her way to the witness stand, smiling softly at the men and women as she passes the jury box.

She locates Sergio and May, seated several rows behind Ellis and his team. She keeps her eyes glued on them as she answers the questions she rehearsed with Ellis. When prompted, she walks the jury through the events of the night of the fire.

"At the last minute, my friend Jess came in from out of town. I hadn't seen her in several years. We met at the Rolling Rock for dinner and drinks. We got a little out of hand, and I called an Uber to drive me home. I didn't make it to my bedroom. I passed out on the sofa in the living room at the front of the house. Next thing I remember, a paramedic was placing an oxygen mask over my face."

"You don't remember who rescued you from the house?" Ellis asks.

"No, sir." Ollie now knows Sergio was the one who rescued her. But she wasn't aware of it at the time.

Ellis asks her about the divorce, and she tells the truth. That her troubled marriage drove a wedge between her parents and Sergio. "When we divorced, Sergio felt entitled to a portion of my share of the business." Ollie holds Sergio's gaze. "I don't blame him. I was a difficult wife. He deserved compensation for what I put him through."

Ellis pauses a beat to let this sink in. "Please tell the court where you're employed, Miss Hendrix."

Ollie smiles. "I manage the wellness center at Hope Springs Farm, a luxury resort in the mountains of Virginia."

Ellis says, "Walk us through the events that happened at Hope Springs Farm on July twenty-ninth of this year."

"Well . . ." Ollie uncrosses and recrosses her legs. "We had a meeting of key staff members out by the hot springs late that evening. Everyone had left, and I was cleaning up when my brother, Alexander, emerged from the shower area. Everything happened so fast. Before I could react, he clamped a hand over my mouth and pressed a gun to my head. Lucy, our sommelier, came back to get her phone, which she'd accidentally left by the hot springs. Alexander had no choice but to take her hostage as well.

"Alexander insisted we go inside to my office. He had some documents he wanted me to sign. One to disclaim my inheritance and the other an affidavit stating I witnessed my ex-husband start the fire. Which was a lie. I witnessed no such thing."

Ollie takes a deep breath. "When we got to my office, Alexander pointed the gun at me while I tied Lucy's hands with a scarf from my coat closet. He pushed Lucy down on the sofa and instructed me to sit at my desk. I have a panic button hidden beneath my desk. When I rolled my chair up, I pressed the button with my knee. But I had to buy some time for security to get to us." Ollie locks eyes with her brother for the first time. "Alexander has bullied me all my life. I know how to defend myself against him. After pretending to read the papers, I refused to sign them until he told me why he killed our parents."

Ellis clicks a button on a remote control and the surveillance video streams on a large screen mounted to the wall behind the judge. The video shows Alexander as he kicks her desk chair, telling her to sign the papers.

Ollie tosses the pen on her desk. "Nope." She swivels her chair to face him, glaring past the gun in his hand to his face. "Not until I get some answers." She pauses. "Why'd you do it, Alex? Why'd you kill our parents?" she asks in a soft tone.

"I wanted to make some changes, to bring the winery into the twenty-first century. But Dad refused to listen to my ideas."

Ollie asks, "Why didn't you come to me with your suggestions? We could've worked together to make the vineyard more current. You didn't have to kill our parents."

"Not just our parents, Ollie. You were meant to die in that fire," Alexander says and the jurors let out a collective gasp.

Ellis clicks the remote and the screen goes black. "That's it, Your Honor. I have no further questions for this witness."

Jeff Morris has an evil face with beady eyes and sharp canine teeth, and Ollie shrinks back in her chair when he approaches the witness box. He comes at her with questions from all angles. Ellis objects many times. Some are sustained, but most are overruled.

Morris grips the wooden railing and leans conspiratorially toward her. "You must bear an enormous burden of guilt knowing you could've saved your parents if you hadn't been passed out drunk. Tell me, Miss Hendrix, are you receiving treatment for your alcohol addiction?"

Ellis is back on his feet, shouting out to the judge, "He's badgering the witness, Your Honor. Miss Hendrix is not on trial here."

The judge brings his gavel crashing down. "Sustained. I'm warning you, Mr. Morris, you're on thin ice here."

Morris tosses his hands in the air. "No further questions, Your Honor," he says, and struts across the courtroom to his chair.

When the judge excuses Ollie, she walks on unsteady legs toward Sergio and May, who slide over and make room for her to sit between them—a show of solidarity for the jurors. The dam of emotion she'd held back while on the stand breaks and she lets out an audible sob. May puts an arm around her, drawing her in and holding her tight as the tears flow and her shoulders heave.

Ellis calls a few inconsequential witnesses before resting his case. With a quick glance at his watch, the judge announces court adjourned until tomorrow morning at nine. Sergio and May support her arms as they exit the courtroom.

Sergio hales a cab and opens the back door for her. "I need a change of scenery. I promised May I'd take her to Sausalito for dinner at Bar Bocce. And you're coming with us."

"You won't get an argument from me. I'd rather not be alone right now," Ollie says, sliding into the back seat.

They beat the early dinner crowd and are seated right away at a table on the deck. Giving the menu a once-over, Sergio orders a liter of Martin Ray Pinot Noir from the server and several appetizers—crispy artichokes, calamari, and spicy prawns.

Ollie takes in a deep breath, filling her lungs with salt-tinged air. "The air is distinct in California. There's no place like it on earth."

"Have you considered moving back?" May asks.

In a tone of resignation, Ollie says, "I can't come back. Not after everything that happened. I'm happy in Virginia. The crisp mountain air is pretty darn good there as well." She experiences a pang of what she assumes is homesickness. She misses her cozy apartment and new friends.

"You did an outstanding job on the witness stand," Sergio says.

Ollie lets out a humph. "Until I fell apart."

"You held it together until after your testimony," Sergio says. "I was watching the jurors. They believed you. They trust you. Your tears made them more sympathetic toward you."

Ollie folds her hands on the table. "Tell me about your testimony."

Sergio looks away. "I'd rather not talk about it."

Ollie looks at May. "Was it that bad?"

May reaches for Sergio's hand. "He's being too hard on himself. He did a great job."

Sergio stares down at the table. "Except when they played the nine-one-one tape. Morris asked why I hung up when the emergency operator asked for my name. I explained that, because of our divorce, I was persona non grata with your family. And that I worried the police would think I started the fire. Ellis convinced me that telling the truth would prove my innocence. Instead, I think it made me look even guiltier."

Ollie can see the worry lines in his face. Sergio has a chance at a new life with May, a chance to have the family he's always yearned for. If Alexander is acquitted, the district attorney will press charges against Sergio. Because of Ollie, he could go to jail for the rest of his life.

Sergio's phone vibrates the table, and Ellis's name appears on the screen. Snatching up the phone, he rises from the table and steps out onto the adjacent beach.

"I'm so sorry I dragged you into my mess," Ollie says to May.

May thumbs her chest. "I'm the one who insisted Sergio go to the police about Alexander. This situation was eating him up. He never could've lived with himself."

"Now it's come down to Sergio's word against Alexander's," Ollie says.

Sergio returns to the table, the lines in his forehead etched even deeper. "We have a problem. Alexander's girlfriend, who was due to testify for the defense first thing in the morning, has disappeared."

4

PRESLEY

During the three-hour drive to Raleigh on Wednesday, Lucy remains tight-lipped about how she plans to confront the man who date-raped her over thirty years ago. She's putting on a good show, but Presley senses tension brewing beneath Lucy's calm demeanor. Her therapist is certain Lucy is ready to face her rapist. Presley isn't as convinced.

Presley has never seen her mother looking so elegant in a sleeveless black sheath that falls to the middle of her thighs, revealing shapely legs and slim feet in simple black sandals. Lucy has toned down in recent weeks. She's eating healthier and exercising more. As a result, her skin glows, and her mahogany hair shines.

Lucy glances over at Presley. "I almost forgot. I have something for you. It's in my bag on the back seat."

Reaching behind her, Presley retrieves the purse and removes a skinny rectangular package in silver wrapping paper.

"It's from Chris," Lucy says.

Presley stares at the gift. "But he already gave me a pair of hooded towels."

"Those were for the baby. This is for you. It's personal. He didn't want you to open it at the shower."

Presley tears off the paper and removes a dainty silver bracelet with a heart charm. "I love it. What an incredibly thoughtful gesture."

Lucy nods at the gift box. "There's a note inside."

Presley attaches the bracelet to her arm and reads the note from her half brother, a brief message thanking Presley for helping him through a difficult time last summer. She fingers the bracelet, remembering Chris's arguments with his mother during the months before he left for college.

Lucy has suffered so much this past year. She was already fragile from a messy divorce when Presley stumbled into her life last fall. Presley's presence brought back traumatic memories of the date rape and subsequent pregnancy Lucy had experienced in college, and she began self-medicating to relieve her angst. When she crashed over Christmas, she admitted herself to a rehab facility for treatment. Soon after returning to her job as the inn's wine steward, Lucy hit rock bottom for a second time. Not because of the wine. Booze was never her problem. Pain pills were her drugs of choice. Discovering her sister, Rita, was in a relationship with Brian, the man Lucy had been seeing before rehab, brought about a whole new array of emotions she was ill-equipped to cope with. Lucy took her anger out on all of them, most especially her son, Chris. A mental breakdown led Lucy to seek treatment from a new therapist, Dr. Norman, who has made the most dramatic impact on her life to date.

Presley returns her attention to her cell phone. "I can't believe he isn't on social media," she says, searching for Levi Jones for the umpteenth time.

"Our generation wasn't raised on social media like yours, Presley. Try LinkedIn. There's not much information, but you can at least see his photograph."

Presley assesses the job site and searches for Levi Jones in Raleigh, North Carolina. His profile pops up and a handsome man with strong jaw, piercing blue eyes, and silver hair smiles back at her. "He's nice-looking."

"He's a rapist," Lucy says in a dismissive tone.

Presley skims his bio. He's a criminal attorney, which she already knew. Her eyes pop. "Whoa. Did you know he specializes in rape victims?"

Lucy's facial muscles tighten. "I read that. While you're on his profile, grab his address and plug it into your GPS."

Entering the address into her phone, Presley calls out directions to Lucy as they near Raleigh. They locate the renovated brick building in downtown, Lucy parks her minivan in the parking garage, and they ride the elevator to the third floor.

An attractive young woman with pursed lips and dark hair pulled back in a tight knot greets them. "Mr. Jones is on a conference call. Have a seat, and he'll be with you momentarily."

Twenty minutes later, Levi's much friendlier administrative assistant summons them, leading them down a hallway with hardwood floors and Oriental rugs.

They enter the corner office, and Levi comes from behind his desk. His piercing blue eyes narrow as he looks from the index card in his hand to Lucy. "Well, I'll be damned. Lucy Townsend. It's been a long time. You look amazing."

Lucy toys with her strand of pearls. "You remember me?"

Levi smiles. "Of course. How could I forget you? I had the hots for you in college. I was devastated when you broke off our relationship."

Lucy's body stiffens beside Presley. "We didn't have a relationship, Levi. We went out one time." Her pointer finger shoots up. "To your fraternity's Christmas formal. You drugged my drink, date-raped me, and nine months later, I had our baby."

She sweeps an arm in Presley's direction. "Meet our daughter, Presley."

Levi's jaw hits the carpeted floor and Presley's neck snaps as she looks over at Lucy. She should've suspected Lucy would drop a nuclear bomb like this.

To his credit, Levi quickly composes himself. "Why don't we sit down?"

They migrate to the seating area where Lucy and Presley sit side-by-side on the love seat. Lowering himself to the wing chair opposite them, Levi says, "This is a serious allegation, Lucy. Why are you waiting until now to confront me? Why didn't you press charges back then?"

Lucy glares at him. "I had no evidence. You would've denied it, and it would've been your word against mine."

Levi grows silent, and Presley can almost see the wheels turning in his mind. "I had a serious crush on you. I would've known if you'd dropped out of college. Did you put the baby"— he glances over at her—"Presley up for adoption?"

Lucy's gaze falls. "I had no choice. I wanted to put the whole thing behind me and move on with my life."

"There are always other choices, Lucy." Lifting a legal pad from the coffee table, Levi sits back in his chair and crosses his legs. "Start at the beginning. Why do you think I date-raped you?" His lip is curled as though he finds the idea distasteful.

Lucy wrings her hands in her lap. "I had a couple of drinks at the beginning of the night. But I remember nothing that happened after dinner. Three months later, when I'd missed a couple of periods and my jeans grew tight, I put two and two together. I was a virgin. You're the only one who could've been her father."

Levi scrawls something on his legal pad and sets down his pen. "I never drugged your drink, Lucy. I liked you too much to take advantage of you." He casts Presley an apologetic look before turning his attention back to Lucy. "You were a willing participant. You consented to having sex with me."

"I don't believe you," Lucy says with a flash of anger in her dark eyes.

"That's your prerogative. But I have higher moral values than that. In fact, some of my fraternity brothers were involved in such a date-rape incident in college, and I turned them into the campus police. That event is the reason I became a sexual abuse attorney."

Judging from the meltdown taking place on Lucy's face, this is not what she expected to hear.

An awkward silence settles over the room. Presley is curious about the event, but now is not the time to press for details. "Do you have any children?"

Levi shifts his focus to her. "I do. A daughter and two sons." His face brightens as though a lightbulb has switched on in his head. "They would be your half siblings."

Presley's heart skips a beat. She has brothers and a sister.

Levi continues, "Their mother passed away a few years back from cancer. Her death has been hard on them."

Presley presses her lips thin. "I know what that's like."

"I'm sorry. Your adoptive mother?" He has a gentle manner about him, and Presley imagines he treats all his clients with such kid gloves. She can't, however, imagine him ever date-raping anyone. Even decades ago, as a frat boy. He doesn't seem the type.

"Yes. She died eighteen months ago from cirrhosis of the liver."

Levi grimaces. "That must have been difficult for you."

"It wasn't all bad. Renee was a highly functioning alcoholic. One of the top country music producers in Nashville." Presley's face warms. "I'm sorry. I don't know why I'm telling you all this."

Levi leans forward in his chair. "Please don't apologize. I

want to hear about your life. What about your adoptive father? Is he still alive?"

A memory of her father buying her an ice cream cone pops into Presley's head. "He was a wonderful dad. Unfortunately, he died from cancer when I was a small child." She shakes off the memory. "My adoptive parents gave me an excellent life, a privileged life. Despite all Renee's problems, she taught me some valuable life lessons."

"Good. I'm glad." Levi's voice is soft, his tone genuine. Presley has acute instincts about others. Right now, her people reader is telling her Levi Jones is the real deal.

His eyes travel to her swollen belly. "When is your baby due?"

"October eighteenth." Anticipating his next question, she adds, "We've decided not to find out if it's a boy or a girl."

"My wife and I were surprised with our three as well." He glances at her ring finger. "What does your husband do?"

"He's a country music singer. You may have heard of him. Everett Baldwin. He's new to the country music circuit."

Levi drops his smile, as though he's heard the rumors of Everett's affair. "Of course, I've heard of him."

Another long moment of awkward silence passes before Lucy stands abruptly. "We're in from out of town. We should head back soon."

Presley and Levi stand in unison.

"Back to where?" Levi asks. "If you don't mind me asking."

Presley answers, "To Hope Springs, Virginia."

"Ah, yes. I keep hearing about Hope Springs Farm from my friends. Is it as luxurious as everyone says?"

"Very much so. We both work there." Presley loops her arm through Lucy's. "Lucy is the sommelier, and I'm head event planner and assistant general manager."

His lips turn up in a smile of approval. "Very nice." He

checks his watch. "We have a lot to talk about. I'd love to take you ladies to lunch before you go."

"I'd like that," Presley says, curious to know more about her father and his children.

"Sorry, but we can't. Our mission here is complete." Lucy's chin quivers and tears fill her eyes. "I've been struggling since Presley came back into my life last fall. My therapist suggested I confront you about the rape. Now that I've done that, we can all move on." Lucy bolts out of the office without looking back.

Levi gives his head a bewildered shake. "I can't believe what just happened here. I'm going to need some time to process all this. But I promise you, I didn't rape her."

Presley doesn't know how to respond. It's his word against Lucy's. Lucy doesn't remember what happened that night. But this man has made a career out of finding justice for victims of sexual assault.

"If I'd known she was pregnant, I would've . . ." his voice trails off.

Anger flashes through Presley at the thought of what might have been. "Would've what? Would you have married her?"

Levi holds his hands out as if to say, who knows. "Maybe. I cared about her. I would not have let her go through that alone. Especially when it was my baby."

"I should go," Presley says, but makes no move to leave this intriguing man who is her biological father.

"Make sure she gets home safely." Levi grabs a business card from the brass holder on his desk and presses it in Presley's hand. "I'd love to hear from you."

"Thanks." Slipping the card into the pocket of her maternity dress, Presley hurries out of the office without looking back.

She catches up with Lucy at the elevators. They don't speak while they wait for the elevator, but Presley stands close enough to Lucy to feel her body trembling. She's a ticking time bomb. Presley prays she makes it to the car before detonating.

The elevator doors part, and they join the throng of workers headed out of the building for lunch. Exiting the elevator on the garage level, they almost make it to the car when Lucy erupts in a fit of sobs. Presley takes the keys from her and helps Lucy into the passenger seat.

Going around to the driver's side, Presley accesses her MAPS app and navigates the car out of the garage and through the downtown streets to the highway. Lucy's blood-curdling shrieks rattle Presley. Every nerve ending stands at attention. She makes it twenty miles outside of town before she reaches her saturation point. Time for tough love.

"Geez! Lucy! Chill out! You're scaring me. No one died. The world isn't ending. If you don't calm down, I'm taking you to Roanoke. Is that what you want? To be readmitted to the psychiatric hospital?"

Lucy cries harder.

Presley tightens her grip on the steering wheel. "Seriously! I thought the meeting went well. Levi seems like a decent guy. Someone else drugged you that night. That should make you feel somewhat better," she says, although truthfully, she has no clue what Lucy is going through.

Lucy bangs her fist on the door panel. "But I consented to having sex with him."

"So what?" Presley tosses one hand in the air while keeping the other on the steering wheel. "He's a handsome guy. And he seems like a nice person. You told me yourself you were attracted to him before you thought he raped you. But he didn't drug you. You and Levi were both victims."

Lucy's sobbing subsides, but tears continue to stream down her cheeks.

"Whatever happened is in the past, Lucy. You have to find a

way to go on with your life. You were doing so well. Don't let this drag you back down. It's over. Dead and buried. I'm getting ready to have a baby. I'm scared, and my husband is MIA. I need your support."

Swiping at her eyes, Lucy draws in an unsteady breath. "Okay. I can try."

They drive for another ten minutes before Presley says, "Are you hungry? Because I'm going to faint if I don't eat."

"I don't have much of an appetite, but we need to feed my grandchild." She points at a building off in the distance ahead. "There's a truck stop. Let's stop there."

Presley parks the car, and they enter the restaurant—a no-frills diner with Formica countertops and wooden booths.

"It's crowded," Presley says under her breath to Lucy. "Must mean the food's good."

They wait five minutes for a booth to open up. When the gum-smacking waitress appears, Presley orders a grilled chicken sandwich with sweet potato fries. And Lucy, without looking at the menu, asks for a BLT.

After the waitress leaves, Lucy unrolls her flatware and places the napkin in her lap. "Thank you for what you said in the car. I really needed to hear those things. I'm sorry I fell apart on you like that. I've been so worked up about today. I let my emotions get the best of me."

Presley is saved from having to answer when the waitress delivers their sweet teas.

Lucy tears the paper off her straw, jabs the straw into her tea, and takes a long sip. "I feel oddly relieved, like an enormous burden has been lifted. I'll never know who drugged me that night. There's no one for me to blame. No focal point for my anger. After all this time, my emotions are finally spent. The well is empty. And I can begin filling it again. This time with happiness. I'm blessed to have you. And Chris. And I'll soon have a grandchild. No more looking back. Only toward the future."

Presley punches the air. "That's the fighting spirit."

Lucy grabs her purse from the bench beside her. "I must look a mess. I'm going to powder my nose."

Presley picks up her phone and absently scrolls through social media. There's a new photograph of Everett and Audrey Manning circulating on the various platforms. He has his arm around her waist, and she's pressing her body against his. She enlarges the photo and studies her husband's image. His eyes are red-rimmed and his face slack. Is he drunk? When she last saw him in July, Everett admitted to having a few beers occasionally, but he'd promised it was under control. He'd struggled with alcohol addiction before they met. The partying culture on the tour circuit could easily make it a problem again. Question is, does Everett have the courage to seek help?

Sliding into the booth opposite her, Lucy says, "Is something bothering you, Presley? Your face is pale. Do you feel okay?"

Presley yearns to talk to someone about Everett. But that someone isn't Lucy. Too much animosity has passed between them in recent months. And, after what she witnessed in the car a few minutes ago, Presley has concerns about Lucy's mental stability. She's afraid if Lucy goes off the deep end again, she might turn on Presley.

Presley places her phone, screen down, on the table. "I'm fine. Just tired."

She slips her hand into her dress pocket and fingers Levi's business card. She only just met the man, but his easy manner instills confidence in her. In a few days, she'll call and ask him about his children. She has a sister and two more brothers, and she's dying to know more about them. Will she one day get to meet them? She has much to look forward to. She can't let the unresolved problems in her marriage get her down.

5

STELLA

On Wednesday afternoon, I arrive early to pick up Jazz from gymnastics. Time permitting, I like to sneak in before class ends to watch the girls tumble. Today, however, I find Jazz sitting on the bench alone while the other girls perform handsprings and somersaults across the mat.

Coach Frazier paces up and down alongside the mat, bellowing out instructions to the girls. He's in his late fifties now. But according to rumor, he was a gifted gymnast in his youth, until a serious shoulder injury ruined his dreams of going to the Olympics.

Coach spots me and motions for me to join him at the end of the mat. "Why isn't Jazz participating? Is she not feeling well?"

"We have a problem. One of the other girls is bullying her. I'm not sure which one, and none of them are talking. I won't tolerate this type of behavior. It disrupts my class."

Anger and sadness descend upon me at once. How dare these little divas be ugly to my Jazz. "What're you going to do about it?"

"I think it's best for Jazz to take a break from the class until this storm blows over."

Fury pulses through my veins. "Wait. What? You're punishing my child when she's the victim here?" The words slip out of my mouth before I can think about them. When did I start thinking of Jazz as my child instead of my sister?

Coach looks down his nose at me, seemingly incensed I would argue with him. "I don't have time for children's politics, Mrs. Snyder."

When I tilt my head to look at him, he turns away. Since when am I Mrs. Snyder? Coach has always called me Stella until now. "You and I both know Jazz is the most talented in the group. She has what it takes to go far. The others don't."

"You're getting way ahead of yourself. These kids are only in second grade." He takes me by the elbow and walks me toward the door where Jazz is now waiting with her backpack. "Jazz can come back once they've worked out their differences. In my experience, kids this age never stay angry long."

I stop walking and face him. "Do you have any idea what the problem is?"

"I have no clue. It might have something to do with race, since Jazz is the only black kid in the class."

"I'd be willing to bet your hunch is correct, Coach Frazier. And you just made matters so much worse by expelling her from the class. If I didn't know better, I'd think you're the racist." Spinning on my heels, I continue on to the door. As I grow nearer, I see big tears spilling from Jazz's eyelids. "I'm sorry, kiddo. I don't know about you, but I could use a hot fudge sundae."

Jazz manages a weak smile.

Taking her backpack from her, I hold out my hand, and we leave the gym together. Jazz is silent on the way to the Dairy Deli. I look at her in the rearview mirror. "Guess what? I have a surprise for you. I've arranged for you and me to have our first guitar lesson on Friday afternoon."

Her face lights up. "Together?"

"That's right. Just you and me."

Tiny lines appear on her forehead. "Who's gonna teach us?"

"His name is Julius Jackson. He has a studio behind his house off Main Street near the college."

"Can we take lessons twice a week?"

I snicker. "Right now, we'll be lucky if we get one lesson a week. Julius is booked solid with a long waiting list. He's fitting us in as a favor to Billy."

She scrunches up her face. "Billy?"

"Yep. Julius knew our father. Not only were they friends, Julius taught Billy to play the guitar."

Jazz's golden eyes shine. "Cool! What guitar are you gonna play, Stella?"

I return my full attention to the road. "I kept one of Billy's for myself. I'll show it to you when we get home." I park behind the Dairy Deli, and we get out of the Wrangler.

We're waiting in line to order when Jazz asks, "Can I really get a hot fudge sundae? Won't it spoil my dinner?"

I wink at her. "We'll ignore the rules this once. We'll just eat a small dinner."

We take our ice cream treats to a table for two by the window. "Do you wanna talk about what happened at gymnastics?" I ask, digging my spoon into the ice cream.

Jazz's lower lip sticks out in a pout. "Sophia's mean. We're not friends anymore."

This doesn't surprise me. Sophia is the know-it-all in the bunch. "How's she being mean?"

Jazz sticks her finger in the gooey chocolate fudge sauce and licks it. "She doesn't want to hang out with me because I'm black. Her mom says she has to be nice to me, but she uninvited me to her birthday party." She lets out a snort. "I don't want to go to her dumb pottery painting birthday anyway."

The birthday party is this weekend. Jazz received the invitation weeks ago. She's already bought Sophia a gift. My blood boils. I long to strangle Sophia, even if she is a kid. "Jack was talking about taking Angel on a picnic hike in the mountains on Saturday, Jazz. If it's still warm enough, we can swim in the river."

"That sounds way better than Sophia's party." Jazz stabs her ice cream with a vengeance. Regardless of what she says, her feelings are hurt about being left out of the party. But she perks up at the sight of her classmate, a little black boy named Asher, playing pinball in the adjacent arcade. "May I please have some money to play games?"

"Yes, you may." I dump change out of my wallet into her outstretched hand. "But don't leave the arcade."

I watch her cross the ice cream parlor and tap Asher on the shoulder. He smiles at her and moves over to make room for her at the pinball machine. I remember all too well how it feels to be bullied. I was the daughter of lesbian mothers before same-sex marriages were widely accepted. My classmates teased me mercilessly, but I learned to stand up for myself, and Jazz will too.

I startle when Presley sneaks up behind me and says, "Boo!"

I press my hand against my racing heart. "Geez, Presley. You scared me. What're you doing here? I thought you were in Raleigh."

"We got back a few minutes ago. I came straight here. The baby has a sweet tooth." She eyes my empty sundae dish. "Whoa. You must have had a serious craving."

"Remember, I'm eating for two." I push away the dish. "I brought Jazz here to cheer her up. She's having a tough day."

"Hold that thought," Presley says, with finger pointed at ceiling. "Let me place my order, and then I want to hear about it."

She joins the line at the counter, returning a few minutes

later with a small scoop of mint chocolate chip ice cream in a cup. I explain to her about Jazz being bullied and the coach kicking her out of gymnastics class.

"What a jerk!" Presley licks ice cream off her spoon. "I'm not an attorney but sounds to me like you have grounds to sue the coach for racial discrimination."

"I would if I didn't think that would make matters worse for Jazz. That little brat Sophia invited Jazz to her birthday party this weekend. Now she says Jazz can't come."

Presley's mouth falls open. "What a little . . ." Her gray eyes travel to the arcade where Jazz and Asher are having fun playing pinball. "She's such a good kid. I can't imagine anyone being ugly to her."

"Kids can be brutal. Jazz will have to learn to take up for herself. Unfortunately, that's easier said than done." I sit back in my chair. "How did things go with your father?"

Presley pauses before answering. "Unexpectedly. Turns out, he specializes in sexual assault. Levi denied Lucy's date-rape allegation. He claims he's not the one who drugged her drink that night. He also insists Lucy consented to having sex with him."

I blink in surprise. "Do you believe him?"

"I do. He's amazing, Stella. I felt a strong connection with him. Not only is he handsome, he has a gentle and sincere way about him."

I smile. "So that's where you got it from."

Her face takes on a dreamy quality. "Maybe."

"And how did Lucy respond to his assertions?"

"She fell apart. Flew out of the office. I think her reaction was more about pent-up nerves. It took a lot of guts for her to confront him. She had a good cry in the car. After that, she appeared much better. She has an appointment with her therapist tomorrow. Dr. Norman will help her sort out what she learned." Presley crosses her fingers. "I think the worst is finally behind us."

"I hope so. You have all been through so much this past year." I fold my hands on the table. "Did you find out if you have any half siblings?"

"Yes!" Presley moves forward in her chair. "A sister and two brothers. But our visit was so short, I didn't have a chance to ask him more about them. He didn't tell me their names, so I can't look them up on social media. But Levi gave me his contact information. I'll call him in a day or two. I really want to know him better."

"I'm so happy for you, Presley. I wish I'd known my biological father."

Presley drops her smile. "I'm sorry, Stella. I'm being insensitive."

"Not at all, Presley. You have plenty of reason to be walking on air."

"I do." Sadness falls over Presley's face. "And I don't. Have you seen the latest photo of Everett and Audrey Manning circulating social media?"

Because I don't know what else to say, I respond with a somber nod. She's my friend. I won't lie to her.

Presley pulls out her phone and finds the image on Twitter. "It's the strangest thing. He has his arm around her, and she's falling all over him. But that's not the worst thing about the photo. I'm pretty sure Everett is drunk."

"Seriously? You're more worried about him being drunk than sleeping with this girl?" I jab my finger at her phone screen.

Presley's eyes glisten with unshed tears. "Call me naïve, but I honestly don't think he's sleeping with her."

"I don't think you're naïve, Presley. You know your husband better than anyone." I've never known Presley to misjudge anyone before. For her sake, I hope she's not wrong this time.

"Everett doesn't like to talk about it, so you probably don't know about his drinking problem."

I shake my head. "No. I didn't know."

"His problem stems from his abusive father and dysfunctional upbringing. A couple of years before coming to Hope Springs, before that music video that launched his career went viral, Everett nearly died from a terrible beating in a bar fight. His mother helped him get clean."

"I'm sorry," I say, frowning. "I see why you're so concerned. Is there anything you can do for him?"

"Not when he ignores my calls and texts. Everett has shut me out on purpose." Presley rubs her swollen belly. "The baby is my primary responsibility right now. If Everett comes to me for help, I'll be here for him. Until that time, I'm trying not to worry about him."

"I can't imagine how difficult that must be for you." I reach across the table for her hand. "You don't have to go through this alone, Presley. I'm here for you. Whatever you need."

Presley swipes at her eyes. "Thank you. I really need my friends right now."

Jazz appears at the table. "Hi, Presley."

Presley smiles at her. "Hey there, you. You're looking as stunningly beautiful as ever."

Jazz's cheeks turn rosy. "So are you. Is the baby moving? Can I feel your tummy?"

Presley takes Jazz's hand and places it on her stomach up near her ribs. "Actually, he or she is on a sugar high right now. Feel that?"

Jazz's eyes go wide, and a slow smile spreads across her lips. "Whoa. That's so cool." With her hand still on Presley's belly, she looks over at me. "How long before I can feel our baby move?"

"A couple more months." I smile to myself. Jazz will have plenty to feel with twins kicking around inside me.

With Presley now occupying Jazz's abandoned chair, Jazz crawls into my lap, which she hasn't done in months. "Guess what, Stella? Asher is taking guitar lessons too. And guess who his teacher is?"

I tap my chin, pretending to consider her question. "Julius Jackson?"

"Yes! And he loves him," she says, exaggerating her words.

Jazz's smile melts my heart. If only I could take away her troubles and make her happy all the time.

6

OLLIE

The afternoon hours on Wednesday drag on as the defense calls to the stand a seemingly endless list of witnesses, none of whom provide compelling testimony to prove Alexander's innocence. Morris is buying time, waiting for his star witness to show up. But when Judge Barrett dismisses court for the day, Dana Reese is still missing.

Ollie shares an Uber with Sergio and May on the way back to the hotel. "What happens when the defense runs out of witnesses to call?" Ollie asks.

Sergio says, "Unless Dana reappears overnight, the defense is already out of witnesses. Both sides will present their closing arguments in the morning, and the case goes to the jury."

"And then the waiting begins," Ollie says under her breath.

May gives Ollie's thigh a reassuring pat. "Wanna grab some dinner with us tonight? We have reservations at Californios."

Ollie has heard good things about the restaurant's contemporary Mexican cuisine. But she doesn't want to wear out her welcome with her ex-husband and his fiancé. "Thanks. But I wouldn't be very good company. You two have fun, and I'll see you in the morning."

The Uber pulls up in front of Ollie's hotel and she jumps out before they can argue. Hurrying up to her room, she changes into yoga pants and a tank top and hits the pavement. With much to think about, she race-walks for miles.

Ollie doesn't know what to make of Alexander's girlfriend's disappearance. Dana may have been with Alexander early in the evening on the night in question. But not later on, when he was busy setting the fire that killed their parents. Is she protecting him because she loves him? Or did Alexander threaten her into testifying on his behalf? If so, did she go into hiding to avoid perjuring herself? What if she refused to lie under oath and he harmed her? Alexander is in jail, but he could pay someone to do his dirty work.

Ollie grabs a taco from a taqueria in the Mission District before heading back to the hotel, changing into pajamas, and reading in bed until she falls asleep. She wakes early the following morning to discover a dense fog has settled over the city. She heads up to the hotel's gymnasium and spends an hour working off nervous energy on a recumbent bike.

She's grabbing a coffee from the lobby when Sergio calls. "Dana Reese has resurfaced. I don't have any details except that she'll be testifying against Alexander."

Ollie lets out an audible gasp. "No way."

"Yep. Ellis wants to see us as soon as possible. We'll pick you up on the way to the courthouse in thirty minutes."

Ollie heads to the lobby elevators. "I'll be ready."

Twenty-five minutes later, dressed in a black pantsuit with her hair still wet from the shower, Ollie exits the hotel as Sergio and May are arriving in an Uber. They don't speak during the drive. When they arrive at the courthouse, Ellis is meeting with Morris in the judge's chambers, and they aren't able to speak to him before court reconvenes at nine. As they take their now familiar seats behind the prosecution, Ollie risks a glance at the defense. Their faces are set in stone. They are devastated by this unexpected turn of events.

Dana Reese is a stunningly beautiful woman with silky black hair and emerald eyes. When Ellis questions her regarding her whereabouts the night of the fire, Dana's eyes remain on the jurors, never once straying to Alexander.

"We had dinner at Ad Hoc in Yountville. Alex was being a jerk, as usual. He was picking on me about my appearance. My dress revealed too much cleavage. I was wearing too much makeup. The relationship wasn't working for me. So, I invited him back to my house after dinner with the intention of breaking up with him. But when we got there, he refused to come inside. He said he had something he needed to take care of."

"Did he say what?" Ellis asks.

"No, and I didn't ask. I was secretly relieved. I really didn't want him in my house." Dana hesitates as she composes herself. "When I heard about the fire on the news the next morning, I tried reaching out to him, but he never responded. I'd never met his parents, but I attended the funeral for Alexander's sake."

Ellis converses with Dana in a soft voice, as though she's the only one in the room. "Did you speak to him at the funeral?"

"I never got a chance. There were too many people. I didn't hear from him for two weeks. He'd just lost his parents. I figured he needed his space. And I wanted to buy some time. I hated to break up with him while he was in mourning. When he invited me for coffee, I agreed to meet him. I couldn't put it off any longer."

"Where'd you meet him?" Ellis asks.

"At Costeaux in Healdsburg. I arrived before him and snagged a table on the patio. Alex was twenty minutes late. When I asked how he was coping, he said he was living in hell."

Ellis narrows his eyes. "Were those his exact words?"

"Yes. I remember specifically. He said, 'I feel so guilty. If I'd been at the estate instead of shacking up with you, I could've saved them.'"

The courtroom erupts in murmurs, and Ellis cocks an eyebrow. "How did you respond?"

"I reminded him he'd dropped me off at my apartment that night after dinner. He asked me if I was sure. And I told him I was positive. He appeared as though he didn't remember. Now I know it was an act." Dana pauses a beat. "Anyway, Alexander got mad and called me a liar. I told him it was over between us and left the coffee shop." She tucks a strand of silky hair behind her ear. "I didn't hear from him for nearly a year. Then, in late July, I found him waiting in the parking lot outside my office building when I was leaving work. He said if the police question me about the night of the fire, I was to tell them he slept at my place and left the following morning. I asked him why he needed an alibi. And that's when he threatened me. He told me, if I didn't lie for him, he would kill me."

"You're sure those were his words?" Ellis asks.

"Positive." Dana shudders. "I'll never forget the look in his eyes. He meant it."

"How did you respond?" Ellis asks.

"I told him he was out of his mind. I got in my car and drove off." Dana's shoulders slump. "The next night, I went out for drinks with friends. When I got home, a man attacked me with a knife." She touches her fingers to her cheek. "He cut my face, not deep enough to need stitches but enough to leave a scar. A reminder. He said if I testified against Alexander, he would come back and slit my throat." Dana begins crying, silent tears streaming down her face.

"Did you get a look at this man?" Ellis asks.

"No. He was wearing a mask." Dana produces a tissue from her pocket and wipes her face. "These past few weeks have been torture. I didn't want to lie under oath, so I disappeared. I've been staying at a friend's beach house. This friend convinced me to contact you, Mr. Ellis." She looks straight at the jury. "On the night in question, I was with Alexander early in the evening, but after nine o'clock, I do not know his whereabouts."

Ollie studies the jurors. Their faces are soft with compassion. They believe her.

"I have no further questions, Your Honor," Ellis says, returning to his seat at the counsel table.

Judge Barrett gives Morris the nod, and he goes after Dana like a rabid pit pull. She sits with her back ramrod straight as she answers his questions in clear and concise sentences. She never falters, never wavers. Ollie has watched plenty of courtroom dramas on television and finds Dana to be as compelling a witness as she has ever seen.

After closing arguments, Judge Barrett gives the jury instructions and dismisses them to begin deliberation. Ollie leaves the courtroom with Sergio and May in tow.

Pausing on the steps in front of the building, Ollie asks, "What now?"

"We wait," Sergio says. "Anyone up for lunch on the waterfront?"

May presses the back of her hand against her forehead. "You two go ahead. I have a headache. I need a nap."

Ollie waits for Sergio to argue with her. When he doesn't, Ollie senses he has something important to talk to her about. After dropping May at her hotel, Sergio instructs the taxi driver to take them to Hog Island in the Ferry Building Marketplace. It's after two o'clock, the lunch crowd is dwindling, and the hostess seats them right away at a table outside.

Without consulting Ollie, Sergio orders a bottle of rosé and two dozen raw oysters from four different west coast locales. They discuss Dana's testimony while they wait for the server to bring the wine.

"What do you think will happen to Dana?" Ollie asks.

"I assume she'll go into witness protection."

When the wine arrives, Sergio relaxes back in his chair with glass in hand. "What is your plan for the immediate future? Will you wait for the verdict in San Francisco?"

Ollie sips the crisp wine and licks her lips. "Only until tomorrow afternoon. I'm driving up to Healdsburg to meet with a couple of realtors on Saturday. Once the estate attorney gives me the green light, I'll be putting the vineyard on the market."

This piques Sergio's interest. "Are you sure you don't want to rebuild?"

"I'm positive. There's nothing left for me in California except terrible memories."

Sergio's lips part in a sympathetic smile. "There are plenty of good ones too, Ollie."

"I know." Ollie places her hand over her heart. "I've stored those away for safekeeping. But right now, I need to escape the past. I'm forging a new life in Virginia. I want to build something for myself. I'm just waiting for the right opportunity to come along. Until then, I'm happy working at Hope Springs Farm."

"Your happiness is the most important thing."

The server delivers their oysters, and they dig in. "Once you have a price, I'd like to make an offer on the vineyard," Sergio says.

This doesn't surprise her. Sergio has always loved the estate. The land is part of her soul, and she trusts him to preserve it. "I'll consider your offer on the property, but I'm retiring the brand."

Ollie expects him to argue. The brand is more valuable than the land. Instead, he says, "I think that's wise. Your family is the Hendrix brand. It belongs to you. You may decide to use it in Virginia." He slurps down an oyster. "Besides, May and I have a concept for our own brand, something more contemporary."

They discuss his ideas while they finish the oysters and wine. They're both a little tipsy, and Sergio is considering ordering another bottle when the phone vibrates the table with a call from Ellis. They stare down at the phone as though it's a hot potato. "Do you think the jury's back already?" Sergio asks.

"I don't know." Ollie eyes the phone. "Answer it."

Sergio accepts the call and tentatively lifts the phone to his ear. Ollie sobers up as she watches the color drain from his face.

"We're on the way," Sergio says, ending the call.

"The jury has reached a verdict." Sergio waves their server over. "You grab a taxi while I pay the tab."

Ten minutes later, they are on their way, zooming back uptown toward the courthouse. "Did you call May?" Ollie asks.

Sergio shakes his head. "She doesn't want to be present for the verdict. She says it's not her place."

"That's ridiculous. She's been in the trenches with us all week. I consider her a friend. I want her to be there."

Sergio taps his phone's screen. "I'll call her now."

Ollie presses her head against the window. Alexander is a menace to society. He deserves to be punished for killing their parents. But, as she stares out at the passing buildings, the years slip away and the brother who bullied her for much of her adult life is forgotten. She remembers the little boy she taught to ride a bicycle, the younger brother who once idolized her. When had things gone so wrong for him? If Alexander is convicted, he'll likely serve two life sentences. Ollie will never see him again. Her parents are gone, and now her brother. She's all alone in the world.

They take their seats in the gallery in the courtroom with no time to spare. May joins them as the jurors are filing back into the box. Sucking in a deep breath, Ollie stares straight ahead, at the back of Ellis's chair, while the foreman renders the verdict. Guilty on two counts of premeditated murder.

7

CECILY

Jameson's is hopping on Friday night. A local girl is having her wedding on the lawn on Saturday, and her out-of-town guests, a rowdy crowd, are staying at the inn. After a surf-and-turf dinner, they serve champagne with crème brûlée for dessert. The toasting goes on for hours, and the guests are on their way to being very drunk when they head across the lobby to Billy's Bar around eleven for more partying.

"I could use a drink myself," Fiona says to Cecily as they are cleaning up and prepping for breakfast on Saturday.

"No kidding. Why don't you run down to Billy's and grab us a bottle of champagne."

"Great idea! I'm on it." Fiona hurries out of the kitchen and returns a few minutes later with a grim expression and no champagne.

Cecily looks up from the recipe she's studying. "What's wrong?"

"Lyle is in the bar. He's really drunk, Cecily."

"Ugh! This is the last thing I need tonight." Cecily storms out of the kitchen, calling over her shoulder to Fiona. "Call security!"

When she reaches Billy's, she fights her way to the bar where Lyle sits on a stool at the end, hurling loud insults at Parker, who is slinging drinks as fast as possible. Parker pretends to be unfazed, but his stony expression tells Cecily he's furious.

Cecily stands behind Lyle, listening to his drunken rant. He's too oblivious to realize she's there.

"You're not good enough for her, dude. Cecily deserves better. She deserves me." Lyle jabs his chest with his thumb. "We're getting back together. She told you that, right?"

"That's it! You've had enough." Cecily hauls him off the stool. "You're going home."

He wraps his arms around her and smothers her face with kisses. "With you. I'm going home with *you.*"

His breath smells rancid, like beer and vomit. She shoves him off her. "Like hell you are."

Parker comes from behind the bar. "Hey, man! Get your hands off her."

"Says who? You?" Lyle pokes Parker's chest. "Bring it on, bitch. I'm not afraid of you."

Parker takes Lyle by the arm and drags him out of the bar. Cecily follows them out into the lobby where she spots Ed, the night security guard, heading their way from the reception hall. She pries Parker's fingers off Lyle's arm. "He's drunk, Parker. Let security handle it. You're needed at the bar. Get back to work."

Parker's face is flushed with anger. "After I take this punk outside and permanently shut his big mouth."

"You're better than that, Parker. Where's the pride in beating up a drunk man?"

Ed approaches with beefy arms swinging at his side. "Is there a problem here?"

Cecily pushes Lyle toward Ed. "Please escort this guy out of the building. He's drunk and causing a scene."

Ed studies Lyle from head to toe. "Is he a guest in the hotel?"

Cecily's face warms. "Unfortunately, he's my ex-fiancé."

"In that case, he's outta here." Ed grips the back of Lyle's neck and marches him through the lobby toward reception.

When Cecily takes off after them, Parker yells, "Hey, Cess! Where're you going?"

She turns around and walks backward. "To make sure he leaves the building. I'll be back in a minute." Spinning around, she increases her pace to a jog.

Lyle causes another scene at the front entrance when he threatens to drive home. "Forget it, Lyle. I'm calling you an Uber." Cecily snatches his phone from him and taps on the screen to access the app.

Ed says, "Don't bother, Cecily. No driver will take him. He's too drunk."

Cecily plucks the car keys out of Lyle's hand. "Then I'll drive him myself."

Ed steps in front of her, arms folded. "I can't let you do that. It's not a good idea."

"He's harmless. I know where he lives. I'll drive him home and walk back." Brushing Ed out of the way, Cecily takes Lyle by the arm and leads him to the parking lot.

On the way through town, Lyle blabbers on about how much he loves her and how much he misses her. "You're so pretty," he says, fingering a lock of her hair.

She swats his hand away. "Don't touch me, Lyle. I'm driving you home. That's it. Nothing's gonna happen between us tonight. Or ever again."

She drives past the brick fences that mark the entrance to Jefferson College and through the neighboring streets to the yellow Cape Cod she once shared with Lyle. She parks his truck on the curb, gets out, and walks around to the passenger side. She holds onto Lyle as he stumbles up the sidewalk. Unlocking the front door, she walks him over to the sofa and pushes him down.

From the top of the stairs comes a strange voice. "Lyle, is that you?" And a guy Cecily's never seen before comes barreling down in athletic shorts and no shirt. He freezes when he sees her. "Oops. Sorry. I didn't realize you're with someone."

Lyle's new roommate is cute with seriously nice abs. But his hair is too long, and he has Lyle's arrogant frat boy way about him.

Cecily backs away from the sofa toward the door. "I'm not *with* him. He was too drunk to drive, so I gave him a ride home. Can you take it from here? I don't want him following me."

A smirk appears on the guy's lips. "Doesn't look like he's going anywhere to me."

Cecily follows his gaze to the sofa where Lyle is fast asleep with his mouth wide open. "Thank God."

Fleeing the house, she books it down the sidewalk and out of the neighborhood. Ten minutes later, she's in front of Town Tavern on Main Street when Fiona's fire engine red Toyota Celica pulls to the curve beside her. The passenger window rolls down. "Cecily! I've been looking everywhere for you. Get in."

Cecily climbs into the car, and Fiona drives off. When Cecily tells her what happened, Fiona says, "Are you outta your mind? What were you thinking giving him a ride home?"

"What was I supposed to do? He couldn't drive himself, and he was too drunk for an Uber. If I let him walk, he would've ended up in a gutter."

Fiona shakes her head as though in disbelief. "For someone so worldly, you're extremely naïve when it comes to men. Lyle is trying to sabotage your relationship with Parker. And you pay him back by giving Lyle a ride home? Stay away from him, Cess. He's bad news."

Cecily slinks down in her seat. "You're right. I didn't want anything to happen to him. We were engaged to be married. I still care about him." She realizes with a start that she was always cleaning up after him and taking care of Lyle when they were together. Lyle doesn't need a wife. He needs a mother.

Fiona drums her fingers on the steering wheel. "Where's your car?"

"I walked to work this morning. Can you drop me at Stella's?"

Fiona turns on her blinker and heads toward Stella's. "Sure! But you'd better text Parker. He's worried about you."

Cecily sends off a quick text to Parker, telling him she's on her way home. *See you tomorrow.*

Fiona whips into Stella's driveway, and Cecily hops out, blowing her friend a kiss. "You're the best, Fi. I owe you one."

Upstairs in her apartment, Cecily closes and locks the door behind her, reminding herself to talk to Jack about a dead bolt.

She washes her face, brushes her teeth, and climbs into bed in her bra and panties, pulling the covers up under her chin. Exhausted from a hard day's work, she falls asleep the minute she closes her eyes.

———

Parker is waiting for her on the kitchen's back porch when Cecily arrives at work the next morning. He hands her a coffee. "Morning. I understand you gave Lyle a ride home last night. How'd that go?"

"It was fine."

"Lyle was talking some serious smack last night. I can't believe you drove him home. He could've attacked you," he says in a concerned tone.

"But he didn't." Parker follows Cecily around the back of the building to the herb garden, and they sit together on the bench. "What was Lyle saying last night?"

"He tried to convince me you two are getting back together."

Cecily rolls her eyes. "Puh-lease. That's an insult." Her shoulders slump. "I'm embarrassed I was ever with him to begin with."

Parker grins at her. "But you were. Which means he can't be all bad. He seems a little off in the head now." He taps his temple. "And I'm not just talking about him being drunk."

Cecily responds by sipping her coffee. She's not ready to admit she's been thinking the same thing about Lyle.

Parker rests his arm on the bench behind her. "The issue isn't what he was saying. The issue is you, Cecily. You've been telling me for weeks you're over him. Yet your actions don't support your words."

Cecily studies his handsome face. She adores him. She's head over heels in love with him. If she doesn't commit to a relationship soon, she could lose him.

She exhales a deep breath. "Let's get through the wedding today. And tomorrow, we'll talk."

"I'm holding you to it." He gets up and pulls her to her feet. They go inside to the kitchen, which is already in full swing with waitstaff serving guests breakfast and catering crew preparing for the afternoon wedding.

The hours pass in a blur of activity, but their efforts come together under the massive tent on the lawn. Food tables occupy one end of the tent, and at the other, a stage is set for a popular swing band. Parker has organized a round bar in the center. The weather is ideal with sunny skies and temperatures in the low seventies.

Guests migrate down to the lawn from the stone terrace following the ceremony. Cecily is putting last-minute touches on the tiered ice sculpture raw bar when she spots Lyle coming toward her.

"What're you doing here?" Cecily says in a tone that lets him know she's not happy to see him.

"I'm friends with the groom. He was one of my players."

Cecily surveys the crowd. "Is Coach Anderson here?"

"Somewhere, I guess."

Returning her attention to the raw bar, Cecily plucks an errant shrimp tail out of the display. "I hope he wasn't in Billy's Bar last night when you showed your ass. I don't think your boss would have been impressed with his assistant coach."

"So what? I drank too much." He places his hand on his chest. "I'm nursing a wounded heart."

"Ha. You wounded *my* heart when you cheated on me."

"I made a mistake," he says. "I've apologized a gazillion times."

She turns to face him. "You can apologize a gazillion more, and I still won't forgive you."

"We'll see about that," he says under his breath, and holds up a glass of clear liquid. "I'm drinking water today. I'm not planning to stay long."

"Good. Now, find someone else to bother. I'm trying to work here." When she walks off, he grabs her arm to stop her.

"I understand you met my new roommate last night. Pete told me you drove me home. You were looking out for me, which is evidence you still care about me." When he tries to finger her cheek, she smacks his hand away.

"Hardly. I was preventing you from killing someone. Or yourself. For the record, Lyle, you and I are never getting back together. So you might as well move on."

"Can we at least talk about it?"

"There's nothing to talk about," she says, and hurries away, leaving him alone at the edge of the tent.

The bride and groom arrive, and the party kicks into gear. The crowd is lively and the band talented and engaging. Throughout the evening, Cecily makes countless trips between the tent and the kitchen, and by the end of the night, she's ready to collapse. It's well past two in the morning when she and Parker walk together to the parking lot.

Parker aims his key at his Tahoe, clicking his doors unlocked. "I'd say let's grab a drink, except I'm too exhausted to lift the glass to my lips."

"I know what you mean," Cecily says, collapsing onto the passenger seat.

On the short drive home, Parker says, "I have some chores to do in the morning. What say we hike up to the overlook tomorrow? It's a perfect place to have our talk."

"I'd like that," she says in a soft voice.

"I'll swing by and pick you up around two." He pulls into Stella's driveway and takes the car out of gear.

Cecily resists the temptation to hook her arm around his neck and kiss his luscious lips. Why is she depriving herself when being together is what they both want? Tomorrow, when they go for their hike, she'll express her concerns about romance ruining their friendship. Parker has a knack for looking at situations from every angle. If he can ease her fears, she'll commit to giving romance with him a try.

She imagines the afternoon as she's getting ready for bed. They'll hurry home from the lookout and spend the rest of the afternoon making crazy love in her treehouse apartment.

On Sunday morning, Cecily rushes through her chores with sex at the forefront of her mind. She soaks in a hot bath, washing every crevice of her body and shaving her armpits and legs. She blow-dries her honey blonde hair and takes extra care in choosing her attire, as though she's going to a cocktail party instead of hiking. Exercise is sexy. And seducing Parker is on her agenda.

Promptly at two o'clock, when she hears his footfalls on the steps, she swings the door open and greets him with a smile. Her lips turn downward at the sight of Lyle coming up the steps behind him.

"What do you want, Lyle?"

"I left my glasses here the other night," Lyle says.

Cecily gawks at him. "What night? You've never been in my apartment."

Lyle brushes past Parker and enters her apartment. Cecily is on his heels. "What're you doing? You can't just barge into my home."

Lyle enters her bedroom, as though he's been there many times before. He checks the nightstand and then drops to the floor on all fours. He reaches under the bed and pulls out the glasses he wears for distance seeing when he drives.

Cecily stares at the glasses, too stunned to speak.

Lyle gets to his feet, adjusts the glasses on his face, and strides out of her apartment, winking at her as he passes.

Parker turns to her. "What the heck, Cecily?"

"You don't seriously believe him? That was a total setup. He must have broken in while I was at work yesterday and hidden the glasses under the bed."

Parker tosses his hands in the air. "I don't know what to believe anymore. You keep blowing me off for a reason. I'm thinking maybe you *are* still hung up on him."

"I can't believe you think that." Cecily is suddenly mad as hell. At Lyle for sabotaging her relationship with Parker. And with Parker for pressuring her into a commitment she's not ready for.

"I'm tired of these childish games you're playing, Cess. Let me know when you're ready for an adult relationship."

When he storms out of her apartment, she slams the door behind him. She's done with men. She doesn't have time for romance anyway. She falls back against the door. Except that she'd make time for Parker. She *is* ready for the next step. If that's true, why did she let him leave?

She places her hands on the side of her head and tugs at her hair. "Ugh!" she cries out to the empty apartment. "What is wrong with me?"

Then it dawns on her. Maybe she's not ready for an adult relationship. Maybe she's not ready to be an adult.

8

PRESLEY

Another week goes by with no word from Everett. Presley picks up the phone countless times to call him but immediately puts it down. His concert was on tour in Maryland over the weekend. He'll be in Washington on Wednesday, and Richmond next Friday. He'll be performing only two hours away from Hope Springs, yet he hasn't invited her to come to the concert or made arrangements to drive up and see her, his *very* pregnant wife. His actions, or inactions, are very telling. With every passing day, her faith in their marriage diminishes.

At least Presley has plenty to keep her busy. She's leaving her cottage, headed out to make her Monday morning tour of the grounds to assess the damage from the weekend, when she spots Ollie emerging from the main building, coffee in hand.

Presley steps in line with her on the sidewalk. "Welcome home. When did you get back?"

"Late last night," Ollie says, flicking a hank of her dark hair over her shoulder.

"I heard about the verdict. I can't imagine what you must be going through. I'm sure your emotions are conflicted."

"That's putting it mildly," Ollie mutters.

Presley's fingers graze Ollie's arm. "Why don't you take a few days off to get your head straight?"

"I can't. Our best yoga instructor quit over the weekend. She just up and left with no notice. She moved to Florida with her boyfriend."

Presley's brow puckers. "No one told me about that."

"I'm on my way to meet two potential candidates now. One is a local woman whose resume I've had on file for a while. The other is a guest who overheard one of the fitness instructors talking about the position. Feel free to sit in on the interviews. I'm rattled after my trip and would love your feedback."

Presley checks her calendar. She's free until her one o'clock lunch meeting with Stella. "I can fit that in."

The candidates are waiting outside of Ollie's office when they arrive. The first, the local woman, is in her late forties. While she's a longtime yogi in impeccable physical shape, she's never taught yoga. The second has more experience and would fit in better with the current staff.

Kate, a striking girl with golden hair and blue eyes, is originally from North Carolina and has been teaching yoga since graduating from UNC four years ago. She seems ideal aside from the one red flag—why is she staying at the inn alone?

"What brings you to Hope Springs?" Presley asks.

"I broke up with my boyfriend, and I don't want to stay in Charlotte. I decided to tour the Carolinas and Virginia to see what else I could find."

Presley exchanges a look with Ollie.

Concern crosses Kate's face. "Did I say something wrong?"

"Actually, you said something right," Ollie says.

Presley explains, "Many of our key staff members, including Ollie and me, have landed in Hope Springs for similar reasons. We're searching for something, running from something, or hiding. Stella, the resort's owner and general manager, is all about giving young people with little experience a chance."

Kate's lips part in a kilowatt smile that lights up the room. "Then I fit the mold. Does this mean I get the job?"

Ollie stares down at Kate's resume. "I'll have to check your references first. What is the status of your current job?"

"I'm on unpaid leave. I told them I was considering moving. They won't be surprised if you contact them for a recommendation."

"When could you start?" Presley asks.

Kate stares up at the ceiling while she considers the question. "I'm booked at the inn through tonight. I'll have to find a place to live and get my stuff from Charlotte. Maybe Thursday. Friday at the latest."

"That would be ideal. I'll check your references and get back to you this afternoon." Ollie stands, indicating the meeting is over.

Kate jumps to her feet. "Thank you for your time. I really want this job. I'm a hard worker and a people person."

"I'll keep that in mind." Ollie shows her out, closing the door behind her. She turns back to face Presley. "What do you think?"

"I like her. You should hire her. Stella will approve." Presley stands to go. "Take some time off, Ollie. You need to clear your head." She exits the office before Ollie can respond.

After a quick walk-through of the wellness center, Presley exits the building and strolls over to Cottage Row. When everything appears in order, she starts back toward the main building. She notices Cecily standing outside the barn, staring up at it as though a million miles away.

Crossing the lawn to her, Presley asks, "What're you doing?"

Cecily startles, gripping the fabric of her chef's coat. "You scared me. I didn't hear you walk up."

"What's going on, Cecily? You seem on edge."

Cecily waves away her concern. "I'm fine. I was just scheming for some ideas for the rehearsal dinner we're hosting here weekend after next."

"Let us handle it. After all, we're the event planners."

"I realize that, Presley. I'm strategizing about the food, not the decorations. As you know, the groom's mother wants casual and rustic with a menu to match. I refuse to serve barbecue at a rehearsal dinner."

Presley smiles. "I admire your tenacity. I'm sure you'll come up with just the right courses."

"Thanks for your vote of confidence." Cecily rolls open the door, and they enter the barn. She circles the vast space with her arms spread wide at the vaulted ceiling and original shiplap walls. "We should use this space more often. Especially this time of year. Last year's open house rocked."

Presley thinks back to the event she planned—oyster roast, hayrides, and themed rooms for the main building—to show off the inn's recent renovations to the locals. "I agree. That was fun. We should do that again."

"Only you can transform a smelly old barn into a winter wonderland. Like the wedding you planned for Stella that ended up being your wedding too." Cecily holds her arms as though dancing with a man as she waltzes around the barn.

"My dream wedding," Presley says, more to herself than Cecily.

Cecily stops dancing. "I'm sorry, Presley. I didn't mean to bring up a sore subject. Have you heard from the rascal?"

Presley shakes her head. "Not a word."

"He's playing in Richmond this weekend. Maybe he'll surprise you like he did last time."

With tight lips, Presley says, "I'm not holding my breath."

Cecily plucks a strand of hay from the bales stacked against the wall and points it at Presley. "Everett is one of the good guys. There has to be a legit reason he's acting like a jerk."

"That's what I keep telling myself," Presley says. "You and Everett were close. Did he ever tell you about his alcohol problem?"

"He mentioned it a few times. Enough that I understood it was a real problem in his past."

Presley removes her phone from her jacket pocket and accesses her photos. She holds the phone up for Cecily to see the screenshot of an image of Everett and Audrey Manning. "I'm sure you saw this on social media. Everett looks drunk to me. Really drunk."

Cecily narrows her eyes as she studies the photograph. "You're right. His face is drooping, and his eyes are glazed." She looks up from the phone. "Do you think he's sleeping with her?"

Presley shrugs. "I never thought Everett would cheat on me. But he's certainly acting guilty."

Cecily lets out a guttural growl. "I will strangle him the next time I see him."

"You'll have to beat me to it," Presley says.

They leave the barn, closing the heavy doors behind them, and head toward the main building.

"I've sworn off men for good," Cecily says. "They aren't worth the trouble."

Presley chuckles. "You're lying. You're totally gaga over Parker."

Cecily's hand shoots up. "I am! I admit it. But Parker is ready for a serious relationship, and I'm not. I'm a wimp, Presley. I'm terrified of commitment. I'm afraid marriage and children will interfere in my career. And I'm not willing to take that risk."

"Maybe you're just gun-shy after what happened with Lyle. You've been through a lot this past year with a broken engagement and Lyle cheating on you."

"That's definitely part of it. In hindsight, I never loved him. I was in love with the idea of being in love. I didn't call off the wedding because of Lyle. I called it off because the idea of commitment freaked me out."

"There's nothing wrong with playing it safe, Cecily." Presley thumbs her chest. "Look at me. I rushed into commitment, both in marrying Everett and deciding to start a family so soon. And look where it got me—pregnant and alone."

Cecily hooks an arm around Presley's neck. "I have faith in you and Everett. You were meant to be together. Be patient. He'll come around."

"I hope you're right," Presley mumbles.

They climb the steps to the kitchen porch, and Cecily reaches for the doorknob. "Are you coming inside?"

Presley longs for a cup of the inn's specially blended ginger tea. But she's been procrastinating on calling Levi long enough. "I wish I could. But I have some things I need to take care of."

Cecily's smile fades. "I understand."

"What is it, Cess? I get the feeling there's something you're not telling me."

Cecily's body tenses. "Lyle's being a jerk. He wants me to give him another chance. I've made it clear that's not happening. But I'm not sure he got the message."

Presley doesn't press for details. She can tell by the firm set of her jaw, Cecily will say no more. "If you ever need to talk, you know where to find me."

"Right back at you," Cecily says, and disappears inside.

Presley's on her way back to her cottage when she receives a text from Ollie. *Kate's reference checked out. I hired her. She starts on Friday.*

Even though she encouraged Ollie to hire her, Presley has doubts about the young yogi. Kate's bubbly personality will win the guests over, but her recent breakup makes her vulnerable.

Then again, Presley was lost and searching for new meaning in her life when she first came to Hope Springs. She laughs out loud to herself. What is she thinking? She's still lost and searching.

At the cottage, Presley makes a cup of tea and takes it outside to the rockers on the porch. She tries Levi's cell, but the call goes straight to voice mail. She leaves a brief message, asking him to call her back at his convenience. Twenty minutes later, she's finishing her tea while watching guests meander around on the lawn when her phone vibrates with his call.

When she answers, he blurts, "Presley! I'm so glad to hear from you. I've been thinking about you."

Presley's heart warms. "I've been thinking about you as well."

"How is Lucy?" he asks.

"As far as I can tell, she's doing well. We went for a long walk yesterday afternoon. She finally seems at peace about what happened in college."

Levi sighs. "If only she'd told me the truth back then, things might have been different."

An awkward silence passes between them. "If you don't mind me asking, I'm curious about the event in college that motivated you to become a sexual abuse lawyer."

Levi clears his throat. "Well . . . let's see. It was a Saturday night during the fall semester of my senior year. I'd taken Elena, the girl who would later become my wife, out to dinner to celebrate her birthday. Elena had to study for an exam on Monday, so I dropped her off early and stopped by my fraternity house on my way home. The football team was playing away that weekend, and many of the students had left campus. I had in mind to shoot some pool with some of the guys, but when I got there, I heard loud music coming from a room upstairs."

Levi pauses a beat. "I barged in on three of my fraternity

brothers gang-raping a freshman, a real pretty girl. Poor thing was passed out cold. We later learned they'd drugged her."

Presley gasps, her hand flying to her mouth. "That's awful. I can see how that would've made a lasting impact on you." She pauses a beat. "I'd love to know more about your children. My half siblings. Will you tell them about me?"

"I don't talk to my sons much. They're busy with their lives in DC. I may wait and tell them at Thanksgiving when we have more time together. But I mentioned you to my daughter. She seemed excited at the prospect of having a half sister. But she's been going through a rough patch lately, and I'm never really sure what's running through her mind."

Presley's heart sinks. Doesn't sound like she'll be meeting her half siblings soon. If ever.

"I'd like to reach out to Lucy," he says. "Do you mind sharing her number?"

Presley hesitates. She's not sure if Levi calling Lucy is a good thing. But who is she to make that decision? "I'll send it to you as soon as we hang up."

"Thanks, Presley. Listen, I need to run. I have an appointment in a few minutes. I'm thinking of coming to Hope Springs Farm for a weekend. I'm curious to see what the hype is about."

Presley imagines having dinner with her father on the porch at Jameson's with the sun setting over the mountains in the background as they linger over dessert. "I'd like that. But you'd better plan it soon. The baby is due October eighteenth."

"So soon? That's only a few weeks away."

Presley rubs her tight belly. "Three weeks from today."

"Let me see what I can work out. I'll be in touch soon," Levi says.

Dropping the phone on the table beside her, Presley leans her head against the back of the chair and closes her eyes.

I'll be in touch soon means Presley will have to wait to hear from him. Just as she'll have to wait to meet her half siblings. Levi told her nothing about them. Not even their names. His sons are in DC, but where does his daughter live? What types of careers do they have? What rough patch is his daughter going through? Presley's marriage is on the rocks, and she's getting ready to have a baby. She doesn't need more drama in her life. But her keen intuition warns of more drama heading her way.

9

STELLA

Jazz becomes more withdrawn by the day. She's often sullen and argumentative. She's only happy when she's practicing her guitar or playing with Angel. I try several times to talk to her about what's bothering her, but she shuts me out. Kids should come with a set of instructions. I'm ill equipped to tackle the problems of an eight year old. How will I ever survive raising twins?

At noon on Tuesday, I'm eating a salad at my desk in my office at the inn when I receive a call on my cell phone from an unknown number. I assume it's a telemarketer, but I answer the call anyway in case something has happened to Jack or Jazz or my mothers.

"Stella Snyder," I answer in a tentative tone, prepared to hang up.

"Mrs. Snyder. This is Rebecca Wheeler, Jazz's teacher."

Alarm bells ring in my head. "Did something happen? Is Jazz hurt?"

"Jazz is fine. But I think maybe something is troubling her. I realize this is last minute, but I was wondering if we could talk for a few minutes at the end of the school day."

"Of course. I'll see you at three thirty."

The next three hours drag on. Too distracted for paperwork, I wander aimlessly about the property, putting out small fires and making idle conversation with guests. When three o'clock finally rolls around, I leave my office and walk across the street to the manor house for my Wrangler. I arrive at the school with fifteen minutes to spare. Instead of joining the carpool line, I find an empty space in the parking lot and wait. When I see children emerging from the building, I go inside and down the hall to Jazz's room.

I met Rebecca three weeks ago at back-to-school night. She's pretty in a wholesome way, with strawberry-blonde hair and a trail of freckles across the bridge of her nose. "Where's Jazz?" I ask, expecting to see my sister seated at one of the child-size desks.

"She's down the hall in the art room working on a special project. I told her you would be a few minutes late picking her up. Let's sit down," Rebecca says, motioning me to a row of desks by the window.

When I lower myself to the tiny chair, I pray the rubber band holding my pants together doesn't snap. I make a mental note to shop for maternity clothes soon.

Rebecca pulls up a chair next to me. "Thanks for coming on such short notice, Mrs. Snyder."

"Of course. And please, call me Stella."

Rebecca smiles. "I've always liked the name Stella. And I hope you'll call me Rebecca." She straightens, as though ready to get down to business. "First, I want you to know I'm crazy about Jazz. Not only is she a conscientious student, she goes out of her way to be kind to the other children. It breaks my heart to see how these little devils are treating her."

A chill travels my spine. "Which little devils? And how are they treating her?"

"They refuse to let her eat lunch at their table or join them on the playground. One child, in particular, is controlling the others."

"Sophia?" When Rebecca doesn't respond, I explain what happened in gymnastics.

Rebecca lets out a sigh. "I'm not surprised based on what I've seen in the classroom."

I force back my anger. "I don't understand. These girls have been friends since kindergarten. Why have they suddenly turned on Jazz?"

"Every group of children has unique dynamics," Rebecca explains. "Bullying is often a problem. Some years are worse than others."

Staring out the window at the carpool line, I spot Sophia and her entourage piling into one of the mother's Suburbans on their way to gymnastics. I return my gaze to Rebecca. "Are these girls singling Jazz out? Or are they picking on others?"

Rebecca's pained expression tells me how much she cares about her students. "One other little girl."

"Is she black?" I ask.

"Asian," Rebecca says with her lips pressed thin. "Emily and Jazz are the only two ethnic minorities in my class."

"So, it is about race. I suspected it might be. What about Asher?" I ask about the little boy Jazz introduced me to at Dairy Deli.

Rebecca shakes her head. "Asher is in another class. They go to lunch and the playground at different times."

"What am I supposed to do, Rebecca? Homeschool Jazz?"

"That's certainly an option," Rebecca says. "But Jazz is an outgoing child who thrives in a learning environment. Home-schooling her might be detrimental to her development. Pulling her out of school would teach her to run from her problems."

"That's true. Have you spoken with Sophia's mother?"

Rebecca holds my gaze. "I shouldn't be telling you this. But yes, I spoke with Mrs. Carr yesterday afternoon. She denied my accusations. She insisted her daughter would never do such things. When I cited examples, she blamed me for not having control of my classroom."

"She's not my favorite of the moms," I admit. Lori Carr's abrasive attitude has always rubbed me the wrong way.

"You're smart to avoid her. In my experience, mothers who think their children can do no wrong are dangerous. I suggest we give the situation some time, see if it plays itself out."

"That sounds like a logical approach." My knees ache when I rise out of my chair.

Rebecca stands to face me. "You have my cell number. Contact me if you have any concerns."

"For sure. And you do the same. Jazz means everything to me. I hate seeing her unhappy." We pause in the doorway. "Are you a mother, Rebecca?"

She places her hand on her belly. "I just found out. I'm expecting my first child next May."

"Congratulations. You have a gentle way about you. You'll be a wonderful mother. I'm expecting twins in March." A mischievous smile creeps across my lips. "But I haven't told Jazz yet, so please don't say anything."

She drags her fingers across her lips. "Mum's the word. I'm aware of Jazz's history. She's well adjusted for a child who has experienced such loss at such a young age. I attribute that to you. She worships you. Her face lights up when she talks about you."

I watch Jazz traipsing down the hallway, her pink backpack dangling from her slumped shoulder. "The feeling is mutual."

When she sees me, Jazz runs toward me. "Stella! You're late. We need to hurry, or we'll miss our lesson. Did you bring my guitar?"

"Both guitars are in the car." I gesture at the exit, and we walk hand in hand to the parking lot.

Jazz is noticeably quiet on the way to Julius's. I assume she's thinking about her problems at school, but she surprises me when she asks, "Stella, do I have a good singing voice?"

"Of course," I say, because all children sing like angels. Truthfully, I've noticed nothing unique about Jazz's voice.

"You're just saying that. Turn up the radio," she orders.

"Yes, ma'am." When I turn up the volume, she belts out the lyrics to "Love Story" better than Taylor Swift.

When she's finished, I find her in the rearview mirror. "That was amazing. You've been holding back on me."

"I've been practicing singing while playing the guitar." She sticks out her tongue at me. "I'm Billy Jameson's daughter, after all."

I laugh. "I'm Billy Jameson's daughter too. But I can't sing like that," I say as I pull to the curb in front of the guitar teacher's house.

Julius has converted the detached garage behind his house into a studio, a cool He Shed with leather furniture, worn rugs, and a collection of music memorabilia that rivals Billy's. Rounding the side of the house, we find Julius throwing a tennis ball for his chocolate and white collie.

"Aww." Jazz hurries over to them. "Can I play with your dog?"

"She would love that. *After* your lesson."

"What's her name?" Jazz asks, following Julius into the studio.

Julius's brown eyes are warm when he smiles down at her. "Ella. Named after Ella Fitzgerald. Do you know who that is?"

Jazz shakes her head. "Who is she?"

"She *was* the Queen of Jazz. I want you to write a report about her as part of your homework."

"Homework?" Jazz says, aghast. "I get enough of that at school."

Julius gives her a warning look. "There's a lot more to music than playing an instrument."

"Yes, sir," Jazz says, lowering herself to the edge of the sofa with her guitar.

Julius sinks down next to her. "Have you been practicing?"

Jazz grins. "A lot."

Julius relaxes back against the cushions, folding his arms over his chest. "Play something for me."

I'm supposed to participate in the session, but Julius and I have an unspoken agreement that Jazz's instruction comes first. While student and instructor are immersed in the lesson, I get up and wander around the room, studying Julius's collection of framed concert posters and black-and-white photographs. I'm surprised to see my father pictured in several of them.

Thirty minutes fly by. When Jazz's turn is up, Julius asks if I'd like to play, but I decline. "I haven't had a chance this week to practice." Which is a lie, but I refuse to be shown up by at eight year old.

Jazz leaps off the sofa. "Can I play with Ella now?"

Julius sweeps his hand at the open door. "Help yourself."

I write the check for the lesson and hand it to him. "I knew you taught Billy guitar lessons, but I didn't realize the two of you were friends."

"Oh yeah. Billy and I were tight despite the difference in our ages."

"When is the last time you saw him?"

"Good question." Julius rubs his salt-and-pepper scruff. "A decade ago, at least. When his health failed, Billy became something of a recluse."

We move to the door and watch Jazz romping around the yard with the dog.

Julius says, "I was a young man, younger than you, when I first met Billy. I had a jazz band back then. We played many Friday and Saturday nights at the inn. I taught guitar lessons on the side to earn extra money." He inclines his head at Jazz. "Billy was about her age when he started taking lessons. She reminds me a lot of him. She has his eyes."

I smile. "Yes, she does."

"Although it's too early to know for sure, she may have inherited his talent. He was one of the most gifted musicians I've ever met."

I feel a pang of longing for the father I never knew. "She's certainly into it. That guitar has become an appendage of her body."

"I can tell. I hope she keeps up the good work. Which reminds me, I had a young man cancel his lessons." Julius chuckles. "Football got in the way, if you can imagine that. I have a permanent spot for you on Thursdays, if that works."

"Thursdays are great. Can we start this Thursday? Jazz is having a tough time at school. She needs the distraction right now."

Julius looks over at me with furrowed brow. "I'm sorry to hear that. I hope it's nothing serious."

"The little girls she thought were her friends have turned on her. I'm sad to say it appears to be race related."

Julius hangs his head. "That's a crying shame. Racism is all anyone talks about anymore."

"It's none of my business, but have you experienced much prejudice in your life?"

"Not in many years. Not since the riots during the Martin Luther King era." He laughs. "But we live in a bubble in Hope Springs. At least I thought we did. Until now."

Leaving me in the doorway, Julius walks over to Jazz and bends down to pet Ella. They are too far away for me to hear what he says to her. But she beams in response. A warmth floods me, and I feel as though someone is watching over me. I cast my gaze heavenward. Perhaps Billy guided us to his old friend for a reason. Julius Jackson is just the mentor Jazz needs right now.

Later, at home, Jazz lets Angel out of her kennel and takes her outside to potty. I access the Sonos app and click on my Billy Jameson playlist. My father's smooth voice fills the room from the ceiling-mounted speakers. I move over to the window and look out onto the terrace. Jazz is leaning against the knee wall, playing her guitar and singing to an attentive Angel, her ears twitching and tail thumping against the blue stone. I smile to myself. Who said a dog was a man's best friend?

I cross the room and pull up a stool at the kitchen island. I'm staring off into space, lost in thought, when Jack arrives home a few minutes later.

"You're a million miles away. Did something happen?"

I eye the stool next to me. "Sit down and I'll tell you." I explain about my meeting with Jazz's teacher and the things Rebecca told me about Sophia's mother.

"You need to stay as far away as possible from Lori Carr," Jack says. "She's trouble."

My neck snaps as I look over at him. "Why do you say that? Her daughter's been here for playdates dozens of times. You've never mentioned anything about Lori before."

"Because I didn't want my feelings about the mother to interfere with the girls' friendship."

"Tell me what happened. Did you do a construction project for the Carrs?"

"Yep." Jack settles back in his chair. "I remodeled their master bath a few years back. We designed the renovations around this fancy spa tub Lori had to have. But the spa tub was back-ordered, and I suggested we hold off on construction until we received the fixture. But Lori insisted we start right away. So, we gutted the bathroom. Months later, when the vendor informed us they'd discontinued that model tub, Lori became furious. She blamed me, as if I controlled the vendor. She was so rude about it, I refused to complete the job. And she took me to court. The judge ordered me to finish the project. That was the longest month of my life."

I shake my head in disgust. "I honestly don't understand what makes some people tick."

Jack gets to his feet and massages my shoulders. "As I said, stay away from Lori Carr. She'll make your life a living hell. And you don't need that kinda stress. Especially now when you're pregnant with twins."

I hook my arm around him, pulling his face into my neck. "I appreciate your concern, but I'm fine. Better than fine. I feel great. The morning sickness is gone. If not for my rapidly growing waistline, I might forget I'm pregnant."

"But you *are* pregnant." His breath tickles my skin. "And this isn't an average pregnancy. You're carrying *two* babies. And I don't want anything to happen to them or to you."

"Nothing will happen. I promise." I kiss his cheek. "I just hate seeing Jazz having a hard time. I want to protect her."

"Me too. But we can't be with her every waking moment of the day." Jack straightens. "Where is she, by the way?"

"In the backyard with Angel." I crane my neck to look up at him. "Didn't you see her when you pulled into the driveway?"

"No." He looks around the corner into the family room. "Angel's in her kennel."

"She is?" I slide off the stool to my feet and hurry down the hall to the bottom of the stairs. "Jazz! Are you up there?"

When she doesn't answer, I book it up to her room. Several

drawers in the chest are open, with articles of clothing spilling out. And the contents of her backpack—math book, spiral notebooks, and an assortment of pencils—are scattered across the floor.

Returning to the head of the stairs, I yell down to my husband. "Jack! She's not in her room. And her backpack is gone. I'll search the house if you go look for her outside. And be sure to check Cecily's apartment. Jazz knows how to shimmy the lock."

I look under beds and in closets, but Jazz is nowhere to be found. I'm frantic when Jack comes back inside. A solemn shake of his head tells me he didn't find her.

"Should we call the police?" I ask, pacing circles in the kitchen.

"Not yet. Let's think like Jazz for a minute. If she were going to run away, where would she go?"

In unison, Jack and I say, "The inn."

"We need to search the entire property." Jack points at my phone on the counter. "Call Martin and get his people on it."

My hand is on the phone when it rings with a call from Presley. "Have you by any chance seen Jazz? She's missing."

"She's here with me. She showed up on my doorstep a few minutes ago."

"Thank God." I collapse on the barstool. "I was worried out of my mind."

"Jazz overheard you and Jack talking. She knows you're having twins, Stella."

I palm my forehead. "We should've been more careful. Is she very upset?"

"She was. But I calmed her down. She's not upset about the twins. Her feelings are hurt because you didn't tell her."

"She's had so many changes in her life. One baby is enough. I was going to tell her. I wanted to find the right time."

"You don't have to convince me, Stella. I get it."

I reach across the counter for my car keys. "I'll come get her."

"No! Let her stay. She wants to spend the night with me. And I'm fine with it. I'd love the company."

I have a burning need to see Jazz, to make sure she's okay. "What's she doing now?"

"She's upstairs in the nursery, checking out all the baby gadgets."

"Oh good. Hang on a second." Holding the phone to my chest, I turn toward Jack. "Jazz overheard us talking. She knows about the twins."

His chest deflates as he lets out a deep breath. "Poor kid."

"Do you think it's okay for her to spend the night with Presley? Or should we bring her home and talk to her about the twins?"

"She loves Presley. It would probably do her good to spend some time with her."

I return the phone to my ear. "She can stay. But give her a hug and a kiss from me and tell her I love her more than anything."

"Will do. I'll have her home in time to go to school in the morning."

"Thanks, Presley. I'll be here if you need me." I end the call and set the phone on the counter.

I plant my elbows on the counter with face in hands. "We should've told her. What was I thinking keeping something so important from her?"

"No one blames you, Stella. You did what you thought best." Jack massages my shoulders. "Jazz needs to know she's part of the family, no different from the twins. I heard from our attorney today. The adoption will be final the last week in October. Let's do something special to celebrate. We should have a party for her with a few friends and family."

"You're brilliant. I love that idea." I hop off the barstool to face him. "Thank you for loving Jazz as much as I do."

"Are you kidding me? She's an amazing kid. How can I not love her? Besides, she's a part of you."

I place his hand on my baby bump. "Soon, we'll meet *our* babies. They're part of both of us."

He leans in and kisses my lips. "Our family will be complete."

I look up at him. "Complete? No way! We're just getting started. We have this whole big house to fill up."

He wraps his arms around me. "I like the sound of that." He nibbles on my neck. "Since we have the house to ourselves tonight, what say we go to bed early. Like now."

"Yes. Let's," I say, my voice husky with desire.

He scoops me up and carries me up the stairs.

10

PRESLEY

Presley returns to the nursery to find Jazz holding up a onesie. With huge eyes, she looks from the tiny garment to Presley's baby bump. "Your stomach is ginormous. I don't understand how two babies will fit in Stella's belly."

"That's the miracle of childbirth, kiddo. Isn't it amazing? A woman's belly expands as the baby grows. And after it's born, her stomach shrinks back to normal." Presley rubs her hand across her swollen abdomen. She doesn't express her concern about flabby skin and stretch marks.

Jazz neatly folds the onesie back in the drawer and closes it. "Do you think Stella's babies will look alike?"

"That depends. There are two different types of twins, fraternal and identical."

Jazz wrinkles her nose as though she doesn't understand.

"It's confusing. I'll try to explain." Presley leads Jazz over to the bed, and they sit side-by-side on the edge of the mattress. "Sometimes when the mama's egg is fertilized, it divides into two equal halves. Because they are from the same egg, they have the same characteristics. These are identical twins."

"Which means they'll either be boys or girls."

"Exactly. But in the second scenario, the mama's body produces two separate eggs that are fertilized. They can be different genders. Which means you could have both a brother *and* a sister."

Jazz places her hand on her chest. "But I'm the aunt. The babies will be my nieces or nephews."

"Technically. By blood you're the aunt. But when your adoption is final, by law, you'll be their sister. That's pretty cool when you think about it. Not many people get to be both aunt and sister."

"Like Stella is my sister, and she'll soon be my mama," Jazz says.

"Correct. You have unique family dynamics. Which makes your family special."

Jazz's lower lip quivers. "Why didn't Stella tell me we're having twins?"

"Because she didn't want to overwhelm you. Adjusting to one baby is a lot. Having two babies in the house will be chaotic at first."

Jazz swipes at her teary eyes. "How will it be chaotic?"

"Well . . . babies require constant care. They cry a lot, constantly need to have their diapers changed, and need to be fed frequently. But Stella is lucky." Presley leans into Jazz. "She has you to help her."

"Ugh!" Jazz falls back on the bed. "I don't know about this, Presley."

Presley turns to look at her. "You don't know about what?"

"I'm not sure I want two babies."

Presley laughs out loud. "There's nothing you can do about it. God is giving you two siblings because he knows you're going to be an outstanding big sister. The good news is, you'll have plenty of time to get used to the idea."

Jazz is silent as she inspects her surroundings. "Your nursery is cozy. Can I sleep in here?"

"Sure! If you'd like. Or, I have a king bed in my room. You can sleep with me."

"I like it here." Jazz's eyes flutter closed.

Presley nudges her. "Don't get too comfy. We haven't eaten dinner yet. I'll let you decide. We can either have food delivered or we can eat at Jameson's."

Jazz sits up straight and bounces off the bed. "I vote for Jameson's! Can we go now?"

"Sure!" Presley checks her watch. "I can't believe it's seven o'clock. No wonder I'm starving. Let's go." She holds her hand out and Jazz pulls her to her feet.

Presley grabs a light sweater from her room, and they head up the hill to the main building. When Presley adds her name to the waiting list at Jameson's, the hostess says, "It shouldn't be too long."

Presley follows Jazz across the lobby to Billy's Bar, where most tables and all barstools are occupied. "Can we go inside for a minute?" Jazz asks.

"I don't know, sweetheart. A bar is not an appropriate place for a young girl."

Jazz presses her hands together under her chin. "Please, Presley. We won't stay long. I want to see Billy's wall."

"Okay," Presley says, reluctantly. "But only for a minute."

Entering the bar, they skirt the crowd and make their way over to the banquette where Billy's collection of guitars, album covers, and swag from famous musicians takes up the entire wall. No customers are sitting on the banquette, and Jazz climbs on the bench for a better view.

She points at a framed black-and-white photograph. "Look! There's Julius. He's my guitar teacher."

Presley moves in for a better view. Billy Jameson and a handsome black man in his fifties sit on stools, playing their guitars. "Wow! How cool is that? Your guitar teacher used to jam with your father."

"Julius taught Billy to play the guitar when he was my age. Do you think I can be a famous musician when I grow up?"

Presley helps Jazz down off the banquette. "You're one of the most determined people I know, Jazz. I think you can accomplish whatever you set your mind to."

When they return to Jameson's, the hostess shows them to a table on the porch. The sun has begun its descent over the mountains, and a cylinder propane heater protects them against the chill in the air. When the server arrives, they order a pizza to share and two side salads.

When the waitress leaves, Jazz's attention is drawn to the interracial couple and their young children at the table next to them. Dragging her eyes away from the family, Jazz asks, "What color will your baby's skin be, Presley?"

"We'll have to wait and see. He or she may have pale skin and auburn hair like me. Or it may have skin that tans easily like Everett."

"Wait a minute." Jazz sits up straight in her chair. "You mean white people have different colored skin? I thought it was all the same."

"Nope. We're just like African Americans. You have lovely caramel skin while others are deep brown like dark chocolate."

"Sophia doesn't want to be my friend anymore because I'm black. Even though I'm not black, I'm caramel."

Presley places her hand on top of Jazz's small one. "The color of a person's skin isn't important, Jazz. What matters is what's inside, in our hearts and minds. And you have a beautiful heart and a brilliant mind. Just keep being your sweet self, and Sophia will come around."

Sadness falls over her face. "I don't wanna be Sophia's friend anymore. I have a new friend. His name is Asher. He's in the other class, and I don't get to see him very often, but he's also taking guitar lessons from Julius."

"How cool is that! You should invite him over for a playdate. Tell him to bring his guitar, and you can jam together like Billy and Julius."

Jazz considers this. "Good idea!"

Cecily appears with their food. "A little birdie told me my two favorite people were here."

"We're having a sleepover," Jazz blurts.

Cecily appears wounded. "You didn't invite me?"

"You can come." She casts an uncertain glance across the table at Presley. "Is that okay?"

"Of course, it's okay. The more the merrier," Presley says, and winks at Cecily.

Cecily slides into the chair beside Jazz. "Thanks for the invitation, but I can't tonight. I've gotta work late. How about you come to my place for a sleepover on Sunday?"

Jazz comes out of her chair. "Yes! That'd be great. Can Parker come too?"

Cecily's smile fades. "I'll have to check. He may be busy. But we'll do something super fun for dinner. Maybe we'll walk to Lucky's Diner for a greasy hamburger."

"Yay! I love Lucky's." Jazz's expression turns serious. "Did you know Stella's having twins?"

Presley gives Cecily a warning shake of her head, and Cecily takes the cue. "Twins? That's amazing. Aren't you lucky? You're getting two siblings for the price of one." She stands to go. "I'd better get back to work. You two enjoy your dinner." She yanks on one of Jazz's pigtails as she passes. "Congrats on the twins. You'll be the best big sister ever."

A grin spreads across Jazz's face as she bites off the tip of a slice of pizza. While they eat, Jazz quizzes Presley about babies.

By the time they return to the cottage, Jazz and Presley are both exhausted and ready for bed.

Presley asks, "Did you bring your pajamas? If not, you can borrow one of my T-shirts."

Jazz unzips her backpack and pulls out a long-sleeved pink nightgown. "But I forgot my toothbrush."

"That's okay. One night won't hurt. I'll give you some tooth-paste, and you can use your finger."

While Jazz is in the bathroom, Presley quickly changes into her pajamas. Her little houseguest is already in bed, under the covers, when she returns to the nursery. Jazz eyes the book, a worn copy of *The Secret Garden*, resting on her blanketed chest. "Will you read some to me?"

"Will I ever? This is one of my all-time favorites. Are you reading it for school or for fun?"

Jazz moves over to make room for Presley. "Stella reads to me every night. We take turns picking the books. This was her choice."

Presley slides in beside Jazz's warm little body and reads out loud until she hears Jazz snoring softly beside her. Closing her eyes, Presley immediately falls into a deep sleep, waking hours later with a start. She sits bolt upright in bed, raking her fingers through her hair. She was dreaming of crying babies, hers and Stella's and Cecily's. She smiles to herself at the image of Cecily with a baby. She hopes they're still friends when Cecily finally gets married and starts a family.

Presley slips from beneath the covers and goes downstairs to the kitchen for a cup of chamomile tea. Her conversations with Jazz from the previous evening come back to her. Poor kid is obviously struggling. She lost her mother less than a year ago. Her friends are being jerks. The situation with Stella being her sister, soon to be her mother and soon to be having twins must be confusing. If only there was something they could do to let Jazz know how special she is.

The idea comes to Presley out of the blue. She's so excited about the prospect, she has a hard time falling back asleep. She finally dozes off and wakes at daybreak to the sound of little feet pitter-pattering on the hardwood floors. Grabbing her robe, Presley walks out into the hall as Jazz is coming out of the bathroom.

"Did you sleep well?" Presley asks.

Jazz gives her a shy nod. "Can I go home now? I didn't bring any clothes for school."

"Sure! Let me change really quick. You can ride home in your nightgown."

Returning to her room, Presley changes into exercise clothes. When she emerges ten minutes later, Jazz is waiting for her downstairs by the door. Presley texts Stella from the car, letting her know they're on the way over. Stella is waiting for them in the kitchen with a cup of decaf coffee.

Jazz throws her arms around Stella's waist and buries her face in her belly. "Hello, babies! Can you hear me in there? I'm your sister, Jazz. And I can't wait to meet you."

Stella picks Jazz up and twirls her around. "And they can't wait to meet you!" She sets Jazz down and gives her a playful pat on the bottom. "Now run upstairs and get dressed while I fix your oatmeal."

Stella watches her go and turns toward Presley. "You're a miracle worker. What'd you say to her?"

"We talked girl to girl about twins and skin color and how much care babies require. I know a way to cheer her up."

"I want to hear it. Talk to me while I fix Jazz's breakfast." Stella motions Presley to a barstool and goes around the counter, removing a package of oatmeal from a box in the pantry.

Taking a seat at the bar, Presley sips her coffee and sets down her mug. "I realize Jazz's birthday isn't until April, but I think we should have a Halloween party at the farm with a hayride and haunted house. We'll invite the entire second grade. We can recruit some of the staff to be the scary characters and have a meet-the-cast reception afterward with cake and ice cream. Jazz will be the star of the show. And Sophia will be green with envy."

"You're brilliant, Presley. I love the idea." Stella stirs water into the oatmeal and places the bowl in the microwave. "Jazz's adoption will be final the last week in October. Jack and I were talking last night about doing something special to celebrate. We won't call the haunted house an adoption party per se. But we'll make certain Jazz understands the purpose of the party. Question is, do you have time to plan it?"

"I'll make time. Besides, Amelia loves Halloween. She'll be all over this."

Stella lowers her voice at the sound of footfalls on the steps in the hallway. "Don't say anything to her just yet. I want to figure out how to tell her. But I will let her know this is your idea. In the meantime, I'll get to work on the invitations."

Presley stands to go. "And Amelia and I will begin coordinating everything else."

Stella comes from behind the counter to hug her. "You're the best, girlfriend. My sister is a lucky little girl to have a friend like you."

"I'm the lucky one. She's a delight, a really great kid."

And Presley is grateful for the distraction of planning the Halloween party. Anything to take her mind off her rapidly approaching due date and wayward husband.

11

CECILY

On Saturday evening, Cecily is greeting Mayor Hanson and his bubbly wife at the hostess stand when she notices an attractive young woman with golden hair perched at the end of the bar at Billy's, shamelessly flirting with Parker. How dare she! Parker belongs to Cecily. With a jolt of reality, Cecily corrects herself. Parker no longer belongs to her, because she pushed him away.

After showing the VIPs to their table, Cecily passes through the kitchen to her office, slamming the door behind her.

Fiona enters without knocking a few minutes later. "Did you hear about Jazz's Halloween party? I haven't been to a haunted house in years. We're in charge of the food for the haunted house and the reception. How gross would it be for the kids to stick their hands in giant bowls of cold noodles and Jell-O?"

Cecily doesn't look up from the stack of vendor receipts she's studying. "Sounds good."

"I want to make a cool cake for the reception. Maybe a sheet cake in the shape of a haunted house."

"That'd be cool," Cecily says, her eyes on her work.

Fiona jabbers on. "Did you volunteer to be an actor? You and I can be a team. Like Frankenstein and his bride."

"I'm fine with that," Cecily says, making a note on a receipt.

Fiona claps her hands. "Earth to Cecily! You're not listening to me. What's the matter?"

Cecily tosses her pen on the desk and falls back in her chair. "Some bitch is at Billy's Bar, making moves on Parker as we speak."

Fiona drops her smile. "Who's the bitch?"

"I have no clue. Go find out and let me know." Cecily flicks her wrist at the door.

"I'm on it," Fiona says, and charges out of the office.

Cecily calls after her. "She's sitting at the end of the bar nearest the lobby."

Picking up her pen, Cecily tries to refocus on her work, but the image of the girl with the golden hair flirting with Parker keeps popping into her mind. She jumps to her feet. She can't be alone with her thoughts right now. Leaving the office, she wanders around the kitchen, barking orders at her line cooks while she waits for Fiona to come back.

Fiona is gone for nearly forty-five minutes. She returns in a giddy mood.

"What took you so long? It's Saturday night. In case you haven't noticed, we're a little busy around here," Cecily says, spreading her arms at the bustling kitchen.

"You're the one who sent me on a mission. Which I can proudly say I accomplished. The girl in question is Kate, our new yoga instructor. She's beautiful and supercool. The good news is, Parker isn't into her at all."

"Good to know. Now get back to work." When Cecily stomps off toward her office, Fiona follows her.

"Seriously, Cess. Parker loves you. He's clearly miserable without you. Why are you torturing him?"

"I told you. I've sworn off men. He'll find someone else. Someone better suited for him."

"Parker offered to help coordinate the haunted house. He's dressing as a zombie. He told me about a cool costume website." Fiona comes behind the desk. "Let's check it out." When she tries to get at the computer, Cecily shoves her away.

"Look, Fiona. I need to finish these tonight, before we close." Cecily lifts the pile of receipts on her desk. "Besides, I'm not really into Halloween. I agreed to do the haunted house for Jazz's sake. Buy my costume for me, and I'll pay you back. But do it some other time, because there's work to be done in the kitchen right now."

"I understand," Fiona says, and slinks out of the office.

The dinner crowd slowly dwindles, and the last party leaves around ten o'clock. The servers and cooks, eager to get on with their nights, file out shortly thereafter. Her paperwork complete, Cecily doesn't know what to do with herself. This is the first Saturday in months the inn isn't hosting a wedding. She isn't ready to go home. She longs to drink red wine with Parker and discuss life. But, as she feared, she's lost her best friend.

Alone in the kitchen, Cecily leans against the counter, scrolling through her contacts. Amelia has gone on a date with a guy she met on Hinge. She's had enough of Fiona and her talk of Halloween. Presley is too pregnant to have fun. She clicks on Ollie's number. The call goes directly to voice mail. Oh well. She'll go home, put a mask on her face, and watch a rom-com.

She grabs her purse from her office and heads off toward the lounge. She's curious to see who's in Billy's Bar, if the new yoga instructor is still hitting on Parker. She strolls casually by, pretending to be looking at her phone while she checks out the action in the bar. The crowd has thinned, and only a handful of occupants remain. Parker is at the far end of the bar, watching a football game with a rowdy group of guys. The yoga instructor, who hasn't moved from her earlier position, is chatting up a guy standing beside her with his back to the lobby. While she can't see his face, the guy looks a lot like Lyle from behind.

Cecily moves past the bar's entrance, pausing just beyond the doorway to spy on them. The guy leans toward the yoga instructor, propping his elbows on the bar and fingering a lock of her golden hair. It is definitely Lyle! Looking past Kate, Lyle squints in Cecily's direction. She shrinks back against the wall. Her heart pounds. Did he see her? An encounter with Lyle is the last thing she needs tonight.

Cecily hightails it through the lobby to the reception hall and out the front entrance. The night air is cool, and the stars are bright, and she takes her time walking across the street. She's in the driveway, passing Stella's back door, when she hears footsteps running behind her. She spins around to face Lyle.

He stabs a finger at her face. His breath reeks of alcohol, and he slurs his words when he says, "I saw you watching me, talking to Kate. She's a hottie. Admit it. You're jealous, aren't you?"

"Nope. The only thing I feel is relief to be over you. Now, please leave. I have to be somewhere."

When she tries to walk off, he grabs her and presses her against Jack's truck. She lets out a shriek and pushes him away. "Get off of me."

"Come on, Cecily baby. Give me another chance. I don't care about Kate. I love you."

"I said, get off of me." Cecily shoves him harder.

Stella's back lights come on, illuminating the terrace and driveway, and Jack emerges from the house through the french doors. His right arm is bent, his hand gripping a pistol pointed at the sky. He moves to the edge of the terrace. "Cecily, is that you? What's going on out here?"

Cecily crosses the terrace to Jack. "Lyle followed me home. He's had too much to drink."

Lyle tosses his hands in the air. "Since when is drinking too much a crime? What're you gonna do, Jack? Shoot me?"

"Don't tempt me. You're trespassing on private property. And you're clearly very intoxicated." Jack shifts his gaze to Cecily. "Has this happened before?"

She gives him a solemn nod.

"Do you want me to call the police?" Jack asks.

Cecily looks over at Lyle, who is weaving back and forth as he struggles to stand up straight. He's still a teenager, trapped in a young man's body. "That's okay. I'll drive him home."

"Not alone, you won't." Jack digs a set of car keys out of his pocket. "We'll take him in my truck. Come on, buddy. You're going home." Gripping Lyle's arm, Jack marches him over to the passenger side.

Cecily slides into the back seat, giving Jack directions as they drive up Main Street. She smacks Lyle's arm. "I'm not joking, Lyle. This is getting old. If it happens again, I'm calling the police. You need to accept that it's over between us."

Lyle's head falls forward, his chin hitting his chest.

"Is he passed out?" Cecily asks.

Jack risks a glance at his passenger. "Apparently." His gaze shifts to Cecily in the rearview mirror. "This is serious, Cecily. We can drive him to the police station, explain to them what transpired. I witnessed the scene."

Cecily looks away from the mirror, staring out into the campus's dark neighborhood. "Lyle isn't dangerous. He's immature. He needs to grow up."

They pull up in front of the house behind Lyle's truck and another SUV, which Cecily assumes is his roommate's. Jack helps Lyle out of the truck, and they walk him to the door. The knob is locked, and Cecily rings the doorbell. When no one comes, she rings it again and pounds on the door. His roommate comes flying down the stairs. He's shirtless, like last time, but his hair is mussed and there's a fresh hickey on his neck.

Pete throws open the door. "What happened to him?"

"He got drunk and threatened Cecily," Jack says, handing Lyle over to Pete.

"When he sobers up," Cecily says, pointing at Lyle, "give him a message from me. Tell him, if this happens again, I will call the police."

"Understood," Pete says, and closes the door.

On the way home, Jack says to Cecily, who is now riding in the front seat. "You should get a gun."

"No thanks. I'm scared of guns."

"Then here." He opens his console and removes a can of mace. "Keep this with you when you're walking back and forth to the inn."

She takes the mace and puts it in her purse. "Thanks."

"You can call me anytime, day or night. I'm not just your landlord. I'm your friend." He grins at her. "Besides, Stella will kill me if anything happens to you."

Cecily responds with a thin smile. "She would. But nothing's going to happen to me. I've been meaning to ask if you'd install a dead bolt on my door."

"Yes! Of course. I should've done that when you moved in." Jack's brow is pinched in concern for the rest of the drive. Upon their arrival at home, he insists on walking her to the garage. "I never realized how dark it is back here. In addition to the dead bolt, I'm going to install a motion-sensor light and security camera."

"That's unnecessary," Cecily says, halfheartedly. She would feel better having both.

Jack wags his finger at her. "No arguing. Consider it done."

She kisses his cheek. "Thanks, Jack. I owe you one. Maybe we shouldn't tell Stella about this. She already has enough on her plate."

Jack doesn't hesitate. "I don't keep secrets from Stella. Besides, if there's a threat of danger on the property, she should know about it."

Cold dread washes over her. "You're right."

Cecily climbs the stairs to her apartment, waving down at Jack before entering. She leans against the door. Although she truly believes Lyle is harmless, he's a loose cannon right now. And there's no telling what he might do. She's putting Stella and Jazz in danger by living here. But she has nowhere else to go. Staying with Presley or Fiona or Ollie would jeopardize their safety as well. If she and Parker were together, she could move in with him until the situation blows over. She longs to feel his muscular body against hers, to fall asleep in the safety of his arms. But they aren't together. They aren't even friends.

Cecily goes into her room and dives onto her bed. For the first time in as long as she can remember, she cries herself to sleep.

12

STELLA

J ack and I wait for Jazz outside the Sunday school building after church on Sunday. She prefers the children's service in the small chapel over big church. We often go with her to the informal service, but today, we had a visiting minister who delivered an inspirational sermon on forgiveness.

Jazz, the first kid to file out of the building, skips along beside me on the way to the car. "Can I join the children's choir? Practice is after school on Wednesdays. Emily's mom lets her walk over from school since it's so close."

My ears perk up at the name Emily. Isn't she the Asian girl in Jazz's class? "Do I know Emily?" I ask nonchalantly.

"I dunno," Jazz says, hunching her shoulders. "She's in my class at school. The choir lady says I might get to sing a solo in the Christmas performance."

"Did the choir lady hear you sing today?"

Jazz bobs her head. "I sang really loud so she'd notice me. She says I have a pretty voice."

We all pile in Jack's truck. When he starts the engine, country music spills from the radio and Jazz sings along to Miranda Lambert.

Jack looks over at me with eyes wide. "Wow. She does have a nice voice."

I wait until the song ends before lowering the volume and turning around in my seat. "Are you still game for a picnic?" I ask Jazz.

"Yes! Can we go to your friend's farm, Jack? You know, the one with the big field and large stream?"

"You bet," Jack says. "I've already okayed it with Roy. He's out of town this weekend. The farm is all ours. I've already got our fishing gear packed."

Jazz punches the air with both fists. "Yay!"

We stop at the manor house to change out of our church clothes. While Jazz and Jack load the fishing gear in the back of the truck, I pack the food I made earlier into a basket—egg salad sandwiches, grapes, and chips.

Angel jumps into the back with Jazz and we head off. The mood in the car is festive during the twenty-minute drive. When we arrive at the property, Jazz tosses the Frisbee for Angel while Jack and I spread out the blanket and set up our picnic.

"So, Jazz," I say, handing her a sandwich. "Jack and I have some exciting news. Your adoption will be final the last week in October."

Wrinkles appear on her brow. "Do I have to do anything or talk to anyone?"

"Nope. Jack and I will sign the papers, and you will officially be our daughter. We thought we'd celebrate with dinner at Jameson's on Sunday. We'll invite Opal and Brian, of course. And anyone else you'd like to include."

"Hmm." Jazz stares up at the sky. "What about Cecily and Presley and Ollie? And Fiona and Amelia. And Parker, of course. He makes everything more fun."

I laugh out loud. "In other words, we'll invite the entire staff. If all goes as planned, Presley will have had her baby by then and can come." I take a bite of sandwich. "Speaking of Presley, she came up with a great idea. What do you think about having a Halloween party with a hayride and haunted house for your class?"

Jazz pops a chip in her mouth and crunches loudly. "But my birthday is in April."

I cross my eyes at her. "I know when your birthday is, silly. This is just a Halloween party. The barn is perfect for a haunted house, and we're fortunate to have a large spread of land for the hayride. We thought it would be a fun treat for your friends."

Jazz stares at the sandwich half in her hands. "I don't have any friends."

"What about all those people who volunteered to be the scary actors in the haunted house?"

Jazz stops chewing. "Who?"

"Cecily and the others you want to invite to your adoption party."

Her face lights up. "Really? They want to be scary actors?"

"Not only that, they're designing all the props for the haunted house. And Fiona's making a special cake for a meet-the-cast reception afterward."

Jack nudges Jazz with his elbow. "You have to admit that sounds way cool."

"I guess." Jazz stuffs the last bite of sandwich in her mouth. "Is it just my class or the whole second grade?"

"The whole grade," I say.

"Good. Asher can come." She selects the biggest brownie from the Tupperware container. "Can I put the fishing rods together now, Jack?"

"Sure! Just be careful," Jack says.

Scrambling to her feet, Jazz runs over to the truck, lowers the tailgate, and removes the fly-fishing tubes from the bed. Jack and

I watch her twist the pieces of the rods together and thread the line through the metal guides.

"She's getting good at that," Jack says.

"She has an excellent instructor. You're a natural-born teacher, Jack, and Jazz is eager to learn. I love how the two of you enjoy your time together on the water."

"Just wait until I have a son. I'm going to teach him to clean my guns, bait my hooks, and change the oil in my truck."

I roll my eyes. "All your dirty work, in other words."

"Isn't that what kids are for?" Jack gobbles down the rest of his sandwich and crawls over to me, stretching out on the blanket and resting his head in my lap. "Have you talked to Cecily today?"

"No, why?" I ask, smoothing back his wiry chestnut hair.

Jack closes his eyes and folds his hands over his chest. "Lyle followed her home last night from the inn. He was drunk and caused a scene in our driveway. Cecily and I drove him home. I think maybe we should call her to check on her."

"Wait! What?" I lift Jack's head out of my lap. "Are you saying Lyle was stalking her?"

Jack sits up. "Yep. And apparently it's not the first time."

I lift my fingers to my lips. "We need to do something about the doorknob on her apartment."

"It's on my list for first thing in the morning. Along with installing a motion-sensor light and a security camera. I'm worried about Cecily." Jack tucks a strand of my unruly mahogany hair behind my ear. "But I'm worried about you and Jazz more. I'm wondering if maybe she should find other housing until this problem with Lyle goes away."

"Other housing? Are you kidding me? Where do you suggest she live?"

"My first thought was Cottage Row," Jack says.

I give my head a vigorous shake. "No way! It's too secluded."

"You could comp her a guest room. She'll have plenty of security at the inn."

"Never mind the inn is booked solid for at least two weekends in October." I furrow my brow. "Wonder why she isn't staying with Parker."

"I wondered that too. I didn't mention Parker last night, and she didn't bring him up."

"Cecily is my best friend. If she's not safe in her apartment, she can move into the manor house with us."

Jack considers this option. "That's not a bad idea. You should mention it to her."

"I will." I give Jack a gentle shove. "Jazz is waiting for you. Go catch some fish while I call Cecily."

"Yes, ma'am," Jack says and scurries off.

I click on Cecily's number, and she answers, slightly out of breath, on the third ring. "Cecily, are you okay?"

"I take it Jack told you about last night. You don't need to worry about me. I'm fine." I hear hard sole shoes on pavement and the slamming of a car door.

"It doesn't sound like you're fine. Why don't you move into the house with us until this thing with Lyle blows over?"

"I appreciate your concern, Stella, but I can take care of myself."

When I hear her car engine start, I ask, "Are you going somewhere?"

"I'm going to talk to Lyle, to warn him if he doesn't leave me alone I'm calling the police."

Alarm creeps up my spine. "You shouldn't go alone. Wait and let Jack go with you."

"I don't need Jack to fight my battles for me." She pauses, and when she speaks again, her tone is softer. "That doesn't mean I'm not thankful for what he did last night."

"What's going on with Parker?"

"Thanks to Lyle, Parker and I are not currently speaking."

Getting to my feet, I pace back and forth beside the blanket. "Cecily, this isn't cool. You need to do something about him. Do you want me to talk to Martin, to have him banned from the inn?"

"That's not a bad idea. Although it might piss Lyle off and make matters worse. We don't need to ban him from the inn, but we can put Martin on alert, so that he is on the lookout for Lyle creeping around the grounds."

"That would make me feel better." A breeze sends chills across my bare arms. "Be sure to call me after you talk to Lyle."

"So, you're my mother now?" Cecily asks in a sarcastic tone.

"Someone needs to look out for you, Cecily."

She lets out a sigh. "I know. And I'm grateful to you and Jack. I'm just in a rotten mood. I'm so angry at Lyle. I want to kill him."

"Don't do that! He's not worth going to jail over."

"Don't worry. I have no intention of going to jail."

I pocket my phone and go to Jack's truck for my sweatshirt. Stretching out on the picnic blanket, I roll up the sweatshirt and place it under my head. When I hear Jack fussing at Angel to get out of the way, I call her over to me and we snuggle together. The warm sunshine makes me drowsy, and I soon drift off to sleep. The sound of Jazz's squealing wakes me sometime later.

Angel and I hurry over to the stream where Jazz is dancing on her toes in excitement while Jack removes the fly from the mouth of an enormous mountain trout. "Can we keep it?" Jazz asks.

"No. But you can hold the fish, and Stella will take your picture." Jack places the fish in Jazz's hands and shows her how to hold it.

I snap at least a dozen photos of Jazz with the fish before Jack helps her return it to the water.

"Let me see," Jazz snatches my phone from me. "Will you post it on Instagram?"

"Get your fishy hands off my phone." Laughing, I take the phone away from her. "I don't have cell service out here. You can look at the pictures later, and we'll post one together when we get home."

Jazz retrieves her rod. "Come on, Jack. Let's catch some more."

When Jazz and Jack return to fishing, Angel and I go for a long walk around the farm. Angel is barking up a tree at a squirrel, and I'm admiring a field of sunflowers when Cecily calls me to report about her confrontation with Lyle.

"He was cutting the grass when I got there," Cecily says. "He acted like it was no big deal. I'm not even sure he remembers it. He made a point of telling me he has a date with Kate, our new yoga instructor, tonight. Should I warn Kate about him?"

"Good question. If you say anything to her, she might accuse you of being the jealous ex."

"You make a good point, Stella. Anyway, if I'm lucky, they'll hit it off and Lyle will stop harassing me."

"Fingers crossed." I make a date to have coffee with Cecily this week before hanging up.

I return to the stream to learn Jazz and Jack have caught three more fish each. An exhausted Jazz falls asleep on the drive home. It's nearly six o'clock when we arrive. Jazz is feeding Angel, and I'm helping Jack unload the truck when I receive a call from Jazz's teacher.

"Sophia Carr has accused me of dropping the f-bomb in class," Rebecca says. "I've been suspended, pending an investigation."

My mouth hits the counter. "Hold on a sec. Did she actually say the F word?"

"She said I cursed, that I used the really bad word that starts with *f*. I never use that word. I would certainly never say it in front of children. But Principal Murphy is taking Sophia's word over mine despite my exemplary track record."

I drop to the barstool. "Why would he do that?"

"Because he's tight with Sophia's mother. Lori Carr is president of the parents' association. Last year, she raised enough money to replace all the playground equipment."

"I see."

"I'm fighting the charges. In the meantime, the class will have a substitute. Which brings me to the main reason I'm calling. Delores Ramsey is an inappropriate choice for second graders."

I grip the phone tighter. "How so?"

"Let's just say she isn't a warm and fuzzy person. Our classroom dynamics are challenging enough with Sophia ruling the roost. I've warned Mrs. Ramsey about the situation. She'll either put Sophia in her place or she'll take her side. Which could be devastating for Jazz and a few others."

My stomach turns and bile rises in my throat. "Okay. Thanks for the heads-up, Rebecca. Let me know if I can help you. And take care of yourself. Your baby's health comes first."

I end the call and slam my phone down on the counter. Spinning around in my seat, I stare out the window at Jazz and Angel playing tug-of-war with a dog toy in the backyard. I debate whether to tell Jazz about the substitute tonight, as we've had such a pleasant day and I hate to ruin it. I'll wait and tell her on the way to school in the morning. No sense making a big deal about it. Who knows? Jazz might even hit it off with Mrs. Ramsey. But a nagging feeling in my gut warns me that won't happen. I sense instead that the situation in Jazz's second grade class is about to go from bad to worse.

13

OLLIE

Ollie feels herself spiraling deeper and deeper into depression. Her anxiety is crippling. She can't eat or sleep or perform a simple task like reviewing minutes from the staff meeting she'd missed on Friday. A meeting she missed because of a panic attack that set in minutes beforehand. She texted Stella, explaining she wasn't feeling well, and went home where she spent the afternoon in bed under the covers, hiding from the world she's no longer sure she wants to live in. Stella has been amazingly understanding about her situation. But Ollie hates taking advantage of her boss's good-heartedness. If she doesn't get a grip soon, she's liable to fall off the cliff. And no one will be there to catch her. Her parents are dead. Her only sibling is in jail for killing them.

Ollie sees her therapist twice a week. Dr. Grant is pressuring her to go on antidepressants. But Ollie wants to manage her emotions without medication. Although lately, her coping mechanism—exercising away her anxiety—isn't helping. She's come to terms with her parents' deaths. Accepted that her brother is a murderer. But her primary source of anxiety—the brutal reality that she's all alone in the world—plagues her twenty-four seven.

Ollie's lost the only home she's ever known. The vineyard, the land that is as much a part of her as her own skin, will soon belong to Sergio. While she loves the friends she's made in Hope Springs, the wellness center gig is just a job. She doesn't feel challenged. She isn't working toward a promotion. She's just hanging out in limbo, living in a tiny apartment with bare furnishings. Money is the only thing she has plenty of. But she doesn't feel right about spending her inheritance when her parents aren't here to watch her enjoy it.

Ollie returns her attention to the meeting report. She reads the bulleted notes over and over, retaining no information. Swiveling around in her chair, she stares out at the mountains, at the leaves on the trees beginning their transition from green to yellow, orange, and red.

Lost in thought, she's startled when Kate barges into her office without knocking. The new yoga instructor helps herself to the chair in front of Ollie's desk and begins rambling on about the class schedule.

"I can't believe we're not offering a sunrise session. The sun coming up over the mountains is breathtaking. I saw it with my own eyes this morning. The lawn might be soggy, but the end of the pier would be ideal. What do you think of having a water yoga class, either in the pool or the hot springs at sunset?"

Ollie folds her hands on her desk. "First, Kate, you can't just barge into my office without knocking. I could've been in a meeting."

"Oops. Sorry," Kate says, pressing her fingers to her tight lips. "We had an open-door policy at my old job."

"And we have one here as well. As long as the door is open, which mine definitely was not."

Kate rises from her chair. "I'll come back another time."

"No. Sit back down. Let's finish the discussion, since you started it. I like your ideas for sunrise and sunset sessions. If you'll write up the description, including the times and locations, we'll highlight the classes in the daily newsletters we leave in our guest rooms during turndown service."

"Cool! I'll do that," Kate says, bobbing her head, her golden ponytail dancing around her shoulders.

"You might also talk to Presley and Amelia. We have weddings booked most weekends this fall. Our brides may want to organize special sessions for their bridesmaids."

Kate's swinging ponytail slows. "What's Presley like? I can't believe she's married to Everett Baldwin. I'm sure you've heard the rumors about his affair with Audrey Manning?"

Ollie has heard the rumors about Everett. But her allegiance is to Presley. "I pay little attention to social media, and I don't listen to gossip."

"Of course you don't. Presley's your friend." Kate sits back in her chair, as though settling in for a chat. "What about that Cecily girl? What's she like? I went out with her ex last night. He seems like a nice guy."

Irritation crawls across Ollie's skin. "Cecily is not a *girl*, Kate. She's on the short list of up-and-coming chefs in the country. As for Lyle, I'd be careful if I were you. Cecily ended their engagement after he cheated on her." She cocks her head to the side. "As the saying goes, once a cheater always a cheater." Ollie gets a warped sense of satisfaction watching the color drain from Kate's face. "I trust you can see yourself out."

Kate jumps to her feet and bolts for the door.

"And next time, knock," Ollie calls out as she watches her go.

Kate has no sooner cleared the doorway when the walls close in on Ollie. Her chest constricts, and she has trouble breathing. Grabbing her purse, she leaves the wellness center and heads toward the employee parking lot. Ollie needs a release, but she lacks the energy to exercise. She's growing more lethargic by the day. She even drove to work this morning, which she usually only does in stormy weather.

She peels out of the parking lot in the ten-year-old Camry she purchased when she first came to town. Even the car feels wrong. She's always owned sporty vehicles like Land Rovers and 4Runners. Her current life is a bad fit. She's been in Hope Springs since April. Why is she just figuring this out now? Because she'd been desperate. And Stella had welcomed her with open arms.

Ollie heads up Main Street, passing the college and continuing onto the rural highway leading deeper into the mountains. She usually drives toward Charlottesville on these mind-clearing outings. Today, she's in the mood to explore. Perhaps that's a good sign. Perhaps that means she's ready to move on with her life.

She rolls down all the windows and cranks the volume on her classic rock station. As she travels the winding mountain roads, her mind wanders. Where would she go if she left Hope Springs? She loves her new friends. But they have significant others and babies on the way, while she has zero personal life. After her disastrous marriage, romance is the last thing on her mind.

Ollie enters the tiny town of Lovely, home to the famous Love-Struck Vineyards. Love-Struck is the largest and most well-known vineyard in Virginia. They host more weddings than Hope Springs Farm, although their wines only receive mediocre reviews.

Several blocks of charming shops and eateries line Magnolia Avenue, the main thoroughfare in town. Ollie parallel parks in front of Ruthie's Diner. She'd skipped breakfast, and she's suddenly famished. The interior is what one might expect of a small-town diner, seating upholstered in red pleather and black-

and-white checked flooring. Taking a seat at the lunch counter, she peruses the laminated menu and the specials offered on the wall-mounted chalkboard. The offerings are traditional with a surprising modern flair.

An attractive middle-aged woman with blonde hair piled high on her head arrives to take her order. She's wearing a black polo, khaki pants, and a name tag that identifies her as the owner. "What can I get you, hon?"

"I'll have the coconut curry chicken soup, please. And a glass of sweet tea."

"Excellent choice." Ruthie scrawls the order on her pad. "I'll get that for you right away." She disappears through swinging doors and returns a minute later with the soup and tea. "I haven't ever seen you before. Are you from around here?"

Ollie sinks her spoon into the soup and blows on it. "I'm from Hope Springs. I was out for a drive when hunger pangs got the best of me." She tastes the soup, and experiences the combination of curry and chicken explode in her mouth. "This is delicious. How long have you been in business?"

"I've worked here most of my life. When I purchased the place a few years back, I changed the name from Love's Diner to Ruthie's." Ruthie snickers. "We have enough love in this town already."

Ollie laughs. "I noticed. Why is that?"

"The Love family established the town in the late eighteen hundreds. They were a large family, obviously enamored with their name."

"What's the population of the town?" Ollie asks, crumbling saltine crackers into her soup.

"Around a thousand, give or take a few. There ain't much here. Tourism is our primary industry. We have a bank and a Food Lion. All the other businesses are designed to take money from the tourists. We have to go to Hope Springs to see the doctor or to shop at Walmart." Ruthie leans back against the counter, folding her arms over her chest. "But we like it this way. Us locals are a close-knit bunch. We don't mind strangers, as long as they only stay a few days."

Ollie sips her tea, working hard not to purse her lips at the sweetness. "I assume there's plenty of lodging for said tourists."

"I wouldn't say plenty. We only have one hotel, the Red Robin Inn, and it's booked solid every single weekend. The same family who owns Love-Struck Vineyards owns the inn. When they renovated a few years back, they fancied the decor. Now they call themselves a boutique hotel. The tourists love the changes. But the makeover set the bar higher for the rest of us. All the eateries are sprucing up, renovating their dining rooms and making their menus more current."

A customer at a table behind Ollie catches Ruthie's attention, and she excuses herself. While she finishes her soup, Ollie watches Ruthie mingle with the locals and tourists. She has a warm and easy way about her that makes Ollie want to be her friend.

After paying her tab, Ollie strolls down both sides of Magnolia Avenue. She categorizes the town as casually elegant. It reminds her of many of the small towns in the wine country.

Ollie returns to her car, but instead of heading back to Hope Springs, she continues on in the opposite direction. Five miles outside of town, she spots the impressive brick gates announcing the entrance to Love-Struck Vineyards. On a whim, she turns down the winding tree-lined road and drives about a quarter of a mile until a stately stone building comes into view. She gets out of the car and follows the signs to the tasting room, a large reception room with worn hardwood floors and a stone fireplace. Patrons are gathered around four long counters, critiquing the wines as they taste.

Locating an empty stool, Ollie informs the server she'd like to sample the white wines. While she waits for her setup, she observes the other staff members as they pour wines and answer questions. They're mostly young and clean-cut and knowledge-able about wine.

When her parents were alive, Ollie traveled all over the world with them, tasting wines. She finds the wines clean but shallow. *Meh* would be her word to describe them. But what Love-Struck lacks in the quality of their wines, they make up for in facilities. The winery is a true wedding destination with immaculate grounds—offering widespread lawns for cere-monies or tented receptions—as well as multiple banquet rooms providing the flexibility to host a variety of events from intimate gatherings to large formal functions.

When Ollie leaves Love-Struck, she ventures farther into the countryside. Just beyond Love-Struck is another much smaller vineyard with a For Sale sign posted out front. A black split-rail fence borders the vineyards along the highway and down the driveway leading to a gray farmhouse with black shutters and a yellow front door. Past the farmhouse is a large barn, much like the one at Hope Springs Farms. Pulling off the road near the entrance, she gets out of the car without turning off the engine. She walks over to the fence and inspects the fruit on the grapevines. The plants are some of the healthiest Ollie has ever seen. Curious to know more about Foxtail Farm, she tugs her phone out of her wallet and searches the internet for the realty company. Her connection is slow, but she finds the basic infor-mation. Privately owned. Over a hundred acres of vineyard, including the three-bedroom farmhouse, barn, and winery. Which she can't see from the road but assumes is behind the barn. Despite the price being reasonable, the property's been on the market for eighteen months. There's a reason such a steal has been on the market for so long. She snaps a few photographs of the entrance and gets back in her car.

Ollie can't stop thinking about the vineyard on the drive back to Hope Springs. In her office at the wellness center, she researches Foxtail Farm. The same family has owned the property since the late eighteen hundreds. Two decades ago, Foxtail produced several notable blends of red wines, one even winning an award, but she can't find any recent information regarding the brand.

In two weeks' time, once she completes the sale of her family's vineyard in California to Sergio, she'll have the resources to make an offer on a small vineyard like Foxtail. The idea scares the heck out of her, but she's also intrigued. The thought of building a future for herself gives her the first rays of hope she's experienced in a very long time.

14

PRESLEY

Presley, waiting for Rita to finish with a guest at the check-in counter, spots Lucy emerging from the elevator and crosses the reception hall to greet her. "I called you several times yesterday, to see if you wanted to go for a walk." She'd been worried when Lucy never responded to her voice message.

Lucy hesitates, refusing to meet Presley's gaze.

Presley tilts her head as she looks more closely at her mother. "Lucy? Is something wrong? Are you avoiding me?"

"No! It's nothing like that." Lucy straightens, holding her head high. "You might as well know, I went to Raleigh for the weekend."

Presley draws her head back. "What for?"

Lucy's lips part in a mischievous smile. "To see Levi. We've been talking on the phone a lot lately. On the spur of the moment, he suggested I come for the weekend. And so I did."

Presley's eyes pop. "Wait a minute. Are you saying you had a romantic weekend with Levi?"

In a snippy tone, Lucy says, "I didn't stay with him, if that's what you're thinking. I booked a hotel room. But we had a blast.

We went out to dinner on Friday night and to the UNC football game on Saturday."

Presley experiences a pang of jealousy. She would've appreciated the opportunity to see Levi again. "Does this mean you two are seeing each other now?"

Lucy's face reddens. "We definitely have chemistry. He's a super nice guy. I can't believe I ever accused him of date-raping me."

Presley stares down at the ground. "Did he ask about me?"

"Of course. He wants to come to Hope Springs soon to see you."

"Did he talk about his children?" Presley asks in a hopeful tone.

"Not much," Lucy says. "I get the impression he wants to keep his two lives separate for now."

Presley lets out a breath she didn't know she'd been holding. "I guess I don't blame him. I can see where he might need some time to adjust to the situation."

Rita comes from behind the check-in counter with her purse slung over her shoulder. "Sorry that took so long. We should go. Are you ready?"

"Yep. My car is out front." Presley turns to Lucy. "Wanna come to my checkup with us?"

Lucy looks at her watch. "I wish I could. But I have a meeting with a wine distributor in an hour. Let me know how it goes."

"Will do," Presley says, and the women part ways.

Presley says little during the short drive to the medical office building. How random would it be if her biological mother and father got married after all these years?

"You're awfully quiet today," Rita says as they walk through the parking lot to the building. "Is something on your mind?"

"I'm fine," Presley says, shrugging off her concerns about Lucy and Levi. "I can't believe my due date is almost here. You don't have to come to these appointments with me. I'm a big girl. I can take care of myself."

Rita holds the door open for her. "As your birthing coach, it's my duty to come to the appointments. Besides, I want to be here for you."

"You're the best, Rita. I don't know how I'll ever thank you."

Rita smiles as she punches the elevator button. "We're family, Presley. This is what we do for one another."

They wait thirty minutes before being called to an examining room. After performing the pelvic exam, Dr. Franklin announces, "You're forty percent effaced."

Cold dread descends upon Presley, and her teeth chatter. "But I'm not due for another two weeks."

The doctor places a blanket over Presley. "Don't be alarmed. The baby might not come for another two weeks. Maybe even three. Every woman is different."

"Okay," Presley mumbles, fighting back tears.

"You need to tell Everett," Rita says on the return trip to the inn. "He's the baby's father, regardless of whether the two of you are together."

Regardless of whether the two of you are together. This sounds so ominous, like she and Everett are divorced. Is that where they're headed?

"I'll call him tonight." As much as she dreads talking to him, Presley doesn't have a choice. As the baby's father, Everett has a right to know her body is showing signs that she may be going into labor soon.

Back at the inn, Presley goes to the event planning office and works for the next three hours without taking a break. Her doctor said she could go another three weeks. But Presley can't bank on that. She needs to get everything ready to hand over to Amelia to handle while she's on maternity leave.

Darkness has set in by the time she leaves the office. With no food in the cottage, she goes to Jameson's for a bite to eat. She's sitting alone on the porch, enjoying Cecily's salad special, when Kate plops down in the chair opposite her.

"I'm glad I ran into you. I need to ask you a question. I've been seeing Lyle." Kate rambles on without breathing. "I've only been on one date with him, actually. But it went well, and I think he'll ask me out again. But I'm worried about what Cecily might say. What do you think, Presley? Should I go out with him again?"

Presley feels dizzy from listening to Kate. "It doesn't matter what I think." She spears a forkful of salad. "If you're worried about Cecily, talk to her."

Kate flicks her golden hair over her shoulder. "I figured you'd say that. Problem is, Cecily scares me. I haven't met her yet, but some of the staff in the wellness center say she's mean."

"Cecily isn't mean. She's . . ." Presley stops herself. Cecily can totally be mean sometimes, especially when she doesn't like someone. "She's just Cecily. Reserve your opinion until after you get to know her."

Kate plants her elbows on the table. "I wish I were as cool as you. Look at you! You're getting ready to have a baby, and your husband is having a very public affair with a drop-dead gorgeous woman, but you don't even seem to care. Maybe you don't care. Do you care, Presley? Are you and Everett still in love?"

Presley's hand shakes and the fork clatters to her plate.

Kate clamps her hand over her mouth. "Oh gosh! I'm so sorry. I didn't mean to upset you. I'm notorious for sticking my foot in my mouth."

Presley can't tell whether the tears glistening in Kate's blue eyes are genuine or whether she's a brilliant actress. She's appalled when Kate prattles on.

"I mean, you're this supercool event planner. You're gorgeous and so put together. You don't seem like the type to let a man walk all over you."

Presley freezes with the fork in midair. "My marriage is none of your business. If you'll excuse me."

She pushes back from the table and takes her half-eaten salad to the kitchen. "Can I get this to go?" she asks, handing her salad plate to Cecily.

"Sure." Cecily studies her. "Are you feeling okay? You look kinda pale."

"I just had an encounter with our new yoga instructor. I'd avoid her if I were you. She was asking about Lyle. I think she's interested in him."

With a grunt, Cecily says, "She can have him."

Presley follows Cecily to the counter by the window and watches as she transfers the contents of her plate to a take-out container.

"Here," Cecily says, holding the container out to her.

"Thanks." Presley turns toward the back door. "I should go out this way, so I don't run into Kate again."

Cecily steps out onto the porch with her. "Are you sure you're okay? Did Kate say something else to upset you?"

Presley looks away, staring out across the lawn. "She accused me of letting Everett walk all over me. Is that what everyone thinks, Cecily? That he's cheating on me, and I'm letting him get away with it?"

"You shouldn't worry about what people think, Presley. You know Everett better than anyone else."

Presley's shoulders sag. "So, you do think he's walking all over me."

"Not at all. Your friends love you. And we support you." Cecily embraces her. "Don't worry. One of these days, Everett's going to show up out of the blue with a legitimate explanation for his behavior."

"That's what I think too." Presley pushes her away. "I'm trying to wrap up some things before the baby comes. If possible, I'd like to meet with you and Stella before the end of the week."

"I'm available at your disposal. Just let me know when."

Presley leaves and walks back to her cottage. She's finishing her salad at the kitchen table when a Google alert appears in her inbox. She set her alerts to notify her of breaking news relating to Everett. She clicks on the alert, linking her to a celebrity gossip website. The top post in the newsfeed claims Everett has mysteriously canceled the rest of his tour.

Presley skims the article. The sudden announcement comes from his manager, Wade Newman, who offers no explanation regarding the cancellation.

Picking up her phone, she calls both Everett and Wade. When neither answers, she leaves urgent messages, asking them to get in touch with her immediately.

Presley dumps the rest of her salad into the trash can and goes upstairs. She changes into her pajamas and gets into bed with a legal pad and pen. While she waits for Everett and Wade to call, she makes a long list of things she needs to accomplish before the baby comes.

At midnight, when there's still no word from Everett or Wade, she sets her phone on silent and turns out the light. To hell with Everett. He must know she's worried sick about him. Clearly, he no longer cares about her. And Presley has let him walk all over her for long enough.

15

STELLA

Jazz bursts into tears when she climbs into the car after school on Tuesday. When I ask her what's wrong, she cries harder and sobs hysterically on the way home. Nothing I say soothes her. She doesn't quiet down until she buries her face in the thick fur at Angel's neck.

I sit cross-legged on the floor beside them. "Hey, kiddo. Are you ready to tell me what happened?"

Jazz sniffles. "Mrs. Ramsey hates me. She's so mean."

I stroke her hair. "Can you be more specific?"

"She accused me of talking during class and made me stand in the corner. I wasn't the one talking. Sophia and Kelley were. They sit in front of me."

"I'm not a teacher, but I imagine it's hard to keep track of everything going on in a classroom at once. Did you defend yourself?"

"I tried. But she accused me of lying. And that's not all. We're supposed to do a report on a famous person who's made a difference in our lives. I picked Billy, but Mrs. Ramsey said it couldn't be a family member, even if the family member was famous. When I suggested Simone Biles, she told me I had to report on

Rosa Parks. How could Rosa Parks have made a difference in my life when I don't even know who she is?"

My pulse quickens, and I warn myself to tread lightly until I have the facts. "I agree. That doesn't make much sense."

"Mrs. Ramsey hates me because I'm black."

Is it possible this is true? Or is Jazz being hypersensitive to the race issue. "What makes you say that?"

"Because she's nice to everyone else."

"You don't know that for sure, honey."

Jazz jumps to her feet. "Yes, I do, Stella! Whose side are you on?"

Jazz has never talked to me this way. She's never given me any reason to doubt her either. "Calm down, sweetheart. Of course, I believe you." I pull Jazz into my lap and gently rock her back and forth. "Have any of your friends mentioned the Halloween party? The invitation went out last week."

"Mrs. Ramsey says we can't talk about the party."

"Why? We invited everyone in the whole grade."

Jazz shrugs her tiny shoulders. "I told you she's mean."

My mind races as I decide how to handle the situation. Tugging my phone out of my pocket, I click on Opal's number. She doesn't answer but calls back right away. "I need to run an errand. Any chance you can stay with Jazz for a while?"

"Sure thing, sweet girl! I'm at the farm, painting. I'll be there in a few."

Jazz cranes her neck to look up at me. "Where are you going?"

"Back to the school, to talk to your principal."

"Good! Tell him to fire Mrs. Ramsey."

I laugh. "I wish I had that kind of authority."

"You do, Stella. I've seen you with your staff. You're mean in a nice way." Jazz gets up and pulls me to my feet. "Let's go wait out front for Opal."

Jazz takes off down the hall with Angel leaping along beside her. She's throwing the Frisbee for the dog when Opal arrives a few minutes later. I quickly explain the situation to my grandmother and head back to the school.

The principal's administrative assistant informs me he's in a meeting and is likely to be awhile.

"I'll wait. This is important," I say, and sit down in the chair nearest the door marked Principal Murphy.

Five minutes later, the door swings open and a striking Asian woman emerges. She's tiny, only five-feet tall, with porcelain skin. I look into her chocolate eyes, and she smiles warmly at me.

The woman moves on and Principal Murphy appears in the doorway. In a gruff voice, he says to me, "I understand you're waiting to see me. My time is limited, but I can give you a few minutes."

I size up the principal as he ushers me into his office. He's about my age with a poof of brown wavy hair on top of his head and black converse high-tops on his feet. Tall and thin, he has a goofy way about him, and I can easily imagine him playfully interacting with his young charges. But he's all business when he asks, "What can I do for you?"

"I have concerns about the second-grade substitute teacher, Mrs. Ramsey." I pause, inhaling a deep breath for courage. "I'm worried Jazz is being singled out because of her skin color."

His brown eyes glare at me from behind thick, black-framed glasses. "That's a serious allegation, Mrs. Snyder."

"I'm aware. But let me explain." Seated opposite him at his desk, I tell him about the homework assignment and Mrs. Ramsey's refusal to let Jazz write about our father, insisting instead that she write about Rosa Parks.

"That seems reasonable to me," Murphy says. "Rosa Parks is an important figure in our nation's history."

I gawk at him. "Did you not hear what I said?" I stab his desk with my finger. "Mrs. Ramsey asked the children to report on a famous person who has impacted their lives. Jazz has never heard of Rosa Parks until today."

Murphy folds his hands on his desk. "How long has this child been in your care, Mrs. Snyder?"

I squirm under his intense scrutiny. "Since December. Why does that matter?"

His lips part in a smug smile. "You haven't been a parent for very long then. Are you even her legal guardian?"

I force back my anger. "Yes, I'm her legal guardian. I'm her sister. Both her parents are deceased. And I will soon be her adoptive mother. I'm within my rights to request you look into the matter."

"I get countless complaints every day. I have to pick the ones that concern me the most. This one does not make the cut."

I shoot out of my chair. "Then you leave me no choice but to seek guidance elsewhere." I flee his office before he can question me about the elsewhere. Since I have no clue where that elsewhere might be.

Rushing past the administrative assistant, I hurry down the hallway and out the double doors into the warm autumn day. I'm surprised to find the Asian woman waiting on the covered sidewalk.

She steps in line beside me. "Aren't you Stella Snyder?"

I glance over at her as I continue toward the parking lot. "I am. And you are?"

"Grace Dunn, Emily's mother. My daughter talks about Jazz all the time."

I slow my pace. "Right. Emily from church. They're going to be in choir together. Jazz has spoken of her as well."

"Are you here because of Mrs. Ramsey?" Grace asks.

"Yes." I stop walking and turn to face her. "Are you?"

Grace removes a folded sheet of computer paper and snaps it open for me to see red marks covering the page. "This is Emily's history report about George Washington, the one Rebecca assigned the kids over the weekend. The substitute told Emily to check her facts. I've been through these comments with a fine-tooth comb. There are no errors in this report."

"What did Murphy say when you showed him this?"

"He defended Mrs. Ramsey," Grace says. "She doesn't normally teach second grade, as if that makes it okay."

I take the paper from her, scanning the marked sentences. "This is basic information about George Washington that everyone should know."

"Why are you here? If you don't mind me asking," Grace says, stuffing the math paper back in her oversized bag.

When I repeat the story of tonight's homework assignment, Grace's eyebrows hit her hairline. "That's blatant racial discrimination. Parents are extremely upset about what happened to Mrs. Wheeler. Not just current second-grade parents, but parents whose children had Rebecca as their teacher in the past."

"What do you suggest we do about it?" I ask.

"We need to get all concerned parents together for a meeting."

"We?" I pat my chest. "As in you and me?"

She nods. "Yep."

The thought of addressing a group of angry parents terrifies me. "If you're aware of Jazz's history, you know I'm new to the parenting job. I feel grossly unqualified to lead the charge."

"On the contrary. You're just the right person. Commerce in this town was withering on the vine before you moved here. By renovating and expanding the inn, you've revitalized tourism. You're a celebrity in Hope Springs. Everyone knows and respects you."

I consider what I have to contribute. "We have several conference rooms. How about if I arrange the meeting space, and you do all the talking?"

"Deal. We need to strike while the iron is hot. How does tomorrow evening at eight sound? You book the room, and I'll get the word out."

I check my phone's calendar. There are no conferences at the inn this week. "I can make that happen."

Grace and I exchange contact information and walk together to the parking lot. "Don't worry, Stella. Rallying parents on issues concerning their children is easy. Especially issues concerning their education. I'll come up with a plan of attack tonight and be in touch tomorrow morning."

I watch Grace scurry over to her car, one of those boxy Ford wagons I never cared much for but somehow seems appropriate for this tiny energetic woman. She's a dynamo, the right person to organize our mission. I have no clue what I've gotten myself into, but I feel oddly comforted in knowing Grace is in charge.

I arrive home to find Jazz performing a guitar concert for Opal and Angel on the terrace, her troubles at school seemingly forgotten. She doesn't mention Mrs. Ramsey again until the next morning when, in the car on the way to school, she begs me to let her skip. My heart breaks. I'm tempted to let her stay home and spend the day doing fun stuff with her at the inn. But giving in would set a dangerous precedent. Although it takes every ounce of my resolve, I insist she attend school.

"You have to face this, Jazz," I say as I inch forward in the carpool line. "You're growing up. Learning to confront obstacles instead of shying away from them will make you a stronger person."

Jazz looks at me with wet eyes. "Like you?"

"I've encountered my share of problems. My mothers always made me face them head on."

She swipes her eyes with the backs of her hands. "Okay," she says and opens the car door.

"You have choir practice to look forward to this afternoon. You and Emily be careful walking over to the church. Be sure to look both ways when you cross streets. I'll pick you up after choir practice."

She flashes me a grin, which improves my spirits as I head over to the inn. I make my morning tour of the grounds before settling in at my desk to catch up on paperwork. My stomach is growling for lunch when I receive a call from Grace.

"I've created a network of students and parents," she says. "Word is out about Rebecca's suspension. Parents are furious. We should expect a large crowd at the meeting tonight."

"Should I provide refreshments?"

"That's unnecessary. I imagine most everyone will have just finished dinner. I'm working on the agenda."

"What else can I do to help?" I ask.

"If you have time, you can draw up the petitions. I'm sure you can find templates online. We'll need two of them. One for the broader group of parents requesting the school board conduct an immediate investigation into Sophia Carr's allegations against Rebecca Wheeler. And the second for our second-grade class, petitioning for a new substitute teacher. Turns out we're not the only parents having trouble with Mrs. Ramsey."

"I'm on it."

A beeping sound on Grace's end of the line signals an incoming call. "This is Rebecca," she says. "I'll see you tonight at eight."

A few minutes later, I receive a text from Grace. *Murphy is giving Rebecca pushback regarding her request for an immediate investigation. He claims it could take months. Liar.*

Jazz is on top of the world when I pick her up from choir practice. On the drive home, she sings to me about her new friends and the Christmas cantata, which will take place on Christmas Eve. She volunteered to perform a solo. The competition is steep, but she thinks she has a good chance.

When Jazz asks if she can take voice lessons, we carry on a conversation in song.

Clearing my throat, I sing, "If I can find a voice instructor."

"Mrs. Nichols, the choir lady, teaches voice lessons on the side."

"I'll look into it." I laugh out loud. "Can we talk normal now?"

Jazz giggles. "Yes! You have a pretty voice, Stella. I'm not the only one who inherited musical talent from Billy."

"Ha. You're sweet to say that, but I have little musical talent." We pull into the driveway, and I turn off the engine. "How were things at school?"

Tears well in her eyes, and she says in a curt tone, "Fine. I don't wanna talk about it." She climbs out of the car and hurries inside.

My mind is on the upcoming meeting as I make Jazz's dinner and help her with her homework. When Jack arrives home from work at six thirty, I leave early for the inn as I want to make certain everything is in place for the meeting. I'm an innkeeper. I can't in good conscience allow guests to enter my hotel without offering them some sort of provisions. I've arranged for a self-serve station with an assortment of cookies, hot apple cider, and coffee—both decaf and regular. When I arrive, the staff is setting up the station outside the conference room.

Parents begin arriving a few minutes before eight. I introduce myself as they enter the conference room, and I make many new acquaintances. It's standing room only by the time Grace climbs onto a chair and brings the meeting to order. In a clear and loud voice, she explains the allegations against Rebecca Wheeler. The parents appear outraged. Two attorneys —a man and a woman—volunteer to deliver our request to the school board.

Most of the parents depart, leaving only the parents from Jazz's second-grade class. Noticeably absent are the parents of the girls who were once Jazz's friends. We drag chairs into a circle for a more intimate conversation. Some moms talk openly about what's been happening to their children, both boys and girls, since school reconvened back in September. Apparently, Jazz and Emily aren't the only ones being bullied.

One mother says, "Sophia is the leader. The others are learning the behavior from her. And she's learning it from her mother."

A father chimes in, "Who is the president of our parents' association. Go figure."

"Let's get rid of her," someone suggests.

Grace says, "Let's focus on getting Rebecca Wheeler reinstated first," which is exactly what I'm thinking.

By the time we disperse nearly two hours later, we've exchanged contact information and created a group in the popular GroupMe app. I'm comforted by our numbers. We aren't friends, although we may be by the time this is all over. But we're bonded by our common goals, each of us as invested as the next.

It's almost ten o'clock when I get home, but Jack is waiting up for me. He pulls me down to the sofa beside him. "I'm worried about Jazz. She wasn't herself tonight. I can tell something is bothering her, but she refused to talk about it."

I nestle closer to my husband. "Same thing happened in the car on the way home from choir practice."

He kisses my forehead. "She asked if she could stay home from school tomorrow. But I told her absolutely not."

I let out a sigh. "She tried that with me this morning. She has to face this, no matter how difficult." I rest my head on Jack's shoulder. "Who knew parenting would be so difficult."

Jack chuckles. "Imagine what it'll be like when we have double the trouble."

16

CECILY

On Friday afternoon, Cecily meets for two hours with Presley and Stella at a table on the porch at Jameson's. Cecily, growing bored with Presley's extensive to-do list for upcoming events, says in a joking manner, "Don't worry, Presley. The inn won't fall apart while you're on maternity leave."

Stella gives Cecily a warning look. "Seriously though, Presley. Why are you so worried when you have a team of event planners?"

Presley wears a concerned expression. "Our *team* of event planners comprises two new hires. Amelia's doing a great job, but she's still green, and her attention to detail isn't up to my standards yet."

Stella closes the folder of papers Presley gave them. "I'm certain Amelia will rise to the occasion in your absence. Nonetheless, I promise to stay on top of things."

Presley hands them one last list. "You should have this just in case. But Jazz's Halloween party is the one event you don't have to worry about. Amelia has that buttoned up tight. How are the RSVPs looking?"

"Almost everyone in the second grade is coming," Stella says.

"That's exciting." Presley closes her iPad and slips it into her purse. "Those kids will have a blast. Who knows? Depending on how things go, I may be there."

Concern crosses Stella's face. "What aren't you telling us, Presley?"

Presley sits back in her chair with her tea. "No one can predict when the baby will come. It could still be weeks. But my cervix is effacing. I want things in order, just in case."

Cecily says, "You don't need to worry about us. We've got you covered. Your biggest problem is your baby's missing daddy. Do you have any clue where he is?"

Stella cuts her eyes at Cecily, and Cecily glares back at her. "What? The entire world knows about Everett's mysterious disappearance."

"You could be a little more sensitive," Stella says. "If Presley wants us to know about Everett, she'll tell us."

Presley looks away, staring out at the mountains. "There's nothing to tell. I've left many messages for Everett *and* his manager. Neither has called me back. I feel like a fool for believing in him when he's being such a jerk. But my intuition tells me he's in trouble. I don't understand why he's shutting me out. Maybe he doesn't want me to worry about him with the baby on the way. Nothing makes sense anymore. For now, all I can do is focus on bringing this baby into the world safely."

Stella reaches for Presley's hand. "Everett will eventually surface, hopefully with a logical explanation. In the meantime, you have plenty of support from everyone here. Jack and I are right across the street if you need anything night or day."

Presley gives Stella a sad smile. "I'm fortunate to have you. And Rita and Lucy as well."

Cecily checks her phone for texts. She's furious at Everett for putting Presley through hell. Her attempts at reaching out to him these past few days have also been fruitless. She slams her phone back down on the table. "We should talk about the weather." She locks eyes with Stella. "Are you worried about this tropical storm?"

Presley furrows her brow. "I'm out of the loop. What storm?"

"Hurricane Riley plowed into the Louisiana coast yesterday," Cecily explains. "The remnants are expected to hit the mountains of Virginia over the weekend."

"I heard about Louisiana," Presley says. "But I didn't realize the storm was headed toward us."

"I've been watching the forecast closely. We're supposed to get heavy winds and rain during the overnight hours on Saturday." Stella presses her hands together under her chin. "I'm praying we get through the Newman wedding before it hits."

Cecily crosses her fingers. "Fortunately, it's an afternoon wedding."

Stella says, "Maintenance will be on standby. As soon as the bride and groom leave, they'll take down the tents and store outdoor furniture in the barn."

Cecily stands. "Speaking of the bride and groom, I have a rehearsal dinner to host." She kisses each of her friend's cheeks before returning to the kitchen where her line cooks and wait staff are in full swing.

For the next several hours, Cecily is on her feet, offering assistance wherever needed. Around eight o'clock, she returns to her office in search of her cell phone. But it's not on her desk where she's certain she left it. She wakes up her computer and accesses the FIND MY app, which positions her iPhone near the barn. Strange. She hasn't been outside on the grounds today. Did someone steal her phone? With all the coming and going in the kitchen this evening, anyone could've snuck into her office and taken it.

She grabs the flashlight she keeps in her bottom desk drawer for emergencies and slips out the back door, hurrying across the road to the barn. With head bowed and eyes cast downward, she's scanning the ground for her phone when Lyle appears from nowhere. He startles her, and she drops the flashlight.

He waves her phone at her. "Looking for this?"

"Give me that!" She grabs at the phone, but he holds it over his head, out of reach. "You jerk! Why did you steal my phone?"

"It's the only way I could get your attention. You can have it back after we talk."

"Talk about what, Lyle?"

"About us. Give me another chance, Cess. I miss you." Stuffing her phone in his back pocket, he comes at her, pinning her to the side of the barn with his body pressed against hers. She tries to fight free, but he's too strong. He shoves his hand under her shirt and tugs her bra above her breasts. When he pinches her nipple, she yelps, and he clamps his mouth over hers, thrusting his tongue between her teeth. Much to her surprise, he tastes like peppermint, not booze. The reality hits with a jolt. He's sober. He planned this. He's going to rape her.

She stills herself, letting him rub his erection against her leg until he comes. His body goes limp against hers, and she shoves him away. She snatches the flashlight up from the ground and clomps him over the head with it.

"Ouch! Damn it, Cecily. That hurt."

She thrust her hand out. "Give me my phone, Lyle."

He slaps her phone in her hand. "I hope you learned your lesson, Cecily. If you won't give me what I want, I have no choice but to take it from you."

Cecily races back to the kitchen. She slips in without being seen and locks herself in her office. Collapsing in her chair, she inhales and exhales until her breath steadies. She rests her head against the back of the chair as she replays the scene. Her nipple still smarts, and her lips are bruised. He's got a lot of nerve. *If you won't give me what I want, I have no choice but to take it from you.* She was lucky tonight. He easily could've raped her. Next time he will.

She accesses her contacts and clicks on Lyle's mother's cell number. When she answers, Cecily blurts, "Margaret, this is Cecily."

"Cecily! Good to hear your voice." Margaret pauses a beat. "Or is it? Last I heard, you and Lyle were broken up. Is there a problem?"

"Unfortunately. Lyle damn near raped me tonight. I should call the police, except he obviously has a problem, and I don't want him to lose his job." The sensation of Lyle's erection against her leg rushes back to her. "On second thought, I'm wasting my time talking to you. I'm calling the police."

"Wait! Cecily! Don't do anything rash."

Cecily holds the phone away from her ear while she chokes back the string of expletives on her tongue. "I'm not being rash, Margaret. This isn't the first time. Lyle's been stalking me. I've given him fair warning."

"Let me talk to him. I can convince him to leave you alone."

Lyle adores his mom. If anyone can get through to him, Margaret can. That's why Cecily called her. "You do that. But I'm warning you, if he comes anywhere near me again, I'm calling the police *and* his boss. In that order."

"We wouldn't be having this discussion if you hadn't broken his heart," Margaret says in an accusatory tone.

Anger surges through Cecily. "He cheated on me, Margaret."

"I...uh..."

Cecily lets out a sigh. "You don't know, do you? I figured Lyle wouldn't tell you the whole story. Truth is, we're not suited for each other. I'm grateful we figured it out now. We saved each other a lot of heartache down the road."

"You saved yourself," Margaret snaps. "You were never worried about Lyle's feelings."

"Contrary to what you think, Margaret, this hasn't been easy for either of us." Cecily ends the call without saying goodbye.

Cecily folds her arms on the desk and rests her head on top. Lyle tried to rape her. He's a psychopath. How did she miss the signs when she was engaged to him? She yearns to go home to her apartment, to crawl beneath the covers in her bed and sleep for a year. But she's safer here, in her kitchen, her kingdom, amongst her people.

Cecily stays at the inn late and arrives early the following morning. The day passes in a whirlwind of preparations for the Carpenter wedding. She spends the evening hours rushing back and forth between the tent and the kitchen, making certain the reception runs smoothly. Around eight o'clock, she goes to the walk-in freezer for a box of sausages for tomorrow's breakfast. Ten minutes later, she's still in the freezer, staring at the items on the shelves, having forgotten what she came for, when she hears Parker's voice behind her. "Cecily, are you okay?"

She spins around, her hand against her racing heart. "I was fine until you sneaked up on me." The frigid air makes her shiver, and she wraps her arms around herself.

He presses the back of his hand against her cheek. "You're freezing. How long have you been in here?"

His touch sends a different kind of chill down her body. "Only a minute. I was looking for this." Grabbing a box of sausages, she brushes passed him and exits the freezer for the kitchen.

He follows her over to the counter at the window and stands close while she washes her hands. "Are you and Lyle back together?" he asks in a low voice, almost a whisper.

Cecily jerks her head up. "Hell no! Why would you think that?"

"He was in Billy's a couple of nights ago, bragging about how he'd won you back. He told me he was thinking of asking you to marry him again."

Cecily's eyes narrow. "You're a bartender, Parker. You should know better than to listen to drunk talk."

"That's the thing though, Cecily. Lyle wasn't drinking."

The little hairs on her neck stand to attention. "Then he's delusional, because we are definitely not getting back together. Ever."

Parker turns Cecily toward him. "I'm sorry I pressured you, Cecily. I should've given you more time. But I miss you like crazy. Can we please go back to being friends?"

Cecily hesitates. It would be so easy to walk into his arms. She longs to be with him, as both friends and lovers. But she refuses to drag him into her Lyle drama. "Now is not a good time for me. I'm going through some stuff."

He tilts his head to the side as he stares down at her. "That doesn't sound like a no."

She smiles up at him. "Definitely not a *no*. Just not right now."

"Yes!" He punches the air. "There's hope!"

His adorable smile melts her heart. "I need time, Parker."

"I understand. And I won't rush you. But I'm here for you if you ever need to talk." He kisses her cheek before leaving the kitchen.

The feel of his lips on her skin is like a memento—a reminder that the sooner she can get rid of Lyle, the sooner she can begin her relationship with Parker.

Cecily removes a fresh tray of sushi from the refrigerator and returns to the tent where she remains until the bride and groom leave the reception around ten. Clouds have built in ahead of the approaching storm, but the rain and wind hold off. As the dwindling crowd migrates toward the main building, her staff clears empty trays and strips table linens while the maintenance crew breaks down furniture.

Stella calls Cecily around eleven. "I've been glued to the Weather Channel all night. The storm hasn't weakened as much as they predicted. There's a tornado warning in effect until five tomorrow morning. I'm afraid we're in for a rough night. How are things there?"

"Coming along. They're taking the tent down now."

"I just tried to call maintenance, but no one answered. I hate to create more work for you, but we need to move the furniture in from the porch at Jameson's. Have them stack it on one side of the dining room, so we can use the other side for breakfast tomorrow."

"What about serving a to-go style breakfast buffet in the lobby?" Cecily suggests.

"I like that idea even better. The guests will understand, given the circumstances. And it's less work for your staff."

"We may be short-staffed anyway, depending on how bad conditions get."

"True. You're welcome to stay with us tonight, Cecily. We've set up makeshift beds in the basement. It's not glamorous, but I think we'll be safe."

"Thanks, but I'm exhausted. I'm gonna crawl in bed and sleep through the storm."

"You know where to find us if you change your mind. If you get scared, I'll send Jack for you."

"Thanks. Let's hope it doesn't get that bad."

Cecily slips her phone in her pocket and returns to work. It's eleven thirty by the time the maintenance staff finishes securing the inn to prepare for the storm. Cecily is crossing the street on her way home when the first gush of wind rustles her hair, and a few raindrops splatter her face. She increases her pace. The manor house is lit up like a stadium with lights beaming in the windows, both upstairs and down. The home looks warm and cozy and safe. If she weren't so tired, Cecily would stop in for a glass of wine.

She continues on to the garage, dragging herself up the stairs. The door is unlocked. Did she forget to lock it when she left for work this morning? And the apartment is dark. The lamp beside the sofa that is set on a timer to stay on all night is off. That's odd. The manor house still has power.

There's a flick of a cigarette lighter across the living room in the adjacent kitchen. Lyle's face appears in the dim glow. With a maniacal grin, he says, "Welcome home, darling."

17

OLLIE

A few minutes after midnight, Ollie and Kate are making their way up from the wellness center, their raincoat hoods pulled tight over their heads to protect them from the driving rain, when Presley calls to them from her cottage porch. "Do either of you have cell service?"

Ollie and Kate dart across the lawn to the porch. They pull their phones out of their coat pockets, but neither have service. "The storm is getting bad fast," Ollie yells over the howling wind.

Presley doubles over, her face pinched in pain.

Kate watches her with concern. "Are you in labor?"

Presley waits for the contraction to pass. "Yes! The early stages." She slowly straightens. "I stayed at the reception until the bride and groom left. When I got home, I went straight to bed. I woke up an hour later to pee, and my water broke. You just witnessed my first contraction. It's too early for me to go to the hospital, but I was going to call my doctor to check in."

A strong gust of wind sends them cowering against the house. They hear a loud cracking sound as the top of a pine tree snaps off and crashes to the ground near the porch.

Kate walks Ollie and Presley to the door. "You two wait inside. I'll run over to the main building to see if they have phone service."

Before they can stop her, Kate leaps off the porch, hurdles the fallen tree, and sprints over to the stone steps leading to the main building.

Presley watches Kate's retreating back. "She doesn't know who to call if the phones are working."

"She can at least find out if the phones are working." Ollie holds the door open for Presley. "Let's get inside before another tree falls."

Presley and Ollie stand at the window, staring into the inky night. "You should go home, Ollie. I'm fine here by myself."

Ollie looks sideways at Presley. How can she be so calm when she's about to deliver a baby? Never mind her husband has mysteriously disappeared. "I'm not leaving you, Presley. Besides, I can't get home, even if I wanted to. Kate and I walked to work this morning. We had no clue we'd have to stay so late. But we got caught up in preparing for the storm."

"Have you heard an updated forecast?"

"It hasn't changed. They're still predicting strong winds and rain." Ollie, to avoid alarming Presley, doesn't tell her about the tornado warning. "Is your bag packed?"

"Ready and waiting." Presley gestures at a small rolling suit-case parked beside the door.

"Can I get you something to drink?"

"I'm fine. But help yourself. I have some juices in the fridge and a selection of tea bags."

Ollie would prefer a glass of red wine, but she'll have to settle for tea. She's in the kitchen, waiting for her lavender tea bag to steep, when Kate bursts through the front door. Ollie drops the tea bag in the trash and returns to the living room with her mug.

Kate sheds her sodden raincoat by the door, dropping it on the floor. "No one has cell service, and all the landlines are down. The wedding-turned-hurricane party is in full swing in Billy's Bar. Parker is pouring drinks as fast as he can. That security guy . . .what's his name?"

Presley turns away from the window. "You mean, Martin?"

"He's the one. He says trees are down all over town. Apparently, the ground is saturated from above-average rains this summer."

"That makes sense," Ollie says. "We did have a lot of rain."

Kate continues, "Martin says we're better off waiting out the storm here. I checked with the night desk agent, but there are no rooms available in the main building. There's good news, though. I asked the crowd in Billy's if there were any doctors in the house." She waves a soggy business card. "No doctors, but I found a nurse practitioner—an OB/GYN nurse practitioner."

Relief crosses Presley's face. "That's awesome."

Kate consults the card. "Her name is Maggy McKinney. Since this is your first baby, she thinks you'll probably make it through the night. But she gave me her room number and said for us to wake her if we need her."

Presley's face tightens as her hand flies to her belly. When the pain passes, she drops her hand to her side. "We should try to get some sleep ourselves. I have a spare bed in the nursery, if you two don't mind sharing."

"I think we should stay down here in case another tree falls." Kate circles the downstairs. "Are there any rooms in this house without windows? You know we're under a tornado warning."

Ollie glares at her. "I wasn't going to tell Presley about the tornado warning."

Kate lets out a huff. "Duh. She needs to know, so we can be prepared."

"She's right. We do need to be prepared." Presley surveys the living room. "We're probably safer in here than anywhere. We can pull the sofa away from the wall and build a fort behind it. Let's get the pillows and comforters off the beds upstairs."

Ollie and Kate retrieve the bed linens while Presley gathers flashlights and candles. They've no sooner huddled behind the sofa in their cozy cocoon than the power goes out. Presley lights a pillar candle, placing it in the center of their makeshift bed.

"Do you know if the baby is a boy or a girl?" Kate asks.

Presley shakes her head. "But I have a feeling it's a boy."

Kate ponders this. "That makes sense. Only a boy would be so inconsiderate as to be born during a hurricane. What're you gonna name him?"

Presley plucks a down feather out of the comforter. "I was going to call him Rhett, after my husband. But the way he's been acting, Everett doesn't deserve to have his son named after him."

Ollie and Kate exchange a look, but neither dares question Presley about the trouble in her marriage.

"What if it's a girl?" Ollie asks.

"Maybe Ava or Layla. I haven't given it much thought. But I really don't think it's a girl. I have a sixth sense about certain things."

Kate scrunches up her face. "What do you mean?"

"I refer to my special intuition, my heightened instincts, as my people reader."

Kate sits bolt upright. "Cool! What does your people reader say about me?"

Another contraction saves Presley from having to answer. When it passes, she rests back against a mountain of pillows. Her face is soft in the candlelight. Despite the trouble in her marriage, she loves this baby very much. Ollie says a silent vow to make certain Presley gets the care she needs.

Presley and Kate doze off and on during the ensuing hours, but Ollie never closes her eyes. With the power out, the cottage soon becomes stuffy. But they can't open the windows because of the storm. She listens for storm noises from outside—the sound of falling trees or, God forbid, the approach of a tornado. She goes often to the window, but it's too dark for her to see past the limbs of the downed tree beside the porch.

Ollie thinks a lot about her future during those lonely hours. She's thirty-six years old. The odds of her having a family decrease with every single day. While she's never really wanted children, she yearns for more than a dead-end job and a tiny apartment. An image of Foxtail Farm comes to mind. She hasn't stopped thinking about the vineyard since her trip to Lovely last week. The proceeds from the sale of her family's estate in California are now burning a hole in her money market account, so why not tour the property? As soon as things are back to normal after the storm, she'll call the realtor and set up an appointment.

18

CECILY

Cecily bolts for the door, but Lyle is too fast for her. He was a three-time All-American lacrosse attackman in college. He's adept at maneuvering his way through tight spaces to score goals. Taking her by the arm, he uses the cigarette lighter to guide them as he marches her back across the room to the kitchenette. He hooks an arm around her neck to prevent her from squirming while he lights two candlesticks on the small, round table.

"You're hurting me, Lyle! I can't breathe."

"You're fine. If you don't stop complaining, I'm really going to hurt you." He grabs coils of rope off the kitchen counter and forces her down in the chair, tying her legs together and her wrists to the arms of the chair. He stuffs a red bandana in her mouth, tying it tight behind her head, and then digs her phone out of her coat pocket, smashing it on the counter with her meat cleaver.

"I have a surprise for you." He sweeps his arm at the table where two places are set for dinner with placemats, china, and flatware. "I cooked dinner for you, the chicken chowder you love so much. Remember, I made it once before. I was flattered the renowned chef, Cecily Weber, actually complimented my cooking."

Lyle takes his bowl to the stove and fills it with soup. He returns to the table, sitting down opposite her and slurping soup from his spoon. "But sorry. You're not getting any dinner tonight. I have to punish you. You've been a very naughty girl."

Cecily lets out a string of expletives, but her words come out as groans.

"You're wasting your energy. I can't understand a thing you're saying with the gag in your mouth." He points his spoon at her. "I had to silence you. You left me no choice. I've been trying to talk to you for weeks, but you won't listen." Hanging his head, he spoons more soup into his mouth. "Why'd you tell my mom all those lies about me? I'm not stalking you, Cecily. I'm trying to apologize."

He opens a bottle of red wine, fills his glass, and sits back in his chair. "I made some mistakes. I underestimated how much your job means to you. But I can be the husband you want. See." He lifts his soup bowl and sets it back down. "I can have dinner on the table when you come home from work. I can be all those things you want me to be. If you'll give me another chance."

He sips the wine and wipes his lips with the back of his hand. "I love you. And I know you love me. I truly believe we can make our relationship work." His face goes dark. "You really hurt me when you cheated on me with Parker. Although I can forgive you since we were broken up at the time. If you promise not to do it again. Do you, Cecily? Do you promise not to cheat on me again?"

"You cheated on me first," she yells, but the words are garbled. Cecily warns herself not to argue with him. He's a deranged lunatic. She's terrified of what he has in store for her. Perhaps if she doesn't agitate him, he won't rape or kill her.

He drains the rest of the wine and refills his glass. "You broke my heart when you ended our relationship," he says and rambles on about their breakup.

Cecily tunes out the sound of his voice, listening instead to the storm raging outside—the wind howling through the eaves and the scraping of tree branches against the window. She racks her brain for a way to escape. Best she can tell, he doesn't have a weapon. But he's far stronger than she.

Lyle drinks and pours until the bottle is empty, and he's visibly drunk. He leaves the table and goes to the refrigerator, rummaging for more wine. But there is none. "Don't you have any booze in this dump of an apartment?"

Lyle is slamming cabinet doors when she hears footfalls on the steps outside. There's a knock on the door's window behind her, and a beam of light falls across the floor beside her. Cecily screams for her life. Lyle, his instincts impaired by alcohol, is slow to react. By the time he realizes what's happening, Parker has broken down the door and exploded into the apartment.

Parker tackles Lyle to the floor, and they roll around, crashing into the sofa and overturning the coffee table. A loud cracking sound from outside is followed by a deafening roar as a large oak tree falls on top of the garage. Parker rolls off of Lyle a split second before a tree branch smashes through the window. A piercing scream fills the apartment as the branch pins Lyle to the floor.

Parker scrambles to his feet and hurries over to Lyle. "Dude, are you okay?"

"Hell no, I'm not okay! Get me outta here."

Parker tries unsuccessfully to rescue him from beneath the tree. "We need help." Parker removes the gag from her mouth and unties Cecily from the chair. "Go get Jack! Tell him to bring a saw."

Cecily descends the steps two at a time and races up the

driveway to a darkened manor house. She pounds on the mudroom door as she yells for Jack and Stella to help her.

A disheveled Jack finally comes to the door. "Cecily! What is it? Has something happened?"

"There's been an accident. A tree fell on my apartment and broke through a window. We need your help. Lyle is trapped. Parker wants you to bring a saw."

Confusion crosses Jack's face, but he doesn't question her. He grabs his raincoat and stuffs his feet into his work boots. As they start off down the driveway, Jack calls out against the wind, "I'll grab the saw from the garage and meet you upstairs."

Cecily gives him a thumbs-up and flies up the stairs to her apartment. Parker is kneeling on the floor, attempting to console a hysterical Lyle.

She drops to her knees beside Parker. "Can you tell where he's hurt?"

Parker shakes his head. "I can't tell if he's screaming in pain or freaking out because he's trapped."

Cecily stretches out on her belly with her face pressed to the floor. She can see Lyle's face, the fear in his eyes and blood streaming from a gash in his temple. "Try to calm down, Lyle. We're gonna get you out of here. Jack's on his way with a saw. Where are you hurt? Can you feel your fingers and toes?"

Lyle screams, "Yes! I can feel my fingers and toes. My whole body is in pain."

They hear Jack on the stairs, and he appears in the doorway, pausing to survey the damage. "Good Lord." He enters the apartment and kneels down beside the tree. "Hang in there, Lyle. We're gonna get you out in a minute, buddy."

Parker and Jack walk around the tree, assessing the situation from all directions. "Best I can tell, only one branch is holding him down," Parker says.

"I see that." Jack crawls into the mangled tree branch and begins sawing.

When the heavy branch detaches from the tree, Parker lifts it off of Lyle and drags it across the room. The men gingerly slide Lyle out, and Jack crouches down next to him to evaluate his injuries. Aside from the gash on the side of his face, Lyle's left arm is bent at an unnatural angle, and he's complaining of pain near his rib cage.

"An ambulance is out of the question," Jack says. "I'll have to drive you to the hospital myself."

"No way!" Cecily says. "You're staying here with Stella and Jazz. Parker and I can take him in my car."

Jack doesn't hesitate. "Okay. I'd rather not leave Stella and Jazz alone in the storm." He tugs his keys out of his pocket. "Take my truck. There'll be more room for him in the back seat."

Cecily takes the keys from him. "How will we get Lyle down the stairs?"

"We'll have to carry him," Parker says.

Parker and Jack help Lyle to his feet. Lyle shrieks in agony as Parker gingerly lifts him onto his shoulder and starts down the steps.

Cecily grabs her purse and follows on his heels.

Hope Springs is a war zone with fallen trees and downed power lines. Parker makes several detours, and the trip to the hospital takes twice the normal time. When he pulls to the curb in front of the emergency room, Cecily hops out and hurries inside. Despite the late hour, the emergency room is slammed with people who endured injuries in the storm.

Cecily approaches a nurse at the check-in desk. "A tree fell on my friend. He's seriously hurt. I need help bringing him in."

"Hang on a sec." She barks orders into a phone, and a minute later, three hospital workers in blue scrubs appear with a gurney. Cecily leads them out to the truck where they load Lyle onto the stretcher and whisk him away.

Cecily waits by the entrance while Parker parks the truck. When he joins her on the sidewalk, he opens his arms, and she walks into them. "You saved my life. How did you know I was in trouble?"

"I could tell you were upset about something when I saw you in the freezer earlier. I thought about you all night. I knew I wouldn't be able to sleep until I checked on you. Since the phones were out, I decided to stop by your apartment on my way home."

Cecily rests her head on his chest. "I'm glad you came when you did."

He kisses her hair. "I love you, Cecily. I understand if you don't love me back. But I can't keep these feelings to myself any longer."

She looks up at him. "I do love you, Parker. With my whole heart. Lyle's been stalking me, and I didn't want to drag you into my problems."

A smirk tugs at the corners of his lips. "Mm-hmm. Your stubbornness almost got you killed. Are you ready to report the rat to the police?"

Cecily hesitates. "I'll report him to his mother. Let her deal with him."

Parker holds Cecily at arm's length. "He could've killed you tonight. You have to press charges."

"He needs a mental hospital, Parker. Not a jail cell."

Parker studies her with intense blue eyes. "You're serious about this?"

"Dead serious," she says with chin high. "And don't try to talk me out of it, because I won't change my mind."

A sexy smile spreads across his lips. "Then I'm appointing myself your protector."

"After what happened tonight, I won't say no to having a bodyguard. Especially one with benefits." Hooking an arm around his neck, she pulls his face to hers and presses her lips against his.

The kiss stirs something deep inside of Cecily, and she yearns to surrender to her passion. But she can't until she's certain Lyle is out of danger. Drawing away from Parker, she touches her finger to his lips. "Can we save this for later?"

In a husky voice, he says, "For you, I'll wait forever. Although I hope it doesn't take that long."

The doors slide open and a young doctor in blue scrubs and a white coat emerges from inside the waiting room. "Excuse me, Miss. Are you here with Lyle Walsh?"

Cecily turns to face him. "I am."

"We're taking him in for emergency surgery to stop internal bleeding. We don't yet know the extent of the damage. Are you the next of kin?"

Cecily's stomach knots. "I'm his friend. His parents live in Connecticut. I'll call them."

"That would be great. The surgical waiting room is on the second floor. Someone will update you as soon as we know more," the doctor says and disappears inside.

Cecily searches her bag for her phone. "Ugh. I forgot. Lyle destroyed my phone. I don't have his parents' contact info."

"We need Lyle's phone. I assume he had it on him when the tree fell." Taking Cecily by the arm, Parker ushers her into the emergency room and finds an empty chair for her. "Wait here while I find a nurse to check Lyle's possessions for his phone."

The reality of the situation bears down on Cecily while she waits. *Internal bleeding? What if he dies?*

Five minutes later, Parker returns with the phone and Cecily places the dreaded call.

Lyle's mother answers on the first ring, expecting to hear her son's voice. "Lyle! How's your weather, son? I've been worried sick."

"Margaret, this is Cecily. I'm sorry to say there's been an accident." Cecily explains the events of the evening, leaving nothing out. "He's in surgery now. The doctor says he has internal bleeding."

Cecily hears both fear and anger in Margaret's tone. "This is all your fault, Cecily. If something happens to my son, I hold you personally responsible."

"Your son held me hostage tonight, Margaret. No telling what he would've done to me if Parker hadn't saved me." Cecily casts a soft glance at Parker sitting next to her. "Lyle is mentally unstable, Margaret. He needs psychiatric help. If you won't be responsible for him, I'll have no choice but to call the police and press charges."

Margaret sighs heavily. "That won't be necessary. I'll get a flight out as soon as possible. In the meantime, keep me updated on his condition. Coincidentally, why are you calling from Lyle's phone?"

"Because he smashed mine with a meat cleaver."

19

PRESLEY

Presley, thinking Ollie is asleep, hides her discomfort as long as she can stand it. But when a strong contraction racks her abdomen and she cries out, Ollie sits straight up. "Goodness, Presley! What do you want me to do?"

Presley props herself on her elbows. "I'm not sure. I'm feeling a lot of pressure, like maybe I need to push. I hate to bother the nurse in the middle of the night, but maybe we should." Another contraction hits, she screams, and falls back against the pillows.

Kate is suddenly awake and on her feet. "We need the nurse. I'll go get her." She flees the cottage without bothering to put on her coat.

Ollie moves to the window. "The sun is coming up," she reports to Presley. "It's still raining, but I think the worst of the storm is over."

Presley grabs hold of the back of the sofa and pulls herself up. She's crossing the living room to the window when another contraction stops her in her tracks. She bends over, moaning loudly until it passes. Straightening, she continues to the window. "Do you think we can get to the hospital? I never volunteered for natural childbirth. I want my epidural."

Ollie gives her a sideways smile. "Let's hope so."

Presley is enduring another contraction when Kate returns with the nurse practitioner. "The landlines are back up in the main building," Kate says. "We called nine-one-one. An ambulance is on the way."

"Thank goodness," Presley says as another contraction grips her.

The nurse waits until the contraction passes before introducing herself. "I'm Molly McKinney, nurse practitioner, specializing in obstetrics. Tell me what's going on."

"The baby's not due for another week," Presley says. "But he's decided to come early."

Molly's face softens. "Do you know for sure it's a boy?"

Presley, unable to speak through the contraction, shakes her head.

"Presley has special intuition," Kate says. "Like ESP or something."

"We'll see soon enough." Lines appear between Molly's eyes as she checks Presley's pulse rate. "Have you been timing the contractions?"

"They've been three minutes apart for over an hour," Presley says.

"I need to examine you." Molly surveys the room. "Is there a bedroom down here?"

"The bedrooms are upstairs," Kate says, and Ollie adds, "But we created a makeshift bed behind the sofa. We slept down here in case we had a tornado."

Molly inspects their haven. "This will have to do."

Searing pain rips through Presley, and her knees buckle. "I need to push."

"Hold on. We're not ready yet." Molly helps Presley down to

the bedding on the floor and performs a pelvic exam. "Fully effaced and ten centimeters dilated."

Molly shouts orders at Ollie and Kate. "One of you find some clean towels. The other needs to wait for the ambulance. Check at the front of the main building in case they're lost."

"I'm on it," Kate says and hurries off to locate the ambulance.

Presley is in agony as one pain after another tears through her body. When Ollie returns with the towels, she squats on the floor near Presley's head. "Do you want me to stay with you?"

Presley is suddenly terrified of what is about to happen. "Yes! Please." She reaches for Ollie's hand. "I can't do this alone."

Molly announces it's time to push, and Presley bears down with all her might. The process of breathing and pushing goes on for some time. Kate returns with two young female paramedics, and the three medical experts determine it's too risky to move Presley.

Presley grows weak. She doesn't think she can take much more of the torture. But when Molly says, "I see the head. Give me one more big push," Presley bears down with every bit of energy she has left.

The baby slips between her legs, and Presley collapses back against the pillows. Seconds later, the baby's cries fill the room.

Molly says, "Your intuition failed you this time, Presley. The baby is a beautiful girl with strawberry-blonde peach fuzz like her mama."

Presley looks over at Ollie, who has tears streaming down her face. "Can you see her?"

"Yes! She's incredible."

Molly cuts the umbilical cord and bundles the baby in a towel before placing her in Presley's arms. "What's her name?"

Presley's heart melts as she stares down at the baby. Her daughter. Her sweet little baby girl. "Hello there, sweetheart. I'm your mama. You don't look like an Ava or Layla to me. You're a feisty little one, entering the world during a hurricane." A light-bulb goes off in Presley's head. "What about Riley? Riley Baldwin." She looks over at Ollie. "What do you think?"

Ollie wipes her tears with her shirttail. "A daughter named after a hurricane? I think you're asking for trouble. But I love the name. It suits her."

Molly nods at the paramedics. "Your ride awaits you. Are you ready to go to the hospital?"

Presley reaches for the nurse practitioner's hand. "Thank you so much, Molly. I don't know what we would've done without you."

Molly runs the back of her finger over the baby's forehead. "It was my pleasure."

"What can I do for you, Presley?" Ollie asks.

Presley looks around the messy living room. "My keys are around here somewhere. Please, lock the cottage when you leave. And, if you can find a phone that works, will you please call Rita for me to tell her about the baby?"

Ollie checks her phone. "Still no cell service here. As soon as you leave, I'll call her from the main building."

"My suitcase is beside the door," Presley says to the para-medics as they help her to her feet. One of them carries the baby while the other holds tight to Presley as she shuffles across the room and out the front door.

The ride to the hospital takes less than ten minutes. When they arrive, Presley and the baby are wheeled on the stretcher up to labor and delivery on the second floor. A team of nurses enters her room. One nurse takes the baby from her. "I'll bring her right back as soon as we check her vitals."

Exhausted from her ordeal, Presley closes her eyes while the nurses poke and prod her. She dozes off, and when she wakes again, Cecily is sleeping with her chin touching her chest in the chair beside the bed.

Presley's body aches all over as she struggles to sit up. The battery on her Apple Watch is dead, and she looks around the room for a wall clock. Ten o'clock. She's been asleep for at least a couple of hours. Lifting the covers, she stares down at her flabby belly beneath the hospital gown.

Cecily wakes with a start, her hands gripping the chair and eyes darting around the room. When she sees Presley, she settles back in the chair.

"What're you doing here?" Presley asks.

Cecily rubs her eyes with balled fists. "You wouldn't believe me if I told you."

"Ha. Try me. After the night I had, I'll believe anything."

"Lyle broke into my apartment. He was waiting for me when I got home from work."

The lines in Presley's forehead deepen as Cecily recounts the story of Lyle holding her hostage and the tree falling on her apartment.

"Good grief, Cecily. You're lucky to be alive. Where is Lyle now? I hope he's in jail."

"He's in the operating room, fighting for his life." Cecily stands and stretches. "I should get back. I took a break from the waiting room and went to look at the babies. I ran into Rita and Lucy, who told me about the baby. You did good, Presley. She's adorable. And Riley is a badass name."

Presley laughs. "I wasn't going for badass. But I take that as a compliment, coming from you."

"Have you called Everett yet?"

Presley lowers her gaze. "Not yet. I don't even know where my phone is."

The door swings open and Lucy and Rita file into the room. A nurse pushing the rolling bassinet with her sleeping baby enters behind them, and Parker brings up the rear.

He motions for Cecily. "Come on. Lyle is out of surgery. His doctor wants to speak with you."

"I'll come see you once you get settled at home," Cecily says and hurries out of the room with Parker.

Lucy and Rita ooh and ahh and ask to hold the baby, but Presley insists they wait until she wakes up.

Lucy sits down on the edge of the bed. "I told Levi about the baby. I hope you don't mind."

"Of course I don't mind. How is Levi? Have you seen him again?"

Lucy's cheeks turn a dainty shade of pink. "No. But we talk on the phone nearly every night."

Lucy is obviously smitten with this man. Presley hopes she isn't jumping into a relationship she's not ready for. "Has he told you any more about his children?"

"A little. His sons are both investment bankers in DC. Douglas, the older of the two, has a serious girlfriend. Levi thinks they'll get married. And Adam, the baby, works hard but uses what little time off he has to sow his wild oats."

"And what about his daughter?"

"He rarely talks about her," Lucy says. "I still don't know her name. I can tell Levi is worried about her, though. Every time I bring her up, he quickly changes the subject." Lucy straightens, holding her shoulders back. "Anyway, Levi is planning a trip to Hope Springs for weekend after next. He'd like to see you and meet the baby."

A feeling of warmth overcomes Presley at the thought of seeing her father again. "I'd like that."

The lactation nurse arrives to guide Presley through her first breastfeeding. She shoos Lucy and Rita out of the room. "You can wait outside, although we're liable to be awhile."

"We need to get going anyway," Lucy says. "Stella will need help cleaning up after the storm."

"Speaking of which, can I have the key to your cottage?" Rita holds her hand out to Presley. "When we finish helping Stella, Lucy and I will spruce things up for you and the baby."

"You're sweet," Presley says. "But I can't ask you to do that."

Rita smiles. "You're a new mama, Presley. Take whatever help you can get. Besides, you gave birth there last night. Bare minimum, you have soiled linens to wash."

"That's true. I'm so grateful to have the two of you in my life." She smiles at each of them. "You'll have to get the keys from Ollie. And thank you both so much."

Lucy and Rita kiss Presley's cheeks in parting. "We'll be back first thing in the morning to drive you home," Rita says. "In the meantime, let us know if you need anything."

Presley's throat constricts as she watches them leave. She's not ready to be alone with the baby. She knows little about infant care. What if she does something to hurt her? What if she breaks her?

The breastfeeding session ends with Presley in tears. The nurse gives her arm a reassuring pat. "Don't worry, hon. These things take time. Your milk hasn't come in yet. And your baby isn't interested in eating." She smiles down at Riley, who is sound asleep on Presley's bare breast.

Presley waits for the nurse to leave before returning the sleeping baby to the bassinet. Despite her earlier nap, she's still exhausted. She retrieves her phone from her purse and climbs back into bed to call Everett. When the call goes straight to voice mail, she leaves a curt message about the birth of his daughter.

She sends a text to Everett's manager. *Everett's daughter was born today. Riley Ingram Baldwin. 6 pounds, thirteen ounces.*

Her phone vibrates right away with a call from Wade. "Congrats on the baby, Presley. I've been meaning to call you. Everett is in rehab. He couldn't control his alcoholism, and he crashed during a concert one night."

Presley pauses as this information sinks in. She's not surprised. She suspected alcohol was the problem. "Why didn't anyone tell me?"

"I'm sorry. I've been meaning to call you."

Anger pulses through Presley. "*You've been meaning to call me? You bastard! I've been worried out of my mind. Where is this rehab facility?*"

"Everett doesn't want you to know where he is. He's dealing with some heavy stuff. His career is over, Presley."

"If that's true, I hold you responsible. You pushed him too hard, Wade."

"I may have pushed him hard, but he's a weak son-of-a-bitch."

Presley ignores his comment. "Tell me the truth, Wade. Is Everett having an affair with Audrey Manning?"

"No way, Presley. Everett would never cheat on you. He loves you too much. Gotta run," Wade says and hangs up before she can question him further.

Emotions flood her. Relief that her husband isn't cheating on her. Sorrow that he's suffering from his addiction and that his career might be over. And anger at Wade for keeping this from her and Everett for not confiding in her about his alcoholism.

20

STELLA

My brain fires on all cylinders as I move from the toaster oven to the coffeemaker to the refrigerator. I'm staring at the food items lining the shelves when Jack pulls me out of the way and slams the door shut.

"You're letting all the cold air out, Stella. We need to keep the door closed until the power comes back on."

"I'm sorry." I press my hands against the sides of my head. "I have pregnancy brain worse than usual today. I have so much to do, I don't know where to start."

"I can relate. I need to contact my foremen and check the status of our projects. Fingers crossed, none of them encountered significant storm damage. And I want to get the tree guy on the phone before he gets booked up." Jack removes his phone from his back pocket, confirming that cell service is still out.

I drum my fingers on the counter. "No telling how many trees are down at the farm. The grounds crew can at least deal with the smaller ones."

Jack walks over to the coffeemaker and jabs at the power button. "Ugh. Remind me why we decided not to install a whole-house generator."

"Because we have massive generators that run the inn across the street."

Jack's face lights up. "I bet they have phone service. And food. And hot coffee. I'm starving. Let's go get some breakfast."

"Yes! Let's!" Gathering our belongings, we call Jazz in from the backyard and head across the street to the inn. The reception hall is mass confusion, with hungover wedding guests eager to make their escape from the storm-ravaged resort.

I spot Ollie at the check-in desk, and she waves me over. "You two go ahead to Jameson's," I say to Jack and Jazz. "I'll be down in a minute."

I work my way through the crowd. When I reach the counter, Ollie says, "Did you hear the news? Presley had her baby."

Chill bumps crawl across my skin. "When? Where?"

"Early this morning in the cottage. A baby girl."

My fingers touch my lips. "I can't believe it. How did that go?"

"Mama and baby are fine." Ollie leads Stella across the hall, out of the way of the guests. "Long story short, she went into labor around midnight. The landlines were out in the main building, so we couldn't call an ambulance. One of the wedding guests is a nurse practitioner who specializes in labor and delivery. Kate tracked her down. Little Riley was born around daybreak, just as the ambulance arrived."

"Poor Presley. She must have been so scared. And you're sure they're both okay?"

"Positive." Ollie does a sweeping gesture with her arm. "Presley got right up and walked out to the ambulance with the baby in arms. You would never have known she'd given birth. And Riley is adorable with a wisp of strawberry-blonde hair like Presley's."

I smile, more to myself than Ollie. "*Riley*. How cute. And appropriate. I'll get over to see her later today." I return my attention to Ollie. "How are things here? Have you been down to the wellness center?"

"Not yet. I went home to take a shower, but I'm headed there now. Based on the reports I've received, the damage is minimal. Mostly trash littering the pool deck."

I check my phone as I walk with Ollie to the back door. "Hopefully, we'll get cell service back soon. I'll be around for a while if you need me. Call the front desk and ask them to locate me."

"Will do," Ollie says and exits the building.

I press my face against the glass door. From this vantage point, I can see a tree down in front of the cottage and a bigger one on the lawn behind the barn. Pine straw and pine cones and other debris cover the sidewalks and grass. Cleanup will take at least a couple of days.

I turn back toward the reception hall. "How many reservations do we have for tonight?" I ask one of the desk agents.

"Ten, the last time I checked." Her fingers fly across the keyboard. "We're down to nine now."

"I imagine that number will continue to decrease as the day goes on. If any guests call for updates on storm damage, discourage them from coming tonight. Comp them a room for a future weekend if need be."

"Yes, ma'am," the agent says, as she reaches for a ringing phone.

I leave reception and stroll through the lounge to Jameson's, grabbing a yogurt parfait and sitting down at the table with Jack and Jazz. "Guess what! Presley had her baby last night."

"Really?" Jazz says, coming off the bench a little. "Is it a boy or girl?"

"A girl. Her name is Riley."

"That's cute. Can we go see her?" Jazz asks, her eyes round like gold coins.

"Not today, kiddo. She needs some time to recover. I'm going to stop by the hospital later to check on her. I'll send her your love."

"Aww. Presley told me I could see the baby."

"And you will. As soon as she comes home from the hospital in a couple of days."

Jack leans into Jazz, nudging her with his shoulder. "Wanna hang out with me today while Stella works?"

"Sure!" Jazz's face brightens. Jack always makes everything fun. Even yard work.

"You two have fun. I'll see you back at the house later." I take my yogurt to the kitchen where I find a harried Fiona overseeing a skeletal staff of servers and cooks.

I give Fiona a pat on the back. "Great job on the buffet. Have you spoken to Cecily?"

"Only briefly. She's got her hands full. I hate to pester her with questions. Maybe you can answer them. Are we serving lunch? And what about dinner? We don't have any reservations booked."

"Hmm." I press my lips together as I consider the situation. "Let's close for lunch. Unless any of the staff needs food. After I survey the damage to the property, I'm headed to the hospital to check on Cecily and Presley. When I get back, we'll reassess the situation for dinner."

Fiona's expression softens. "Isn't it so exciting about the baby? I just love her name."

"Me too. The name *and* the story behind it." I give Fiona's arm a squeeze. "Hang in there. We've survived worse."

I exit the back door and take a quick tour of the buildings and grounds. I encounter the groundskeeper and head of maintenance along the way. Both assure me the damage is minimal.

"We should have everything restored to normal by this evening," Mike, the maintenance head, tells me.

"Let's use this opportunity to power wash the porch and clean the windows before putting the furniture back. If it takes another half day, so be it."

"Yes, ma'am. I'd already planned on it!"

Assured that we're on the road to recovery at the resort, I retrieve my Wrangler from the manor house and head toward the hospital. I zigzag through the downtown streets of Hope Springs, detouring around tree services and utility companies who are busy restoring our lives to normal.

At the hospital, I find Presley's room door closed. I hesitate. She's exhausted from being in labor all night and needs her rest. I start to move away when I hear crying coming from within. I crack the door and peek inside. Presley is pacing the room, bouncing the screaming baby as she coos, "Tell me what you want, little one. I don't know what you need."

I enter the room. "Do you want me to get the nurse?"

Presley looks up at me, her face blotchy and eyes swollen from crying.

"Oh, honey. Give me the baby." Taking the bundle from her, I bounce her around until she stops crying. "Why did the nurse leave you alone?"

Presley's shoulders heave as she sobs, "She's my baby, my responsibility. I can't even change her diaper."

I lay the baby on the bed, peel back the blanket, and sniff her diaper. "Whoo-wee. How can such a pretty little girl smell so rotten?" I grab supplies from a nearby table and quickly change the diaper. I swaddle the baby in the blanket and hand her back to Presley. "All clean."

Presley looks up at me with a stunned expression. "Since when did you get to be an expert on infant care?"

"I babysat for spending money in high school."

Presley gets back in bed with the baby. "What do you think

of her name? Riley sounded like a good idea at the time, but now I'm not so sure."

"Her name is all anyone can talk about. Everyone loves it. And the story behind it."

Presley's lips part in a soft smile. "That makes me feel better."

I lower myself to the edge of the mattress. "You're going to need some help at home."

Presley kisses the baby's forehead. "I've hired a nanny. She's on standby, waiting for me to tell her when to start. But I want some time alone with Riley first. We need to get to know each other."

"You'll figure things out. Have you tried breastfeeding yet?"

Presley nods. "It didn't go so well. But I'm not worried. Things will fall into place." She cradles the baby in her arms. "I wasn't crying about the baby, Stella. It's Everett. I just found out he's in rehab."

I let out a gasp. "Oh, no! I'm so sorry, Presley."

Presley stares down at her baby. "I'm honestly not surprised. I expected something like this. But I'm terribly worried, and I have no way of reaching him. His manager won't tell me where he is. He says Everett doesn't want me to know."

"That seems off to me, Presley. You have a right to know your husband's whereabouts."

Presley draws up her knees. "I agree. But what am I supposed to do? Call every rehab facility in the country? They won't give out information against a patient's wishes, anyway."

"There must be a way to find him." I get up from the bed and walk over to the window, staring out at the gray sky while I contemplate her dilemma. An idea strikes me, and I turn to face her. "Maybe Brian can help," I say about my uncle, who is a local attorney. "Would you like me to ask him?"

"Sure. Anything's worth a shot."

"Brian can be very persuasive. If nothing else, he can put pressure on the manager to tell you where Everett is."

"That'd be great. I'll send you Wade's contact info later."

I return to the bed, standing near her head. "You need some sleep. You must be exhausted after last night. I can stay and look after Riley while you nap."

"She's asleep now. Will you put her in the bassinet?" She hands me the baby, and I place her in the bassinet, wheeling it close to the bed.

I tuck the covers tight around Presley. "Anything else I can get you before I leave?"

Presley's eyelids flutter and then shut. "Turn out the light and close the door on your way out, please. And thank you."

I tiptoe out of the room, pulling the door closed behind me. Taking the elevator to the first floor, I'm crossing the lobby to the parking lot when I spot Cecily and Parker. I call out to them and wave them over. "How's Lyle?"

Cecily's expression is grim. "He's out of surgery. But the doctor says the next twenty-four hours will be crucial."

"Please tell me there's a guard stationed at his door."

Cecily and Parker exchange a look. "I'll pull the car around and meet you out front," he says.

Cecily watches him exit the lobby. "I'm not pressing charges, Stella. I care about Lyle. I was engaged to be married to him. I don't think he'll get the mental help he needs in prison."

"But it's not safe for you to live in the same town with him."

"I'm aware. The problem is Lyle's mother. I just talked to her. She's at the airport in Roanoke on her way here. She doesn't understand the seriousness of the situation. She's more worried about Lyle losing his job." Cecily's eyes light up. "That's it." She takes off toward the exit.

"That's what?" I call after her.

"Lyle's boss! His coach will know how to handle the situation."

I hope Cecily knows what she's doing. Something tells me there's more trouble ahead where Lyle is concerned.

21

CECILY

Parker exits the hospital parking lot and heads toward Main Street in Jack's truck. "Shall we go to my place? I don't know about you, but I could use a shower and a nice long nap." He corrects himself. "I'm not suggesting we nap together. I have a spare bedroom."

Cecily squirms in her seat. The idea of being in bed with him makes her female parts tingle. "As enticing as that sounds, I'm too on edge to sleep. Besides, we need to get Jack's truck to him. And there's something I need to take care of."

He glances over at her, his brow furrowed in concern. "What something?" When she doesn't answer, he sighs and returns his attention to the road. "I should've known. It has something to do with Lyle. What're you planning, Cecily?"

"Don't worry about it. It's nothing dangerous. I'll tell you later."

"I'm going to trust you on this, even though my gut is warning me not to." Parker's gaze is steely, but to his credit, he keeps his irritation to himself. "I'll drive to my house, and you can take Jack his truck back."

"That'd be great," Cecily says, staring out the window.

Parker groans when he turns onto his street and sees the large tree branch covering much of his front yard. "There goes my nap," he says as he pulls into the driveway.

"At least it didn't hit your house." She gets out of the truck and goes around to the driver's side. She gives him a quick hug and a peck on the cheek. "Thanks again for saving my life."

He stares down at her with expectant blue eyes. Earlier, after she'd kissed him outside the emergency room, she asked if they could save it for later. By later, she'd meant as soon as they could be alone together. That time has come, but she's too distracted.

"Maybe I'll see you at the inn this afternoon," she says.

The lines in his forehead deepen. "You're going to work on your day off?"

She shrugs. "I thought I'd stop by, to see if they need any help."

"I'm sure they do. I may come later, depending on how long it takes me to clean up this mess." He steps out of the way so she can get in the truck.

Sadness overwhelms her as she watches Parker walk toward his house with head bowed and shoulders slumped. She thinks of what he said earlier at the hospital. *For you, I'll wait forever. Although I hope it doesn't take that long.* She hopes he means it. She wants everything to be perfect when they finally make love.

Backing out of his driveway, she returns Jack's truck to the manor house and gets in her own car. She drums her fingers on the steering wheel. She's been to Coach Anderson's house a few times for team dinners. But Lyle always drove, and she doesn't think she can find it on her own. She remembers she has Lyle's cell phone. Removing it from her purse, she searches the contacts for Coach Anderson. She clicks on his address, engaging the MAPS app, and heads up Main Street toward Jefferson College's campus.

The coach is working in his yard when she arrives. Anderson

is hot for an old dude. In his mid-fifties, he has a full head of dark hair and muscular tanned legs sticking out from beneath his khaki work shorts. He looks up from raking when he hears her car pull up.

She approaches with arm extended. "Coach Anderson, I don't know if you remember me. I'm Cecily Weber, Lyle's ex-fiancée."

He shakes her hand. "Of course, I remember you. What brings you here?"

"I hate to interrupt your yard work, but if you can spare a minute, I need to discuss a sensitive matter involving Lyle."

"That sounds serious." He leans his rake against a tree. "I'm parched. Can I offer you some lemonade?"

"I would love some."

He motions her to the rockers on his front porch. "Make yourself at home. I'll be back in a minute."

Cecily gathers her thoughts while she waits. Is she doing the right thing in coming here? Or should she press charges against Lyle and be done with it? Lyle was out of his mind last night, like a demon had taken over his body. She must try to help him.

The coach returns with two tall Tervis tumblers of lemonade. He hands one to her and sits down. "What's going on, Cecily?"

"Lyle was in an accident during the storm last night. A tree fell on my apartment and a branch broke through a window. He's pretty banged up. Broken arm. Dislocated shoulder. Internal bleeding. He's out of surgery now, but the doctors warn he's not out of the woods yet."

The coach freezes, his tumbler against his lips. He lowers the tumbler. "Poor Lyle. I'm sorry to hear this."

"The thing is . . ." Cecily sucks in a deep breath for courage. "Lyle's been stalking me. He was holding me hostage when the tree fell."

Anderson balks. "That doesn't sound like the Lyle I know."

"He's not himself right now. He needs psychological help. Which is why I'm not pressing charges. But I have to do something."

"Understandably. Your life is in danger. Are you asking me to fire him?"

Cecily shakes her head. "Firing him would only make matters worse. Lyle is mentally unstable. He needs our support right now. I'm hoping his problem is only temporary, that a psychiatrist can work through his issues and set him back on course. If Lyle seeks psychological treatment, would you be willing to help him find another job? In another town somewhere, preferably far away from me."

Coach Anderson chuckles. "That seems like a logical solution to me. You're a good person, Cecily. Most young women I know would turn him over to the police in a heartbeat."

"Nothing good will come from Lyle going to prison." Tears blur her vision as she imagines Lyle behind bars. She almost married him. She can't help but care about him.

"I agree. Although you need to make it clear to Lyle you'll press charges if he doesn't get his act together."

Cecily waits until she trusts herself to speak. "I plan to."

"How would you like me to approach the situation?"

"I haven't figured that part out yet. Lyle's mother flew in this morning. She's unlikely to go along with our plan. She blames me for his problems. She's more worried about Lyle's career than his mental stability."

"That's unfortunate." Anderson gets up from his chair and moves over to the railing. A long moment of silence passes as he stares out at his yard. "Being in a position to help young people is one reason I chose coaching as a profession. You're not alone in this, Cecily. You can count on me. I'll talk to my assistant coach, and we'll come up with a solution."

Cecily goes to stand beside him. "We have time. According to his doctor, Lyle will be in the hospital for several days." She hands him her empty lemonade tumbler. "I'm sorry to burden you with our problems."

"Not at all. My players and coaches are like family to me. I truly want to help." His smile reaches his warm brown eyes, and for the first time in weeks, Cecily feels at ease. She did the right thing in coming here.

He motions her to the sidewalk and walks her to her car. "I'll be in touch."

Cecily slides behind the wheel. "I don't know how to thank you." The trauma of the last twelve hours comes crashing down on her, and she can no longer hold back her tears.

"Hang in there, Cecily. We'll figure this thing out together."

As she's driving off, Cecily realizes she failed to give the coach her contact information. She glances down at Lyle's phone in the cup holder. She can't have the phone in her possession. It's a reminder of the horrors he's put her through.

She drives straight to Lyle's house, and after committing Anderson's contact information to memory, she drops his phone through the mail slot.

On the way to the inn, Cecily is relieved to see a bucket truck in the driveway as she passes the manor house. The rumble of the massive generators powering the building greets her as she walks from the parking lot to the kitchen. Maybe she'll get a room here tonight if the power doesn't come back on at Stella's.

Fiona is alone at the stove. When she sees Cecily, she sets the spoon in the spoon rest and hurries over to greet her. She gives her the once-over. "Did that bastard hurt you?"

"Just my pride." Cecily looks around the room. "Where is everyone?"

Fiona returns to the stove. "Some of the staff showed up for breakfast. But we sent them home when we decided not to serve lunch."

Cecily leans over the pot Fiona is stirring and inhales the aroma. "Smells yummy. What is it?"

"This is Brunswick stew." Fiona points her wooden spoon to a second stockpot on the back burner. "That's beef and bean chili. We're having a party tonight for the staff."

Cecily raises an eyebrow. "Says who?"

"Says Stella. She wants to thank everyone for their hard work, preparing for the storm and cleaning up afterward."

A slow grin spreads across Cecily's lips. A party provides the perfect excuse for her to call Parker. "Stella's impromptu parties are the best. We'll make cornbread and several fresh salads to complement the soups. We'll eat community style in the dining room. If the storm didn't destroy them, there may be some autumn flowers left for the table."

Cecily is standing at the back window, peering out at her garden, when the generators go silent. She turns away from the window. The overhead lights are still on. "The power's back!"

Fiona's phone vibrates on the counter with an incoming call. "Cell service too!" She accepts the call. "She's right here." Fiona holds the phone out to Cecily. "Jack wants to speak to you."

Cecily takes the phone. "Hey, Jack. What's up?"

"We've removed the tree from your apartment. We nailed plywood over the window. It does the job, but it cuts out a lot of your sunlight. I'll order a new window first thing in the morning. It should be here by the end of the week."

"You're the best, Jack! I don't know how to thank you."

"No thanks are necessary. I'm happy to help. By the way, the power just came on over here.

"Awesome! Here too!"

"Good! I'll tell Stella."

Cecily hangs up on Jack and stares down at Fiona's phone screen. "Do you have Parker's number?"

"I should. Check the contacts," Fiona says, putting the lid on the soups.

Cecily locates Parker's number and clicks on it. He answers on the third ring. "What's up, Fi?"

"It's Cecily."

Silence fills the line. "Right. I forgot Lyle destroyed your phone."

Cecily is tired of talking about Lyle. "How's the yard cleanup coming?"

"Almost done. Did you complete your errand?" Parker asks, a hint of sarcasm in his voice.

Cecily notices Fiona staring at her and walks into the dining room for privacy. "Yep. I'll tell you about it later. We're having a party at Jameson's tonight. Stella's orders."

"That sounds like fun," Parker says.

"I just spoke with Jack. The tree has been removed, but I'm sure my living room is a mess." She checks her watch. "It's almost one o'clock. I'm going to clean my apartment from top to bottom and take a shower. Wanna meet back here around four? I'll help you ice down beer if you help me set tables."

"Deal. I'll see you at four."

Cecily returns Fiona's phone to her. "I'm going home for a while. I'll be back later to help you get ready."

Fiona grins at her. "I'll be right here."

Cecily walks on air out to the parking lot. She won't sleep with Parker tonight. Maybe not for days or weeks. But he's back in her life, and despite her trouble with Lyle, she feels like her life is finally on the right track.

22

OLLIE

Ollie drags herself up the hill to the main building. Kate, who is never far from her side these days, walks ahead of her at a faster pace. Ollie tunes out Kate's chatter. The young woman talks incessantly about nothing. Kate's seemingly endless supply of energy exhausts Ollie even more than she already is.

After being up all night and working all day, Ollie is not in the mood for a party, but she feels obligated to attend. The festive atmosphere in the lounge immediately lifts her spirits. The grounds and maintenance workers bypass the bar and head straight for the buffet while others linger over drinks in the lounge.

Ollie and Kate wait in line at the makeshift bar Parker has set up in front of Billy's. When it's Ollie's turn, Parker asks if she prefers beer or wine. "Lucy picked out some very nice wines for tonight."

"Wine sounds good. What are my choices?"

He shows her a bottle with a label from a well-known California vineyard. "We have Cab Sauv, pinot noir, and Chardonnay."

"I'll try the Cab for a change." Ollie normally prefers lighter reds, but a rich wine and a full belly is a recipe for a peaceful night's sleep.

He hands her the glass, and she steps out of the way so Kate can place her order.

"Hey, Parker," Kate says in a flirtatious tone. "Show me those wines again." With no one in line behind her, Kate will undoubtedly drag out the decision about wine in order to have more face time with Parker.

Ollie slips away while she has the chance. She joins Stella and a group of staffers who are sharing war stories about the hurricane. Jack talks of an uneventful night in their basement, leaving out the part where he rescued Lyle from the tree.

Stella turns to her uncle standing next to her. "What about you, Brian? Where did you and Rita weather the storm?"

"We started out in the utility room in my basement." Brian places a hand at the small of Rita's back. "We were nice and cozy when water started backing up through the drain."

Rita coughs into her hand, a gesture intended to mock her boyfriend. "I learned something new about Brian last night. He's paranoid of tornados. He insisted we move upstairs to his powder room, the only room in the house with no windows. When the power went out, with no air conditioning, the bathroom got hot fast."

Brian laughs. "If a tornado had come, you'd be thanking me right now instead of making fun of me."

Rita rests her head on his shoulder. "My hero."

Lucy chuckles. "Well, sister dear, while you were having your lover's tryst in the bathroom, I was spending the evening with *our* parents and their friends at the retirement home. The administration moved all the independent living people to the lounge in the main building. Normally, they don't allow alcohol, but they made an exception because of the storm. Those old people are a hoot. I heard more funny stories about weddings delayed and honeymoons canceled because of past hurricanes. If you're ever looking for entertainment on a Saturday night, I highly recommend Shady Grove Retirement Home."

Ollie smiles to herself. Having never seen Lucy so animated, so genuinely happy, Ollie can't help but wonder if a man is responsible for her sudden mood change.

"I slept right through the storm," Stella's grandmother, Opal, says. "Didn't even crack an eyelid when my neighbor's tree missed my house by inches."

Rita's hazel eyes land on Ollie. "Our stories can't compare to yours. Tell us about Presley's delivery."

Ollie recounts the events of last night without going into much detail. "I never thought I wanted children, but witnessing the miracle of childbirth has given pause to me reconsider that decision."

"You can have one of mine," Stella says in a teasing tone, and everyone laughs.

Ollie glimpses Jazz and Angel racing up and down the lobby. "Those two are having a blast."

Stella chuckles. "Under normal circumstances, I would never dream of letting them run around inside the inn. But since all the guests canceled for tonight, I figure they're not bothering anyone."

Ollie watches the child and dog with longing. She would give anything to be a kid again, even if for just one day. One day to spend with her parents on the estate. Riding horses at daybreak as they inspect the vineyard. Picnic lunches at the edge of the small stream that runs through their property. Roasting marshmallows over bonfires after dinner. Playing kick the can with the neighboring children while their parents drink wine by the fire.

Jazz runs up to the group, jerking Ollie out of her reverie. "Stella! Is school canceled tomorrow because of the storm?"

Stella gives her head a rub. "No such luck, kiddo. I received an email from your principal. School is on for tomorrow."

"Aw." Jazz stomps her foot. "Why can't you homeschool me?"

Stella musses Jazz's hair. "Because I would make a lousy teacher. Are you ready to eat dinner? I'm sure Fiona and Cecily would love to clean up and go home."

We migrate to the dining room, where the other workers have already cleared out. We serve ourselves from the buffet and gather around a long rectangular table. Parker and Kate, who hasn't left his side since they arrived, bring bottles of white and red to the table, refilling glasses before fixing their plates.

Ollie watches Kate and Parker with curiosity. When they return to the table, Kate sits down next to Ollie, leaving an empty chair on the other side of her. Kate flashes Parker a brilliant smile, an invitation for him to sit beside her. But Parker goes around to the opposite side of the table, taking a seat beside Cecily.

Kate's smile fades, and an evil glint appears in her eyes. "So, Cecily. I heard what happened last night. Lyle turned out to be a real loser. I can't believe you were going to marry him."

Stella saves the moment by tapping her knife against her glass. "Let's bow our heads in prayer." She offers a lovely off-the-cuff blessing, thanking God for friendship and the meal they are about to share.

When she finishes, everyone lifts their utensils and digs into their food except Kate, who goes in for the kill. "Seriously, though, Cecily. Where is Lyle now? I hope he's locked up in jail."

Cecily pins Kate against the wall with her steely gaze. "Who are you again?"

Ollie bites her lip to keep from laughing. Cecily knows darn well who Kate is.

Kate straightens, her chin held high. "I'm Kate, the new yoga instructor."

Cecily's lip curls up in distaste. "Right. The yoga instructor. Are you enjoying working here?"

Kate's golden ponytail bounces high on her head. "I love it!"

"That's good." Cecily jabs her spoon at Kate. "If you want to keep said job, I suggest you learn to mind your own business."

The table erupts in suppressed laughter.

Kate appears unfazed by Cecily's warning. "Last night was insane. I've never experienced childbirth. Watching the little baby emerge from her mother's—"

Ollie elbows Kate in the ribs. "We don't need details. We're eating."

Rita sets down her spoon and wipes her lips with her napkin. "I didn't know you were there when the baby was born."

Kate appears incensed. "I'm the one who found the nurse practitioner that delivered the baby. The party was raging in Billy's." She bats her eyelashes at Parker. "Parker helped me stand on the bar. He had to do that finger whistle thing three times to get everyone to listen. I yelled out 'Is there a doctor in the house?'" Kate cups her hands around her mouth for effect. "Molly McKinney raised her hand. She's not a doctor, but she was the next best thing."

"And thank the Lord for her," Ollie says, and everyone begins talking at once.

For the rest of dinner, no one engages Kate in conversation. Ollie feels sorry for her. But she doesn't want to talk to Kate either. She's had enough of her for one day.

Ollie spoons the last of the soup from her bowl. "The stew is excellent, Cecily. I may go back for seconds."

"Help yourself. There's plenty left. But I can't take the credit for it. That's Fiona's secret recipe."

Fiona grins from the other end of the table. "Glad you like it. You should try the chili."

"I think I will," Ollie says, pushing back from the table.

The chili is even better than the Brunswick stew. And the apple crisp Fiona made for dessert is to die for. Fiona is clearly talented. The inn will be hard-pressed to keep her for long.

After dinner, everyone pitches in to help clear the table and do the dishes. Ollie is wiping down the community table when Stella pulls her aside. "How much do you know about Kate?"

"She got a glowing reference from her former employer. And she's an outstanding instructor. The guests love her. She just tries too hard sometimes."

"She needs a filter," Stella says.

"I agree," Ollie says. "I'll talk to her."

When cleanup is complete, Ollie and Kate bid goodnight to the others, exit the main building through the front door, and walk down the long driveway. "We need to talk about tonight. Cecily's going through a hard time. Why would you attack her like that?"

Kate hangs her head. "I don't know. I have a bad habit of sticking my foot in my mouth."

When they reach the end of the driveway, Ollie stops walking and turns to Kate. "You got Stella's attention tonight for the wrong reasons. She's amazing to work for, but she doesn't tolerate inappropriate behavior. From now on, try to think before you speak."

Staring at the ground, Kate says, "I understand. I promise I'll do better."

Ollie gives her ponytail a playful yank. "You're doing a wonderful job otherwise. Keep up the good work."

"Okay. I'll see you tomorrow." With a half-hearted wave, Kate slumps off in the direction opposite Ollie.

For the first time in over twenty-four hours, Ollie is alone with her thoughts as she heads up Main Street toward her apartment. With the storm and the baby coming, she's been too busy to dwell on her own problems. She hasn't had a panic attack since Saturday morning. Hard work has always kept her grounded. But she yearns to be working for herself, not someone else.

She's grateful to find her power and internet have been restored at her apartment. She locates the contact information of the listing agent for Foxtail Farms. She shoots him a brief email expressing interest in touring the property. She wakes the following morning to find his response in her inbox. *Would ten o'clock this morning work?*

She sends off a reply. *Ten o'clock is great. See you then.*

Ollie showers, dresses in gray slacks and a black sweater, and twists her damp hair in a lone braid down her back. After making a brief stop at the wellness center, she heads out of town in her beat-up Camry. If she makes an offer on the vineyard, she'll buy herself a new SUV or pickup truck to celebrate.

When the highway narrows to a country road on the outskirts of Hope Springs, she rolls down the window, letting the fresh hair whip through her hair. She feels a force guiding her, encouraging her to keep searching for her life's purpose. She often senses her parents' presence. She peers over the top of her sunglasses at the crystal blue sky. Are they looking down on her from heaven now?

The listing agent is waiting for Ollie in front of the farmhouse when she arrives. Jamie Hodges has thick blond hair, a boyish face, and pale blue eyes. Ollie guesses him to be in his early thirties. Which is too young for her, but she can enjoy the flirtation.

He unlocks the cheerful yellow front door and steps out of

the way for her to enter. "The house is in good shape, although the bathrooms and kitchen could use a makeover."

The home offers four bedrooms and two bathrooms on the second floor and a living room, dining room, and wood-paneled study on the first. A screened porch extends off the large sunny kitchen. Stepping out onto the porch, Ollie imagines a daybed swing at one end, a pair of wicker rockers, and a small table where she can drink coffee in the mornings. The porch overlooks a fenced garden, which is divided into sections for fruits, vegetables, and flowers.

"Everything is well maintained," Ollie says. "The owner obviously loves this farm. Why is he selling?"

Jamie holds the screen door open for her. "He was diagnosed with rheumatoid arthritis a few years back. The property has become too much for him to manage. His sons live in Arizona. He's moving out west to be near them."

"That makes sense," Ollie says.

Jamie gestures at the buildings off in the distance. "Do you mind touring the grounds on foot? If not, I'll get my car."

"Let's walk," Ollie says, and takes in the surroundings as they stroll down the gravel driveway. Straight ahead is a red barn and a large stone building. "What's the stone building?"

"You'll see in a minute. Let's go through the winery first," he says, and directs her down a wide path to the left.

After a short walk, a building built to match the farmhouse with gray siding comes into view. Inside, the musty smells of oak and fermenting wine greet Ollie, stirring longings for her home and family and long-ago days. Instead of bringing tears to her eyes, her yearnings bring a smile to her face. She has an uncanny sense of familiarity, of déjà vu. She hasn't seen the rest of the property yet, but she knows beyond any doubt that Foxtail Farm will be her new home.

Ollie wanders around the barrel room. "I'm impressed. The facility and machinery are immaculate."

"The owner hasn't made wine in years. He's been selling his grapes to other wineries. However, during the height of his career, he produced several award-winning vintages."

Ollie smiles. "I know that from my research. Do you think he'd be willing to sell his brand? I may update the label to something more contemporary, but I'd like to keep the Foxtail Farm name if possible."

Jamie's lips curve into a smile, and two adorable dimples appear. "I think that would make him very happy."

Jamie and Ollie continue the tour in the old barn, which is full of tractors and farming equipment.

"Wow! This space is amazing." Ollie gazes up at the ancient rafters. "It's a shame to store farm equipment here. The owner obviously didn't get the memo. Barns are for weddings now."

Jamie's laugh has a melodic quality that makes Ollie want to hear it again.

"Follow me," Jamie says, waving her on. "I want to show you something."

Ollie is on Jamie's heels as he wends his way through the tractors to the back of the barn. When he slides open the massive doors, Ollie gasps at the picturesque scene before her. About fifty yards from the barn, the landscape descends into a valley, offering a spectacular view of the mountains.

"Does all this belong to Foxtail Farm?" Ollie asks of the seemingly endless rows of grapevines.

"Yep. Every last acre."

"Be honest with me, Jamie. The farm is a steal at this price. What's the catch? Why hasn't someone already snatched it up?"

"Well, there is one issue you should be aware of."

Ollie tosses her hands in the air. "I knew it was too good to be true."

"Hear me out. Maybe it won't be a deal breaker for you."

Jamie starts, "The owner is Melvin Bass."

Ollie nods. "I read about him online."

"He asked me to be upfront with any potential buyer. The circumstances are a bit unusual." Jamie stares out over the mountains. "Melvin's ancestors settled at Foxtail Farm a decade before the Love family founded the town. When the Loves bought the property next door, they made the Basses an offer on Foxtail. The Basses refused. The two families have been feuding ever since."

"You mean like the Hatfields and the McCoys."

"Exactly," Jamie says with a curt nod. "Melvin can explain more about it if you're interested. He's told me some pretty crazy stories. There have been times, over the years, when things have gotten pretty ugly between the two families."

"I don't understand. Why didn't the Loves snatch up the property when Melvin put it on the market?"

"Melvin won't sell to them. It's a matter of principle." Jamie's smile lets Ollie know he appreciates Melvin sticking to his guns. "Is this a deal breaker for you, Ollie?"

"Heck, no! I'm not afraid of a century-old feud. Makes me want to buy the place even more."

"I like a girl with spunk," Jamie says, his laughter filling the air.

This time, the charming sound of his laughter makes her heart flutter. She reminds herself that he's too young, and she isn't in the market for romance.

"Can I see that building now?" Ollie asks, gesturing at the stone building next door.

"Absolutely."

Jamie closes up the barn, and they walk together to the stone building. One large room with a vaulted beamed ceiling makes up the interior. Ollie circles the room, pausing to admire the enormous stone fireplace. "It's enormous. What purpose does it serve?"

"Many purposes throughout the decades. The original owners built it as a place of worship. At one point, subsequent owners used it as a schoolhouse for neighboring children. Most recently, people rent out the space for meetings and weddings." Jamie chuckles. "I can see the wheels turning in your brain. What would you use it for?"

"A tasting room and cafe combo." She suppresses the flutters of excitement dancing across her chest. "I need to be comfortable with the neighbor situation before I make an offer. Do you think Melvin would be willing to talk to me?"

"Of course. I'll have him get in touch with you as soon as possible." Jamie motions her to the door and locks up behind them.

"If everything works out, will you be running the farm alone?" Jamie asks as they walk back toward the house.

Ollie kicks at the gravel. "Yep. I'm flying solo."

Jamie stuffs his hands in the pockets of his jeans. "Does that mean there's not a special someone in your life?"

Ollie shakes her head. "I'm sorting out some stuff right now. Romance isn't high on my priority list."

He glances sideways at her. "Divorce?"

"Among other things."

"At some point, Ollie, you have to take a leap of faith."

Ollie thinks he's too young to be offering her advice. "That's why I'm here. Baby steps."

More laughter from him, music to her ears. "I hardly call buying a vineyard baby steps."

As they approach the front of the house, he eyes her car with concern. "We should talk about finances. Melvin's been burned a couple of times. I'd hate to get his hopes up if you lack the means to purchase the property."

It's Ollie's turn to laugh. "Never judge a book by its cover, Jamie. Or a person by their clunker of a car." She runs her hand across the hood. "I'm originally from Napa. My parents were killed when our family's vineyard burned last summer in the fires. I'm the sole beneficiary of their estate. I recently sold our vineyard. I can pay cash for Foxtail Farm if I so choose. I'm not saying I will, though. I need to talk to a financial planner first. Bottom line, I have the money."

A slow smile spreads across his face. "With your background, you may very well be the ideal person to revitalize this vineyard."

The dimples appear again. Ollie must limit her interaction with this intriguing man. Resisting him might prove to be a challenge.

23

STELLA

Jazz whines all the way to school. It pains me to listen to her. Not because she's being a brat but because she once loved school. When I reach the end of my rope, I pull the Wrangler to the curb and turn around to face her. "Talk to me, Jazz. I understand you're not happy with school. But you have to tell me why. I need details. Tell me something other than Mrs. Ramsey's mean. I can't help you until I have more to go on."

Jazz clams up like she always does when I press her for information about the substitute teacher. She's keeping something from me. But why? Is someone threatening her? Who could that be? The teacher? The bully? The principal?

"I hate to see you so unhappy, sweetheart." I grab her shoe and give her leg a shake. "Is there someone else you'd feel more comfortable talking to about what's going on at school? Cecily, maybe? Or Jack?"

Her eyes fill with tears, and she looks away. "Can we just go now?" she says to the window.

I put the Jeep in gear and continue on to school. I notice Grace Dunn behind us in the carpool line. I roll my window down and wave at her. Seconds later, my phone pings in the cup holder with an incoming text from her. *Have time for coffee?*

I text back. *Sure. Wanna follow me to the inn?*

She responds. *Right behind you.*

We park side-by-side in the inn's nearly empty parking lot and walk together to the main building. As we pass through the lobby to Jameson's, Grace says, "Why is it so quiet around here?"

"There are no guests in the house. They all canceled last night because of the storm. But that will soon change. We have a small conference starting tomorrow. The guests will be arriving this afternoon."

I stick my head in the kitchen and ask one of the waitstaff to please serve us on the porch, before leading Grace outside to a table for two on the railing.

I sit down opposite Grace and inhale the crisp, clean air. The weather is glorious. The mountain is on fire with orange and gold and red autumn leaves. Behind it, the cloudless sky is a clear periwinkle blue.

"What's it like to own your own inn?" Grace asks.

"It's not all fun and games. But it has its perks."

Cecily appears at the table. When I introduce her to my friend, Grace's eyes sparkle and face flushes as though starstruck.

"I'm honored to meet you. You're quite the local hero."

Cecily chokes out a laugh. "Stella deserves all the credit. I'd still be a barista at Caffeine on the Corner if she hadn't taken a chance on me."

I smile up at Cecily. "We make a good team."

Cecily produces an order pad from her pocket. "What can I get you two? An omelet? Oatmeal? I just took some cranberry orange muffins out of the oven."

"I'm tempted," Grace says. "But I'll just stick with coffee. I'm watching my weight."

I rub my expanding belly. "Since I'm eating for two, I'll have two muffins. And chai tea, please."

"Coming right up." Cecily turns on a nearby space heater before disappearing inside.

Grace watches her go before setting her gaze on me. "So, on Friday, I heard back from both of our petitions. Because of the storm, I haven't had time to reach out to anyone until now. The school board says they'll eventually get around to investigating the charges against Rebecca. But they wouldn't give me an approximate date. I get the impression it won't be anytime soon. As far as the substitute teacher is concerned, Principal Murphy says Mrs. Ramsey is the only one available long term."

"I don't believe him, do you?"

"Nope. He's a liar."

A server returns with our beverages and my muffins.

Grace stirs a sweetener into her coffee. "I had to drag Emily to school, kicking and screaming this morning. I hate seeing her so miserable."

I pinch off a bite of muffin. "Same with Jazz. I don't know how much more of this I can take. We have to do something."

"I agree. But I'm at a loss. The situation is explosive. Something will eventually happen."

"Unfortunately, Jazz and Emily are the fuses."

"Jazz and Emily aren't the only ones. Parents have been blowing my phone up all weekend." Grace removes her phone from her bag and shows me the text messages on her screen. "These have come in while we've been sitting here."

"What're their kids saying?" I ask and stuff the rest of the muffin in my mouth.

"The same thing. Mrs. Ramsey is mean." Grace drops her phone back in her bag. "It's not enough. We need something substantial, something concrete." She steeples her fingers together. "We should have another meeting this week. Just the parents from our class. If we put our heads together, maybe we can come up with a plan. Can we meet here again? I hate to ask, but it's so convenient."

"Sure. We have the conference starting tomorrow. But I'll figure something out. We can meet in the wellness center if necessary."

"If it's a problem, let me know, and I can ask another parent to host. In the meantime, I'll take a poll to see which night works best." Grace glances at her watch. "I need to get going. I have a dentist appointment."

"I'll walk you out," I say, wrapping my second muffin in a paper napkin to take with me.

After seeing Grace to the door, I stop by the check-in desk to speak to Rita. "Have you heard from Presley today?"

Rita's blue eyes shine with excitement. "She called a little while ago. Her doctor's releasing her this morning. Lucy and I are leaving soon to bring her home."

"Wow! That was the shortest hospital stay ever. I wonder if doctors let mothers of twins stay longer."

Rita laughs. "Don't count on it."

"What can I do to help Presley?"

Rita taps her chin. "Hmm. Nothing at the moment. The cottage is clean, and her fridge is stocked. As you know, Presley is not one to ask for help. We should take turns dropping in on her, to make sure she's not overwhelmed. Cecily's bringing her lunch today. Maybe you can stop by sometime this afternoon."

"I'd love that. I'll check in on her before I leave to pick Jazz up from school. In the meantime, I'll be around if anything comes up." I leave the building through the rear exit and take a long stroll around the grounds, making certain everything has been restored to order from the storm.

I spend the rest of the morning and early afternoon in my office. Around two thirty, I pay a visit to the cottage. I gaze into the bassinet at the sleeping infant. "She's really beautiful, Presley."

"Thank you. We're getting the hang of nursing, which is an enormous relief." Closing the cover on her iPad, Presley draws up her legs to make room for me on the sofa.

I sit down next to her. "I saw Brian last night. I talked to him about Everett. He's more than happy to help you with the Everett situation. He was going to reach out to his manager today. He's going to call you as soon as he knows something."

"I hope he gets more out of Wade than I did." Presley picks at a stray thread on her blanket. "I'm sorry you had to witness my meltdown yesterday. But I feel much better today. I'm relieved knowing Everett is safe. I wish he would've talked to me about his addiction. But I understand why he didn't. Everett is a proud man."

"He'll come home when he's ready." I glance over at the baby. "And when he does, he's gonna fall head over heels in love with his new daughter."

A dreamy expression crosses Presley's face. "He will. I just hope he still loves his wife."

I pause, considering my response. "He's a damn fool if he doesn't."

Presley's chin quivers, and I worry she's about to cry.

"Jazz is dying to see the baby. Is it okay if I bring her by later in the week?"

Presley runs the back of her hand over the tip of her nose. "Sorry. Hormones. I would love for you to bring Jazz over. Isn't it adorable how little girls that age are so into babies? Jazz will be an enormous help to you with the twins."

"I'm sure she will." My phone rings and I look down at the caller ID. "Speaking of Jazz, this is her school. I hope nothing's wrong."

When I accept the call, a woman identifies herself as Lana

Butler, the school nurse. I jump to my feet. "Is Jazz okay? Did something happen to her?"

"She's fine. But she had an accident. Banged up her knees pretty good. I'd like to discuss the situation with you in person. Are you available to pick her up?"

"I'll be there in fifteen minutes," I say, and end the call.

I look over at Presley, who is watching me closely, her brow pinched in concern. "Jazz got hurt at school. She banged up her knees. That's all I know." I kiss the top of Presley's head. "I hate to run out on you. I'll check on you later."

I hurry out and break the speed limit on the way to school. Fortunately, I don't encounter any police officers. The carpool line has begun to form at the school. I create a parking space near the building and race down the hall to the nurse's office, bursting through the door. Jazz sits on the side of the cot, swinging her bandaged legs. When she sees me, she holds her arms out. "Stella!"

I pick her up, and she wraps her legs around my waist. "What happened, sweetheart?"

Her legs grip me tighter. "I fell down on the playground."

An attractive woman with milk chocolate skin comes from behind the desk. "I believe someone pushed her down. But she won't say who." She peers at me over the top of her reading glasses. "I'm Nurse Lana. I understand you're Jazz's half sister."

"That's correct. Both her parents are deceased. I'm her legal guardian, soon to be her adoptive mother."

She rubs Jazz's back. "This child is covered in bruises. And I'd like to know how she got them," she says in an accusatory tone.

I gawk at her. "What're you talking about? What bruises?"

"It's harder to see them on dark skin." Nurse Lana pries Jazz out of my arms and sets her back down on the cot. "Show your sister the bruises, Jazz."

Jazz pushes her sleeves up and holds her arms out so I can see the trail of purple marks. I should've suspected something when she insisted on wearing long-sleeved shirts, even on warmer days. "Who did this to you, Jazz?"

Jazz folds her arms across her chest. "I'm not allowed to say."

"You'd better say." I point at the nurse. "She thinks *I* did this to you."

"No, she doesn't." Jazz glares at the nurse. "Do you?"

"The thought crossed my mind." The nurse bends over to look Jazz in the eye. "It's my job to protect you, Jazz. If your sister is hurting you, I need to know."

"Not Stella." Jazz begins crying hysterically. "She wouldn't do that. She loves me. Please don't take me away from her."

"I want to help you, honey. Not make things worse for you." Nurse Lana hands Jazz a tissue. "But, if you don't tell me who's hurting you, I'll have to report your case to social services."

Panic rises in my chest at the thought of losing Jazz. I sit down beside her on the cot and rest my hand on her shoulder. "Remember when you first came to live with me? We agreed we'd always tell each other the truth. I need you to do that now, Jazz. If you don't, Jack and I could be in a lot of trouble. Is the person who gave you the bruises the same person who pushed you down on the playground today?"

Jazz lowers her gaze, and I have to listen carefully to hear her mumbled response. "Sophia. She gave me the bruises. She pushed me down today."

"Oh, sweetheart," I say, drawing her little body close. "Why didn't you tell me?"

"I told the teacher. She said if I didn't keep my mouth shut, she'd give me Fs on all my schoolwork and make me repeat second grade."

Anger surges through me. "Did she use those exact words?"

Jazz nods as she wipes her snotty nose with the tissue.

I glance up at the nurse, whose facial muscles are tight and hazel eyes narrowed. "What're you gonna do about this?" My tone is angry. While this isn't Lana's fault directly, she's employed by this school, which makes her responsible on a minor level.

"I plan to report it to the principal," she says briskly.

I jump to my feet. "I suggest you do that. Right away. Like now." I hold my hand out to Jazz, and we leave the nurse's office.

We're on the way to the car when my phone rings. Grace blurts, "Emily told me what happened. Is Jazz okay?"

"I'm leaving the school now with Jazz. Sit tight, and I'll call you in a few minutes."

I wait until we're out of the parking lot before I say to Jazz in the rearview mirror, "You did the right thing in telling me. I only wish you'd told me sooner."

"Does this mean I don't have to go back to school?" I've never seen her more sullen, more vulnerable. Which is saying a lot considering all she's been through in the past eighteen months.

"Not until we sort through this mess."

"Okay," she says and looks away from my reflection.

At home, I set her up with a snack at the kitchen counter and go outside to the terrace to call Grace. I fill her in on what just transpired in the nurse's office. "I guess I'm homeschooling for the foreseeable future."

Grace lets out a sigh. "I have a feeling you won't be the only one. I've heard from several parents in the past hour. Their kids may not have known about the bullying, but nearly all of them saw Sophia push Jazz today. The parents are requesting an emergency meeting. Do you think we can pull that off for tonight?"

My mind races. "Sure! The conference doesn't start until tomorrow. I'm sure we have a meeting room available."

"Great! I'll get the word out. Let's say eight o'clock. That time seems to work well for everyone."

As I end the call, the french doors open, and Jazz and Angel come barreling out.

"Come here a minute, Jazz. I need to talk to you about something." I sit her down in a lounge chair and explain about the meeting. "Will you give me permission to talk about what's been happening to you? I won't tell them if you don't want me to. But I think your story could help the other children. For all we know, they're experiencing the same treatment from Sophia and Mrs. Ramsey. Maybe, like you, they're afraid to talk about it. Wouldn't you like to help them?"

I'm prepared for pushback. I have my argument ready. Much to my surprise, in a cheerful voice, she says, "Okay. You can tell them. Can I go throw the ball for Angel now?"

I laugh. "Yes, you may."

My heart warms as I watch Jazz and Angel frolic in the colorful leaves covering the ground. Soon the trees will be bare, and we'll have our first snow of the season. Thanksgiving will follow Halloween and then we'll celebrate Christmas. Before long, the twins will arrive and turn our lives upside down. The problem Jazz is having at school is just a blip on the radar. But all these situations we encounter together bring us closer. The adoption papers are just a legality. In my heart, Jazz is already my child.

24

STELLA

Jack is furious when I tell him what happened to Jazz at school. He snatches his truck keys off the counter and marches across the kitchen toward the mudroom.

I dash around him and throw myself in front of the back door. "Wait. Where're you going?"

"To give Lori Carr a piece of my mind."

"Don't, Jack. You'll only make matters worse." I loop my arm through his and drag him back to the kitchen. "We need to handle the situation diplomatically. I have faith Lori and Sophia will both get what's coming to them."

Jack's shoulders sag. "At least let me come to the meeting with you."

"That's fine. Let me see if Opal can keep Jazz," I say, reaching for my phone.

When I explain the urgent nature of the meeting, Opal readily agrees to my request. "Let her spend the night. We'll bake a cake and watch a movie. And since she won't be going to school tomorrow, she can hang out with me in the morning."

"Thanks, Opal. What would I do without you?"

Opal chuckles. "Let's hope you don't find out anytime soon."

Jazz is beyond thrilled at the opportunity to spend the night and day tomorrow with Opal. She begs to take Angel with her, but I refuse. "That's too much to ask of Opal. Jack and I will take good care of Angel while you're gone."

Jazz reluctantly agrees as she heads upstairs to pack her bag.

I feed my family an easy dinner of tomato basil soup and grilled cheese sandwiches. After dropping Jazz at Opal's, we drive over to the inn. When Jack is noticeably quiet, I ask, "What's on your mind, babe?"

His eyes remain on the road. "I can't stop thinking about Sophia. If she weren't a kid, I'd jerk a knot in her. Apples don't fall far from trees, do they?"

I let out a sigh. "Apparently not. What're we gonna do about Jazz's education?"

"We can always send her to the private school in Roanoke," Jack suggests.

I blink hard. "But Roanoke is forty minutes away. The drive would drastically alter our lives."

Jack makes a right-hand turn and drives up to the inn. "We might not have any choice. Unless you're willing to homeschool her. And that won't be feasible once the twins come."

"The best solution is to fix the problem at the elementary school," I say and get out of the truck.

I enter the building and join Grace outside the conference room to greet the other parents. I'm surprised to see Lindsay's and Hannah's moms coming toward us.

"Lindsay told me what happened at school today," Jennifer says. "She is distraught about the situation."

"So is Hannah," Melanie chimes in.

"We want you to know we don't condone that kind of behavior," Jennifer says, and Melanie nods.

"Thank you. It's been a difficult few weeks for Jazz."

Jennifer and Melanie have no sooner disappeared inside the conference room when Rebecca Wheeler and Nurse Lana arrive.

"I heard about the meeting from one of the other parents," Rebecca says. "I hope you don't mind us being here. Lana told me what happened to Jazz today."

I narrow my eyes. "But—"

Lana cuts me off. "After you left my office, I went straight to the principal's office and spoke with Murphy in private. He ordered me to bury the report, not to tell a soul about the playground incident or Jazz's allegations against Mrs. Ramsey."

The nurse glances over at Rebecca. "I needed to talk to someone. Rebecca seemed like the obvious choice." Lana runs her hand over her cropped hair. "This situation is screwed up on so many levels. I'll help you protest, no matter how you decide to proceed. I'm prepared to lose my job if necessary."

"You will not lose your job," Rebecca says. "And I'm going to get mine back."

I smile at them. "I like your attitudes. We're going to need all the support we can get."

"Yes, we are! Let's get this meeting rolling," Grace says, and herds us into the conference room.

Most of the parents sit at the massive conference table. Only a few remain standing near the door. I wonder if they are contemplating an escape.

Grace calls the meeting to order. "We have a real problem in our second-grade class. I've spoken with many of you over the past few days. Our children are unhappy. I'm sure most of you have heard about the event that happened today. Stella will tell you more about that in a minute. But first, I have other disturbing news." She talks about the status of our petitions.

Rebecca raises her hand before speaking. "I've been waging my own war with the school board. I don't understand their reluctance to provide a speedy investigation. This isn't about resources. They could order the investigation to take place tomorrow if they wanted."

"I smell a skunk," a parent calls out from the other end of the table.

When the room erupts in murmurs, Jack finger whistles to quiet everyone down.

"We'll open the floor for discussion in a minute," Grace says. "But first, let's hear from Stella."

I stand up in order to see everyone better. "I'd like to start by thanking you all for coming on such short notice. My daughter, Jazz, gave me permission to tell her story. She hasn't been herself lately. She's always loved school until recently."

Others at the table nod their heads, signaling that they've noticed similar behavior from their children.

I go on to tell them about what happened on the playground today and Jazz's confession to Nurse Lana.

A mother I don't recognize tentatively raises her hand. "Will someone please explain why this Sophia kid is getting away with bullying?"

"Her mother is president of the parents' association," Jennifer explains. "Lori Carr raised money for the new play-ground equipment last year. This year she's organizing a silent auction for the funds to renovate the library. She has Principal Murphy eating out of her hand."

A father bangs his fist on the table. "This is an outrage!"

Another dad stands abruptly. "I'm pulling my kid out of this school until the real teacher comes back," he says, pointing at Rebecca.

Several parents stand at once, their voices a chorus of *Me toos*.

"Listen up!" Jennifer says, knocking loudly on the table. "I've got an idea. What about staging a walkout? Can you imagine

Mrs. Ramsey's face when none of her students show up for class tomorrow?"

Grace looks over at me, her eyes glistening with excitement. "I love this idea. What do you think?"

"I think we should take a vote."

"Yes! Let's!" Grace addresses the table. "Everyone in favor of a protest raise your hand."

Most everyone in the room stretches an arm over their head.

"Those opposed?" Grace says.

The room remains silent.

Grace claps her hands. "We've got ourselves a protest."

The men adjourn to Billy's Bar for a beer while the moms gather in a tighter circle around the table to discuss the details. An hour later, I leave the inn feeling more hopeful than I have in weeks. Jack, Jazz, and I are not alone in our problem. We have the support of nearly every second-grade parent. I finally feel like one of them. I'm no longer the half sister. I'm the mom.

At eight thirty on Tuesday morning, our group assembles beneath the covered walkway between the carpool drop-off location and the main entrance. At nine o'clock, Principal Murphy comes flying out of the building.

"What the devil's going on here?" he demands, his face so red I worry he might stroke out.

I gesture at the picket line. "What does it look like? We're protesting."

He jabs his finger at me. "I knew you were trouble the first minute I saw you."

"I'm not the one causing the trouble, Principal Murphy."

His brown eyes pop behind his black glasses. "What's it gonna take to make you people go away?"

I hold up two fingers. "A new substitute teacher. And an immediate investigation into the charges against Rebecca Wheeler."

"You're wasting your time." He spins on the heels of his Converse high tops and stomps back into the building.

"That didn't go well," Grace says near my ear. "This might be more of a challenge than I expected."

I hold up my picket sign. "It's gonna be a long day for sure."

Protesting is exhausting business. But we're all dedicated to our cause. We take turns making coffee runs, and at lunchtime, Grace and I treat everyone to pizza from Ruby's.

Lori Carr is first in line for afternoon carpool pickup. She parks her car and wanders over to Jennifer and Melanie, who are sitting on a bench, taking a break. I move in closer so I can eavesdrop on their conversation.

"What's going on?" Lori asks.

Jennifer looks at her over the rim of her designer sunglasses. "What does it look like? We're protesting. We're demanding a new substitute teacher and an immediate investigation into Sophia's charges against Rebecca."

Lori ignores the part about her daughter. "Is there a problem with Mrs. Ramsey?"

"Huh!" Melanie snorts. "You know what the problem is."

Lori frowns, but no lines appear on her Botoxed forehead. "Are y'all mad at me about something?"

"We're not *mad* at you," Jennifer says. "We just no longer wanna be your friends."

Lori jumps to her feet. "Fine! Then you're off the silent auction committee."

Jennifer stands to face her. "Fine. I'm not raising a dime for this school until our demands are met."

Lori storms off in a huff.

Seconds later, Sophia bursts through the door and runs to

the car. When the teacher opens the passenger door, Sophia whines to her mother, "Mo-om! I was the only one at school today! All my friends got to stay home."

The teacher slams the car door, and Lori speeds away.

Despite Murphy's efforts to get rid of us, we remain throughout carpool pickup. When other moms find out why we're picketing, they want in on the action, particularly moms of students who had Rebecca as their teacher in the past. By the time the last car pulls through the line, we've tripled our number of protestors. Grace creates a schedule for the next three days, dividing us into groups of ten, with each group working three-hour shifts.

When it's time to go home, Rebecca and I walk with Grace to the parking lot. "What if this continues? We can't keep our kids out of school indefinitely."

"We'll homeschool them," Grace says.

"I volunteer to teach them," Rebecca says, waving her hand.

I shake my head in amazement. "Your enthusiasm is contagious. I'll contribute space for the classroom. We can set up in the barn at the inn."

Grace nudges me. "See! We have a plan in case we need it. But I have a hunch it won't go on too much longer." Mischief tugs at the corners of Grace's lips.

I laugh. "What're you scheming?"

"If I tell you, I might jinx it." She crosses her fingers. "See you bright and early in the morning."

I watch Grace drive off in her minivan. I admire her spunk. Regardless of what happens, I feel like I've made a friend for life.

25

OLLIE

Ollie is pleasantly surprised when Melvin Bass offers to drive to Hope Springs for their meeting. He's already waiting at a table by the window when Ollie arrives at Caffeine on the Corner at ten o'clock on Wednesday morning. She orders a latte from the counter and joins him.

His hair is snow-white and his skin is leathered and lined from the sun. "I figured we're safer meeting here," he says, his voice deep and smooth like Cabernet Sauvignon. "I can't do anything in Lovely without one of the Loves' informants spying on me. I want to protect you as long as I can."

Ollie gulps. "Protect me from what?"

"From their threats. The Love family scared off my two previous buyers. Should you decide to make an offer, I have no doubt they'll come after you."

Ollie cocks an eyebrow. "If I didn't know better, Mr. Bass, I'd think you were the one trying to scare me off."

"Please call me Melvin." He steeples his fingers. "I'm not trying to scare you. I just want you to be prepared. I failed to warn the other buyers. They ran off with their tails between their legs. I don't want that to happen again."

Ollie thinks he has a funny way of *protecting* her. "Are these people dangerous?"

Melvin chuckles. "Eighty years ago, the Basses and Loves would shoot at one another if either crossed the other's property lines. But we've mellowed in the past twenty years."

If he's trying to make her feel better, he's failing. "What kind of threats are we talking about?"

Melvin sits back in his chair with his coffee mug in hand. "Who knows what they'll come up with. Mostly scare tactics intended to frighten you away from the deal. You need to know who you're dealing with, and if you decide to proceed, you should be on guard."

"Why do the Loves want your land so bad?"

"They want to build a resort." Melvin spreads his hands wide in front of him. "Great big thing with concrete towers and a golf course."

"You're joking? A golf course? In the middle of the vineyard?"

"Yep. Can you imagine that?" Melvin presses his lips tight. "Some of them Loves don't have good sense."

Ollie narrows her eyes in suspicion. "And you know this for sure?"

"Yep. The architect's a friend of mine. He showed me the plans. Rumor has it the older Love boys oppose the project. I hear they're fighting amongst themselves over it."

Ollie sips her latte. "What will you do if you can't sell it?"

"I'm not worried. I'll eventually find a buyer," Melvin says with a note of confidence. "Jamie tells me your parents were winegrowers in California."

"That's correct. Hendrix Estates in Napa."

He gives her an appreciative nod. "I know it well."

"I grew up on the vineyard. The business has been in my family for generations. My father was grooming me to take over when the fire destroyed the winery and a large percentage of the crop."

"Then you'll understand this." Melvin glances around, as though making sure the coast is clear. He leans across the table in a conspiratorial manner. "The Loves never understood the true value of my land. It's not the view. Although the view is stunning, particularly at this time of year. The dirt in the valley produces the best grapes in the state. Every vintage that has come from that area of the farm has won awards."

"Really? That's fascinating. Tell me more," Ollie says, and they settle into a conversation about grape growing and wine-making that lasts for over an hour.

Ollie checks her watch. "I need to get back to work."

"Of course. I didn't mean to keep you so long."

They stand together, and Ollie holds her hand out to shake his. "Thank you for taking the time to meet with me. I will probably make an offer. But I'd like to walk through the property again with my contractor. I need to be sure he can make the improvements I envision."

Melvin motions her to the door. "I understand. My time is flexible. You and Jamie schedule the appointment whenever you see fit. I've enjoyed talking to you, Ollie. You have a real understanding of the industry. I hope things work out, for both our sakes." They exit the coffee shop together and part on the sidewalk out front.

Ollie waits until she's a block away before digging her phone out of her purse. She accesses Jack's contact info and clicks on his number. After exchanging pleasantries, she says, "I'm considering making an offer on a vineyard in Lovely. Do you work on projects over there?"

"All the time," Jack says.

"I'd like to get your thoughts on potential renovations. Any chance you're free for a walk-through tomorrow or Friday?"

"Hmm. The next two days are tight for me. I know it's short notice, but I have some time this afternoon."

"Awesome. I'll call the realtor and text you back when I know more. By the way, Jack. This opportunity came up suddenly, and I haven't had a chance to talk to Stella about it. I would never leave her in the lurch. I should have plenty of time to hire and train my replacement."

"Don't worry about Stella. She'll miss you, but she wants what's best for you."

"That makes me feel better. Thanks."

Ollie follows up the call with a text to Jamie. He responds right away. *Does 3 o'clock work?*

She exchanges several more texts with Jamie and Jack before confirming the appointment.

Ollie walks on air back to the wellness center. This opportunity feels right, despite the potential for trouble from the Loves. As the saying goes, anything worth having is worth fighting for.

Her good mood comes to an abrupt halt when she finds Kate sitting behind her desk in her office. "What do you think you're doing?"

Kate cowers, as though afraid Ollie might hit her. "I was waiting for you. I didn't mean to make you mad."

Ollie checks her phone. "Do we have an appointment? I don't have one noted on my calendar."

"I didn't know I needed an appointment to talk to my friend. Or aren't we friends?"

Ollie thumbs her chest. "Foremost, I'm your senior. I closed my door when I left a while ago. You can't just let yourself into my office and help yourself to my chair. Now, get up!"

Kate jumps to her feet. "Gosh, Ollie. I'm sorry."

Ollie grabs her by the arm and marches her across the room to the door. "Get out."

"Am I fired?" Kate asks, tears glistening her eyelashes.

"One more stunt like that, and you will be."

Ollie slams the door, locks it, and returns to her desk, collapsing in her chair. Stella's words from dinner the other night come back to her. *How much do you know about Kate?*

"Not enough," Ollie says out loud to the empty room.

She retrieves Kate's resume from her file and searches the internet for the yoga studio where she previously worked in Charlotte. The manager's name is Sonya Francis. Ollie's eyes travel to the resume. Which is not the name Kate listed as a reference.

Ollie picks up the desk phone's receiver, punches in the studio's number, and asks to speak to Sonya. She waits five minutes for an irritated voice to answer. "Sonya Francis. How may I help you?"

"I'm Ollie Hendrix calling from Hope Springs Farm in Virginia. I'd like to check a reference for your recent yoga instructor, Kate Connor."

After a brief silence, Sonya asks, "Did Kate provide my name as a reference?"

"No. She listed Bonnie Maxwell at the following number," Ollie says, and recites the phone number Kate provided.

"I've never heard of Bonnie Maxwell. And that number doesn't ring a bell. I can't imagine why Kate would list our salon on her application. She left on bad terms. I fired her after she slept with a client's husband. She ruined the client's marriage and her own."

An affair? With a client? Kate never mentioned being married. "How long did Kate work there?"

"Three years," Sonya says. "Don't get me wrong. She's an excellent instructor. She's just a bit odd. I often wondered if she was on the spectrum. If maybe she has Asperger's Syndrome or something. She's socially awkward at times, if you know what I mean."

"I've witnessed that behavior myself," Ollie says, thinking back on some of the strange things Kate has done in the short time she's been at the farm.

Sonya goes on, "Then again, her husband is a perfectly normal guy. He seemed really into her. Until she cheated on him."

"I wish I had better news for you. Kate endeared herself to me at times. She's a good kid at heart. But the client in question is an important member of our community. I had no choice but to let her go."

"I understand. Thanks for the information."

Ollie places the receiver in its cradle and leans back in her chair, staring up at the ceiling and thinking. The night that Presley went into labor, Kate had been so excited, so eager to help. What if something is legitimately wrong with her? She can't help it if the cylinders in her brain don't all fire properly.

This is not a problem Ollie wants to solve alone. And not one she needs to deal with today. Not when she's preparing to make the most important business decision of her life.

Jack gives the Foxtail Farm buildings an inspection worthy of a professional. Ollie follows him around, peppering him with questions, while Jamie sits on the front stoop of the house, conducting business on his phone. Jack checks fuse boxes and squirms his way through crawl spaces. He flushes toilets and examines foundations.

They finish the survey at the lodge. "Everything appears to be in tiptop shape," Jack says. "I've always admired this property. She's a real gem."

"She needs some work though. A diamond in the rough."

Jack folds his arms over his chest. "Speaking of which, tell me what you're thinking about renovations."

Ollie shares with him her ideas for updating the kitchen and baths in the main house. Jack gives her a ballpark estimate and adds, "That could change depending on fixtures, finishes, and appliances."

"I understand." Ollie points a finger toward the lodge. "I'm thinking of converting this building to a tasting room and cafe."

"It would be perfect. You'll need to add on a kitchen. Stella's architect does an excellent job of designing buildings with historic elements to fit in with original structures."

"That's exactly what I need—a new kitchen with all the modern conveniences made to look old." Ollie opens the door and Jack enters the lodge ahead of her.

"The historic vibe is perfect for a winery," Jack says.

"I agree. Although we could use more light." She crosses the room to the rear wall, which features a single metal door. "Can we take out this wall and install sliding glass doors?"

Jack rubs the scruff on his chin as he considers her question. "The less we disturb these ancient exterior walls the better. However, you could install two pairs of french doors that would open onto a covered porch or a terrace or both."

"Yes! I like the idea of having both. We can use the covered porch for three seasons. And a terrace for warmer weather with umbrellaed tables that can easily be moved if we're hosting a wedding."

"Sounds like you have a plan," Jack says.

Ollie smiles. "I think so."

They exit the building and head toward the main house. "How long would it take to do the renovations?"

"Well, let's see." Jack stares up at the deep blue sky. "If we start before Christmas I could have you up and running by summer."

"Which is plenty of time for me to find my replacement for the wellness center and train her."

"Does this mean you've decided? You're going to make an offer?"

"I want to sleep on it one more night. But I think so." Excitement bubbles up inside of Ollie. She's really going to do this. The last year has been full of heartache, but those tragic events have led her to this place, this point in time. She's on the road to a new beginning. And it feels oh so right.

26

STELLA

Our movement continues to expand with an increasing number of parents of older children protesting about our corrupt principal. I'm astonished at their complaints and disheartened an elementary school principal would abuse his position of power. Despite the overwhelming support from other parents, my enthusiasm wanes as the hours and days pass.

At lunchtime on Wednesday, Grace and I are helping ourselves to the sandwich platter Cecily brought over from the inn, when I admit, "I'm getting discouraged. Nothing's happening, and I have a business to run. I can't protest indefinitely."

"We shouldn't have to wait too much longer," Grace says, plucking a half of a ham and cheese sandwich from the tray.

"Shouldn't have to wait for what? What aren't you telling me, Grace?"

"You'll see," she says, a smirk tugging at her lips.

Two hours later, the first moms are arriving for carpool when a news van shows up. "And here she is now," Grace says, beaming from ear to ear.

"So this is what you've been hiding? The news media?"

Grace grumbles, "Took her long enough to get here. I've

been harassing her for days." She loops an arm through mine. "Come with me. I refuse to be interviewed alone."

Mandy Hicks is an attractive brunette from the local ABC affiliate. I stand silently beside Grace as she walks Mandy through the events leading up to our walkout and tells her our lists of demands. Grace's words are well spoken, her points well thought out, as though she spent a considerable amount of time preparing her speech.

"Is the mother of the bullied child here?" Mandy asks.

Placing my hand on my chest, I say, "That would be me."

Mandy gives me the once-over. "You look familiar. Aren't you Stella Snyder, proprietor of the inn at Hope Springs Farm?"

"I am. The child is my half sister. Her adoption is in the works."

Mandy pulls me to the side, away from the other parents. "Would your sister be willing to speak to us?"

"I don't know." My tone is hesitant. "She's so young. And this situation has been really hard on her."

Mandy places a hand on my back, pressing me farther away from the crowd. "Look, I have kids of my own. I understand this is a sensitive issue. I promise I'll be gentle with her. We'll bring a crew to your home. She'll be more comfortable there. I wouldn't go to the trouble if I wasn't convinced her interview will make a big impact on our viewers."

My gut instinct is to decline. But this is Jazz's story. She should decide. "I can't commit without talking to Jazz first."

Mandy brings herself to her full height. I've taken the bait. All she has to do is reel me in. "Where is she now?"

"At the inn with my grandmother. Opal is giving her painting lessons."

Mandy's smile softens her features. "I'm familiar with Opal's work. I have one of her landscapes hanging above my fire-place." She glances at her phone's screen. "I'd like to lead with this story on the six o'clock news. In the interest of time, if you'll give me your address. I'll take my crew to your house and wait for you there. If Jazz won't talk to us, we'll leave. No harm done."

"That sounds fair." We exchange cell numbers, and I explain where I live. "The manor house is right across from the entrance to the farm. You can't miss it. The house is a mini replica of the inn."

Mandy smiles. "I know exactly where it is."

I argue with my conscience as I drive through town on Main Street. Am I exploiting this child by allowing her to tell her very personal story on television? I call Jack for his opinion, but he doesn't answer. Then I remember he texted about a meeting with a client in Lovely. Ultimately, I decide that, if Jazz chooses to do the interview, talking about the situation so openly might be therapeutic for her.

I drive around to the back of the farm and park at the maintenance building near the wellness center. I find Opal and Jazz working at their easels on the lawn under Opal's favorite dogwood tree. Jazz's painting of the lake is quite good, and I tell her as much.

"Thank you," Jazz says. "Maybe I'll become an artist like Opal."

"What happened to being a rock star like Billy?"

Jazz flashes a toothy grin. "I can be both."

"Yes, you can." I crouch down at eye level with her. "So, kiddo, I need to talk to you about something," I say and explain about the reporter. "They want to interview you for the evening news."

Jazz's golden eyes get big. "You mean, like on television?"

"Exactly." I run a finger down her cheek. "You don't have to do this, sweetheart. Talking about what Sophia did to you might be difficult."

Jazz cranes her neck to see Opal behind her. Opal gives her a nod of encouragement.

"I want to do it, Stella. I have nothing to be ashamed of. And my story might help some other kid who's being bullied."

I cut my eyes at Opal, who grins sheepishly at me. My grandmother is full of good advice, and I'm thrilled Jazz feels comfortable confiding in her.

"All right, then." I stand up straight, giving my stiff legs a shake. "We should get going. The reporter is waiting for us at the manor house."

"Are you coming too, Opal?" Jazz asks as we pack up their art supplies.

"Are you kidding? No way will I miss your television debut. I'll follow you over in my car." Opal tosses her art bag over her shoulder, tucks her easel under her arm, and heads off to the parking lot at the main building.

I thumb a quick text to Mandy as we walk back to the car. *We're a go. Be there in a minute.*

On the way to the manor house, Jazz quizzes me about what questions the reporter might ask. "I honestly don't know, sweetheart. If she asks you anything you're not comfortable talking about, don't answer her. Okay?"

"Okay."

Mandy and her cameraman are waiting in the driveway when we arrive. She holds out her hand to Jazz. "I'm honored to meet you. I hear you have a very important story to tell."

Jazz shrugs, as though unsure of what to say. "Can Angel be on TV too?"

"Who's Angel?" Mandy asks.

"My dog. I'll go get her." Jazz runs inside, and seconds later, the golden retriever comes bounding out of the house with tail wagging.

"She's been in her crate for hours," I say to Mandy. "I'll put her up after she goes potty."

"I'm a big fan of dogs. If she can behave, we'll include her in the interview." Mandy circles the terrace. "Let's film out here. It's lovely with the sun filtering through the trees."

Mandy and the cameraman spend a few minutes choosing the right position for the two lounge chairs they've chosen for the interview. They decide to place the chairs at the edge of the terrace with the colorful autumn trees in the background. Mandy sits in one of the chairs and waits patiently for Jazz and Angel to come to her.

Mandy asks Jazz about Angel's favorite toy and what treats she likes. Jazz hardly notices when the cameraman attaches a microphone to the front of her sweater. Jazz and Mandy take turns petting the dog and rubbing her ears. When Mandy sits back in her chair, Jazz tells Angel *down* and the dog sinks to the bluestone pavers at Jazz's feet.

When I look up, I see the camera is rolling. If they decide to use it, the footage will make for a sweet introduction.

Mandy angles her knees toward Jazz. "So, Jazz, I understand you've been having some trouble at school. Can you tell me a little more about it?"

"Well . . ." Jazz's eyes fall into her lap, and I'm terrified she might cry. Then she inhales a deep breath and looks up. "A girl in my class has been hitting and pinching me. I got tired of it and told our substitute. Mrs. Ramsey said to ignore her. I tried that. But the girl started hitting and pinching me harder. When I told Mrs. Ramsey again, she said if I didn't keep my mouth shut about the bullying, she'd give me Fs on all my schoolwork and make me repeat second grade."

Mandy frowns. "That must have been hard for you, going to an adult for help with a problem and having her turn you away."

Jazz bobs her head.

"What happened then?" Mandy asks.

"The girl pushed me down on the playground the other day. I skinned my knees really bad." Jazz pats the knees of her blue jeans. "I had to go to the nurse's office. Stella, my sister soon to be my mom, came to the school, and they made me tell them about the mean girl and Mrs. Ramsey."

"You did the right thing in telling the truth," Mandy says. "Do you understand why you've been out of school these past few days?"

"We're having a walkout." Jazz hunches her shoulders and holds her hands out by her sides. "Whatever that means."

Mandy snickers. "Are you enjoying your time away from school?"

"Sorta. My grandmother is teaching me to paint." Jazz smiles over at Opal, who is standing with me behind the cameraman. "But I like school." Jazz's face falls. "At least I used to. I wish our real teacher would come back. She'll make everything go back to the way it was."

Mandy hesitates, as though debating whether to ask her next question. "Do you know why Mrs. Wheeler is out? Why you have a substitute for an extended period?"

"The mean girl claims Mrs. Wheeler said a naughty word in class. But none of the other kids heard her. I don't think Mrs. Wheeler uses bad words. She's too nice."

"She sure sounds like it. I have a hunch you're gonna get your wish about Mrs. Wheeler."

Jazz presses her hands together as though praying. "I hope so."

"Thank you for talking to us today, Jazz. It took a lot of courage for you to share your story. I know the other children and parents at your school appreciate you coming forward." Mandy looks down at the sleeping golden retriever. "Your dog's personality matches her name. She is an angel."

As if on cue, Angel cracks an eyelid and then closes it again. Jazz giggles and Mandy laughs out loud.

When Mandy tells the cameraman to cut, Jazz jumps to her feet. "Am I done?"

"You're done. You did beautifully, Jazz. Thank you." Jazz runs off with the dog, and Mandy stands to face me. "She's amazing."

My eyes travel to Jazz and Angel in the yard. "Thanks. I think so too."

"We'll open with her segment, and then transition to the footage we took at the school. Our community won't tolerate what's been happening there. I imagine you'll be hearing from the head of the school board before the evening is over."

I let out a breath of air I didn't know I'd been holding. "I certainly hope you're right. Thank you for caring, Mandy. And thank you for being so patient with Jazz."

"It was my pleasure." Mandy checks the time on her phone. "Five o'clock already. We need to hurry back to the station if we want to make the six o'clock news."

I walk Mandy to the driveway and wave as she speeds off in the van.

Jazz comes running up to me. "Can Opal stay for dinner? I want her to watch the news with us. Will Jack be home by then? Can we get pizza from Ruby's to celebrate? Please, please, oh pretty please."

"Yes, yes, and yes. But first you need to feed Angel and take a bath. You're covered in paint."

Jazz frowns. "Where?"

"Right there." I touch the tip of my finger to her nose. "You have yellow speckles all over your nose."

Jazz brushes my hand away and rubs her nose. "Do you think the paint will show up on camera?"

"So what if it does? You're so cute it won't matter." I scoop her up in my arms and carry her giggling and squirming inside.

When Jazz goes upstairs to take her bath, Opal says, "If you call in the pizza order, I'll go pick it up."

"I hate to ask you to do that."

"I don't mind at all. But hurry. We don't want to miss the show."

I smile at her. "Yes, ma'am."

While Opal's gone, I call Grace and tell her about the interview. "That's fabulous news. Principal Murphy's gonna be shaking in his Converse high tops."

"I can hardly wait," I say.

At five minutes till six, I'm seated at the kitchen counter with Jazz and Opal, the television on and a large pizza box open in front of us, when Jack arrives home. "Pizza night on a Wednesday. What's the occasion?"

I pat the empty stool beside me. "Sit down and watch. I don't have time to explain."

He lowers himself to the stool as Mandy announces, "I'm reporting from Hope Springs Elementary, where second-grade parents staged a walkout this week amid allegations of teacher misconduct." The camera direction changes, capturing Mandy from a different angle. "I had the opportunity to speak with one of these young students earlier today."

Jazz's face appears on TV and her interview with Mandy broadcasts in its entirety. Grace's footage follows, and the segment closes with Mandy and Jazz interacting with Angel.

Jazz hops off her barstool, and taking hold of Angel's front paws, they victory-dance around the kitchen.

I remain glued to my barstool, staring blankly at the commercial on television. "Mandy is a genius. That was amazing."

Jack gets up and pours himself a Maker's Mark and water. Sipping his drink, he says, "I'm so proud of you, Jazz. You handled that like a pro."

My phone blows up on the counter in front of me. I scroll through the texts until I get to Grace's. *AMAZING! JAZZ IS A HERO.*

I read the text out loud and Jazz squeals. I'm ecstatic to see her happy again.

Another text from Grace. *Incoming. Wait for it.*

My eyes are glued to the phone for fifteen minutes before she finally calls. "We've won a short-term victory," Grace blurts out. "Our class has a new substitute, a young woman Rebecca endorses wholeheartedly. *And* the investigation into the allegations against Rebecca will begin first thing tomorrow morning. The school board promises to wrap up the investigation in ten days' time."

"Yes," I say, punching the air with my fist. "What about Principal Murphy?"

"The school board is organizing a special committee to look into every single complaint against him. We've done our part, Stella. The rest is up to them."

Grace and I make a date for coffee in the morning before ending the call. I repeat the conversation to the three sets of eyes staring at me, and they cheer in response.

Despite all I've accomplished since coming to Hope Springs, everything pales compared to the way I feel at this moment. I rest my hand on my expanding belly. I've built a life for myself. My guests are important to me. Granting their wishes fulfills me. But raising my family matters most.

27

OLLIE

Ollie leaves her apartment at the usual time on Thursday morning. But instead of heading toward the inn, she walks up Main Street in the opposite direction. At the end of her block, a strange man steps in line beside her. "Are you Ollie Hendrix?"

"Who wants to know?" she asks, casting a quick glance in his direction. He's tall and attractive. She guesses him to be in his late twenties or early thirties.

"I'm Sheldon Love. I'm—"

"I know who you are. I was warned you might pay me a visit."

If he's surprised, he hides it well. "In that case, let's dispense with the pleasantries. I'm prepared to offer you a large sum of money to walk away from Foxtail Farm."

"You're wasting your time. Melvin Bass will never let the property fall into your family's hands."

Love rakes his fingers through his wavy golden hair. "Maybe not. But Melvin won't live forever. And his sons will sign over the property before they put Melvin in the ground."

"I wouldn't be so sure about that," Ollie says, even though

she has no idea what Melvin's sons will do after he's gone. She increases her pace. "I'm not backing down from this deal. The property will be mine in a month's time."

Love hurries to catch up with her. "I wouldn't be so quick to turn down my offer. If you go through with the purchase, my older brothers will get involved. And they aren't nearly as nice as me."

Ollie stops walking. "Are you threatening me?"

"Not a threat. But a warning. I know my brothers. And they will make your life a living hell."

Ollie thinks back to all the years her own brother bullied her. But Alex is in prison now. And Ollie will never let anyone bully her again. "I never shy away from a challenge, Mr. Love. Tell your brothers to bring it on." She inclines her head at him. "Have a good day. I look forward to being your neighbor."

Ollie hurries off, relieved when he doesn't follow her. She arrives for her appointment with her new financial advisor with no time to spare. Harriet Hogan assures Ollie she can easily afford to purchase the vineyard and make the necessary improvements to the facilities. An hour later, Ollie leaves the meeting with a financial plan in place for her future.

Back at the inn, she calls Jamie to tell him she's ready to make her offer. The amount she proposes is slightly less than asking price. She has a hunch Melvin would take even less money. But the farm is already a steal, and she doesn't want to take advantage of him.

Jamie assures her it's a fair offer, and twenty minutes later, he emails the paperwork for her to sign.

Ollie is on pins and needles as she moves through the rest of her morning and early afternoon, waiting to hear back from Jamie. But this kind of stress she can handle. She hasn't had a panic attack since she first considered buying Foxtail Farm. She'll soon be spending her days outdoors, breathing fresh air with the sun warming her face. She can never go home again, to Hendrix Estates where she grew up. But Foxtail Farms is the next best thing.

Five minutes after one, Ollie's eating a quinoa bowl in the cafe downstairs when she receives the call from Jamie. "Melvin accepted your offer. Congratulations. You're going to be a wine-maker again."

Ollie sets down her fork and places a hand on her pounding heart. "I can't believe it. I'm thrilled out of my mind. But I'm also scared to death."

Jamie chuckles. "I would be worried if you weren't a little nervous. You're taking on an enormous venture. But I have faith in you, Ollie. You're gonna be a tremendous success. Melvin thinks so too."

"Really? Did he say that?"

"Really."

Ollie hears laughter in his voice and imagines his adorable dimples. "I'm flattered. That means a lot coming from Melvin."

"Indeed, it does. He's a legend in these parts." Jamie pauses a beat. "Tell you what. I need to get the earnest money check from you. Why don't I drive over to Hope Springs this afternoon, and we can have a drink to celebrate?"

Ollie wonders if he has drinks with all his clients when he closes a deal. But she doesn't care. She suddenly wants to see him again. There's no harm in an innocent flirtation. Even if he is just a boy.

"I'd like that," Ollie says. "How about if we meet in Billy's Bar here at the inn around five thirty?"

"Perfect. I'll see you then."

Ollie is too excited to return to work. Her life is about to change drastically, and she's in the mood to celebrate. Dumping her half-eaten lunch into the trash can, she retrieves her purse from her office and hurries back to her apartment. She gets in her car and drives out to the Ford dealership on the outskirts of town. Two hours later, she leaves the lot in a brand-new gray Bronco Sport.

She takes a leisurely joyride into the mountains before returning to the inn. She's exiting the main building when she sees Presley and Fiona on the front porch of the caretaker's cottage.

Presley waves her over, and Ollie joins them. She looks down at the bundled infant sleeping soundly in Fiona's arms. "She's so sweet. Is she always so good?"

Presley holds up crossed fingers. "So far."

Ollie plops down into the empty rocker. "You look amazing, Presley. Motherhood agrees with you."

Presley's smile lights up her face. "I feel amazing. I'm not ready to go back to work yet, but I'm going to have the nanny come a few hours next week, so she can get used to the baby and I can run errands."

Presley studies Ollie more closely. "You're the one who looks amazing. You're practically beaming. What gives? Have you met someone?"

Ollie doesn't mention Jamie. There's nothing to talk about yet. "I bought a vineyard."

Fiona looks up from the baby. "Shut up!"

Presley holds her hand up for a high five. "That's fabulous, Ollie. Congrats."

"I haven't told Stella yet, so please don't mention this to anyone. I plan to stay on at the inn until I hire and train my replacement." Ollie is suddenly eager to move to Foxtail Farm, to start working the land. She makes a mental note to talk to Melvin about his farm hands. He must have at least two or three employees. She'd like to keep them on, if possible. She certainly can't manage the acreage alone.

Fiona places the baby in the stroller. "Tell us about the vineyard."

"The name is Foxtail Farm, and it's located twenty minutes away in Lovely. The house needs updating, but the winery is in great shape. There's a stone lodge with an amazing view of the mountains. I'm hiring Jack to convert it into a tasting room and cafe."

"That sounds seriously cool," Fiona says. "So you'll be hiring a chef?"

"Along with a lot of other staff as well." Ollie's chest tightens at the thought of all she has ahead of her. She takes several deep breaths until the panic subsides. One step at a time. She can do this.

Fiona stands. "Well, keep me in the loop. I better get back to the kitchen before Cecily comes after me."

Ollie waits until she's out of earshot. "Keep her in the loop about what?"

"She asked if you'll be hiring a chef. Sounds to me like she's interested in a job."

Ollie smacks the chair's arm. "Duh. I didn't pick up on that. So much has happened today, I'm not thinking straight. Do you think she's ready to be a chef?"

"Absolutely! If she's interested, I would hire her in a minute."

"I'll give it some thought. I don't want to rush into anything. My most recent hire didn't turn out so well."

Presley narrows her gray eyes. "You mean Kate?"

"Yep." Ollie tells Presley about the false reference on Kate's resume.

Presley blinks hard. "Kate doesn't seem like the type who would do something like that."

"Come on, Presley. You have to admit she's kinda strange."

Presley considers this. "Maybe. But in a good way. I think she's immature and socially awkward."

"I wouldn't categorize her as immature. She had a legitimate reason for lying. She got fired from her old job for having an affair with a client's husband. Ruined both their marriages."

"Wait," Presley says, gripping the arms of her rocker. "Kate's been married before?"

"Yep. Do you think I should fire her?"

Presley hesitates. "I'm not the best person to ask about that. I have a special place in my heart for her after the storm. I don't know what I would've done if Kate hadn't found the nurse practitioner to deliver the baby."

Ollie's aqua eyes get big. "Right! I forgot about that. So what do I do? Should I tell Stella?"

"Hmm," Presley says, tapping her chin. "Maybe you should ask Kate why she lied first. See if she tells you the truth. If she does, give her a warning and put her on probation."

"That sounds like a solid plan."

Presley stands and stretches. "I'm stiff from so much sitting around. I can't wait to exercise again."

Ollie rests her head against the back of the rocker and inhales the clean mountain air. "Who would've thought I'd end up in the mountains of Virginia? Me, a born-and-raised California girl."

"I know what you mean," Presley says, leaning against the railing. "This place has a way of growing on you. I'm a city girl at heart. But I'm seriously considering staying in Hope Springs. My family is here, and it's a great place to raise children."

"I thought you were dying to get back to Nashville to start your event planning company."

"My plans have changed. I'm thinking of starting a party rental company instead, one that caters to high-end events offering premium linens and authentic Sperry Tents and props like elegant seating arrangements."

Ollie rocks to her feet and stands beside Presley at the railing. "That sounds exciting, Presley. There's definitely a need. We can do business together. I imagine I'll be hosting weddings at Foxtail Farm. On a smaller scale, of course."

Presley gives her a half hug. "I hope that means we'll be friends for a good long time."

Ollie bends over the stroller and strokes the baby's head. "I certainly hope so. I'd love to see this little one grow up."

It scares Ollie a little how perfectly things are falling into place. But life is full of ups and downs. She's had plenty of downs lately. She'll enjoy the ups while they last.

28

CECILY

C ecily is in her office, going through a stack of invoices, when she receives word about a man in Billy's Bar asking to speak with her. "Parker thinks the man's the lacrosse coach at Jefferson College," the barback says.

"I'll be right there," Cecily says, needing a minute to collect herself.

She's been waiting all week for word from Coach Anderson. She thought maybe he'd decided not to go along with her plan. She's called the hospital periodically these past few days, to check on Lyle's condition and to make sure he's not out on the loose.

Inhaling a deep breath, she leaves her office and passes through the kitchen and dining room to the lounge. Anderson sits on the stool closest to the lobby with a beer mug on the bar in front of him. When he spots her, he moves over a stool, and she slides onto his vacated seat.

"I haven't seen Lyle yet," Anderson says. "Although not for lack of trying. You were right about his mother. She's worse than a guard at a state prison. She refuses to let me talk to him. She's accusing you of fabricating allegations against him."

Cecily rolls her eyes. "She's ridiculous. I'm trying to save him from going to prison."

With a grim expression, Anderson says, "That's what we all want, Cecily."

She presses her lips into a thin smile. She's relieved he's on her side. "What're we gonna do?"

"I sent one of my most trusted players to see Lyle earlier today. Sandy is a handsome young man with a winning smile who charmed his way past Madame Prison Guard. Lyle didn't tell Sandy about his plans for the future, except to say he was being released tomorrow."

Cecily plants her elbows on the bar. "Which means I'll have to go to the police in the morning."

"Not necessary," Anderson says. "It means I have to get to Lyle tonight. And I will. Even if it means waiting until midnight for his mother to abandon her post."

From the other end of the bar, Parker winks at her, and she wiggles her fingers back at him. "I'm sorry to put you through so much trouble, Coach Anderson."

"It's no trouble. I only wish I had better news. I would've been in touch sooner, but I didn't have your contact information."

"Lyle destroyed my phone." Cecily flashes her new phone. "I got my replacement in the mail yesterday. If you'll give me your number, I'll text you, and then you'll have mine."

Her thumbs fly across her phone's screen as he recites his number.

Anderson's phone dings on the bar with her text. He peers over to read it and sits back on his stool. "It dawned on me that Madame Prison Guard must be staying here, this being the only suitable hotel in town. Since she knows you're the chef at Jameson's, I imagine she's keeping a low profile."

Cecily smacks her forehead with her palm. "Why didn't I

think of that?" She holds up a finger. "Hang on a sec. I'll be right back."

Cecily leaps off the barstool and hurries through the lobby to reception. She doesn't know either of the desk agents. One is on the phone. She leans across the counter toward the other, reading her name tag. "Hi, Sally. I'm Cecily, head chef at Jameson's. I think a friend of mine is a guest here. Can you tell me if you have a reservation for Margaret Walsh?"

Sally's fingers fly across the keyboard. "Yes, ma'am. She's staying here. But I can't give out her room number."

"I understand. Thanks. And don't call me ma'am again. I'm not much older than you."

A flush creeps up Sally's neck to her cheeks. "Sorry."

"No worries." Cecily is headed back to Billy's when another thought strikes her. She stops in at the hostess stand at Jameson's. "Do we have a guest coming in tonight by the name of Margaret Walsh," she asks Lisa, the head hostess.

"Let me check." Lisa fingers the iPad. "Yep. Reservation for one on the porch at eight thirty."

"Thanks," Cecily says and returns to the lounge to report her discovery to Coach Anderson.

Anderson consults his watch. "It's almost eight now. As soon as I finish my beer, I'll head over to the hospital. If need be, I'll hide out down the hall until I'm certain she's gone."

"Let me know how it goes," Cecily says, standing once again.

"I'll call you as soon as I talk to him."

Returning to the kitchen, Cecily immerses herself in the organized mayhem of dinner preparation to avoid thinking about what's happening at the hospital. Ninety minutes later, her head server summons her to the porch, where a guest is asking for a word with her.

A feeling of dread overcomes her. Either the guest has a complaint, or the guest is Lyle's mother.

Her hunch is correct. Margaret is sipping a glass of red wine on the porch. She points a long, bony finger at the chair opposite her. "Sit."

Cecily's skin prickles with irritation. How dare Margaret order her around on her own turf? She eases into the chair. "How's Lyle?"

"He's being released tomorrow. I'm taking him back to Connecticut with me to convalesce at home. Thanks to you, his future is uncertain. You've ruined his career. And now I will ruin yours."

Through clenched teeth, Cecily says, "You have some nerve threatening me. Your son stalked me for weeks. He almost raped me behind the barn. He held me hostage during the hurricane. And you're accusing *me* of ruining his career. Lyle did that all by himself."

Margaret takes a sip of her wine and dabs her lips with her napkin. "Do you have any evidence of these accusations?"

Cecily glares at her, longing to smack the smirk off the woman's face. "As a matter of fact, I do. A witness who rescued me when Lyle was holding me hostage."

Margaret looks down her nose at Cecily. "I assume Parker is your witness. Do you really want to drag your boyfriend into your problems? The police will never believe him anyway. He's merely corroborating your lies."

Anger burns inside of Cecily. "There are other people who will vouch for me."

"Ah. Yes. Coach Anderson. I don't understand why he's taking your word about these trumped-up allegations. Then again, he's merely a lacrosse coach."

I raise an eyebrow. "As is your son."

Margaret grimaces. "Perhaps now would be a good time for Lyle to consider law school. I've always wanted more for my son, even though he seems content to settle for less than he deserves. Especially when it comes to girls."

Cecily stands abruptly. "Your son needs psychological help, Margaret. I tried to make that happen for him. But you're forcing me to go to the police, which means he will probably go to prison. Is that what you want?"

"I'm not worried. A small-town prosecutor will never win against my high-profile attorneys." Margaret's gaze falls to her dinner plate. "By the way, the lamb was tough as shoe leather. And you call yourself a chef."

Cecily's lungs constrict, and she finds it difficult to breathe. She flees the porch, racing in the dark around the back of the building to her garden. She collapses on the bench, inhaling deeply until her breath steadies.

Her phone vibrates, but when she tugs it free of her pocket, it slips out of her shaking hands, crashing to the gravel path. She bends over to pick it up, relieved to see the screen isn't shattered. But she missed the call from Coach Anderson.

She clicks on his number, calling him back, and he answers right away.

"I spoke with Lyle," the coach says. "He seems genuinely remorseful. And also grateful for the opportunity I offered him. He wants to think about it. He promised to call me in the morning."

"Question is, can he stand up to his mother? He's never been able to before. I just had a run-in with her. You're right. She's turning this on me, making me look like the guilty one."

"My money's on Lyle. He's aware of his crimes. And he understands how lucky he is you're not pressing charges. Try to get some sleep. We'll talk in the morning."

"Thanks for all you've done, Coach Anderson. I'm glad someone believes in me."

"Everyone believes in you, Cecily. Madame Prison Guard will get what's coming to her," Anderson says and ends the call.

Cecily sneaks in the kitchen's back door and pulls Fiona into her office. "I hate to ask you, but can you close up for me tonight?"

Fiona narrows her eyes in concern. "You're pale. Are you sick?"

"Sick at heart. I just had a showdown with Lyle's mother, and I need a drink." Cecily sheds her chef's coat and hangs it on the back of her door. "If anything comes up, I'll be down at Billy's."

Cecily sits at the far end of the bar, and in between him waiting on customers, she feeds Parker snippets of the evening's events. "I'm so done with all this, Parker. It needs to end soon before I lose my mind."

"You won't have to wait much longer." Leaning across the bar, he takes her hand and kisses her fingers. "One way or another, it'll be over tomorrow."

She drinks two more glasses of wine and is more than a little tipsy when Parker walks her home. She yearns to invite him inside. To feel his lips on hers, his hands on her body. Margaret's words rush back to her. *Do you really want to drag your boyfriend into your problems? The police will never believe him anyway.*

"Thanks for walking me home. I'll see you in the morning." Cecily brushes her lips against his before dragging herself up the stairs to her apartment.

After a restless night's sleep, Cecily arrives at work before dawn. She waits for Coach Anderson's call all morning and into the afternoon. Instead of hearing from Anderson, she receives a visit from Lyle around three o'clock. He doesn't ambush her at the back door like the last times. He asks a desk agent to ring the kitchen and let her know he'd like to speak with her.

"Tell him to wait for me in the rockers on the porch," Cecily instructs the desk agent.

Cecily is aghast at the sight of her ex. His left arm is in a sling and his skin is sallow. He was a thin guy to begin with, but now he appears gaunt. When she approaches him, he rises to greet her, but winces in pain and sits back down.

Cecily drops to the chair beside him. She doesn't know what to say, so she lets him take the lead.

"I came to apologize, Cecily. And to say goodbye."

Cecily lets out a breath she didn't know she'd been holding.

"I'm so sorry, Cecily. I was a monster to you." He drags his hand down his face, as though appalled at the memory of the things he'd done. "Thank you for not turning me into the police. You're right. I need psychological help. I'm going home with Mom tomorrow. I'll be starting an outpatient treatment program on Monday."

Cecily's brow shoots up to her hairline. "Does your mom support this decision?"

"She's not happy about it. But I stood up to her for the first time in my life." Lyle chuckles. "She made me promise I'd consider applying to law school once I get my head on straight."

Cecily can't see him as an attorney, but his career is no longer her business.

"Coaching was my way of staying connected to college life," Lyle says. "It's time for me to grow up."

She's relieved to hear him admit what she's been saying all along. "Some people mature quicker than others. You'll eventually get there."

Lyle places his hand on hers. "I wish you a happy life, Cecily. You deserve someone who will treat you like a queen. I've seen the way Parker looks at you. And I think he may be the one."

"I know that wasn't easy for you to say. But I appreciate it." She leans over and kisses his cheek. "I wish you a happy life too, Lyle. Don't give up on coaching just yet. You enjoy it, and the players look up to you. Anderson taught me that there's more to coaching than winning the game. I can see you twenty years down the road, helping a struggling young person the way he helped you."

"Coach Anderson has been an excellent mentor to me. I have a lot to think about in the months ahead." He groans as he hauls his body out of the chair.

Cecily walks Lyle through the building to the front entrance and watches him drive off in his truck. A piece of her heart goes with him. She was once engaged to marry to him. In time, she will forget the bad stuff and only remember the good. At long last, she can put all this behind her and move on with her life.

29

PRESLEY

After spending a lonely Saturday with her newborn, Presley is thrilled when her half brother, Chris, and his girlfriend, Amy, drive over from Lexington to see the baby on Sunday around noon. The weather is unseasonably warm, and Presley suggests lunch on the porch at Jameson's.

"We've already eaten," Chris says. "We grabbed some food on the drive over."

Presley doesn't let her disappointment show. She's eager to resume her life. She reminds herself it's only been a week. It will happen in due time. Today, she'll have to settle for lemonade and cookies on the porch.

Chris can't take his eyes off Riley, but he's afraid to touch her. Amy, on the other hand, is a natural. And Presley is content to let Amy hold the baby.

Lowering herself to a rocker beside Chris, Presley says, "Tell me about college life." She hasn't seen him since August when he left for school.

He talks of the rigorous academics at Washington and Lee and which fraternities he will rush come January. Two hours later, Chris and Amy are saying their goodbyes when Stella and Jazz arrive.

Jazz's face melts when she sees the baby in Presley's arms. "Aww . . . She's so cute. Can I hold her?"

"Of course." Jazz takes a seat in a rocker, and Presley places Riley in her arms. Angel sits in front of her, observing the bundled infant with keen interest.

Jazz looks down at the baby and back up at Presley. "She's so tiny. Does she cry a lot?"

"Not much. Mostly she's sleeps and eats. I'm sure that will change soon."

"Some babies are just good-natured," Stella says. "Maybe she inherited your easygoing personality."

"How're things going at school, Jazz?" Presley asks.

"Great! My teacher's coming back tomorrow."

Presley looks over Jazz at Stella who nods. "The charges have been dropped," Stella says. "The children were questioned one by one. Not a single kid heard Mrs. Wheeler say the dreaded F word."

Presley sits back in her chair. "That's excellent news. I'm so happy for you, Jazz. For your whole class."

"Guess what?" Jazz says. "Principal Murphy is throwing our class a pizza party on Friday. He feels bad about what happened."

Stella chuckles. "He's walking on thin ice with the school board."

"I bet he is," Presley says. "Is the mean girl being any nicer?"

"She's being super nice. I think she got in trouble with her parents. I'll be nice back. But I'm not friends with her anymore. Emily is more fun. Did I tell you? We both got a solo for our choir's Christmas program. Will you come hear me sing, Presley? Please?" Jazz says in a begging tone.

Presley smiles. "I wouldn't miss it."

Presley notices Rita and Brian leaving Jameson's and walking hand in hand toward them. When they reach the porch, Rita peels the baby's blanket back to see her face. "How's my niece today?"

"You can take her?" Jazz holds the baby out to Rita.

"Gladly." Rita accepts the bundle and settles into Jazz's vacated rocker.

Jazz slaps her thigh. "Come on, Angel. Let's go play in the leaves." Jazz scrambles to her feet, and the twosome take off across the lawn.

Presley stands to face Brian. "Have you heard anything about Everett?"

"That's why I'm here. Shall we?" he says, and motions her away from the porch.

Presley's stomach is in knots as she follows him across the sidewalk. They stand under a maple tree, its brilliant orange leaves fluttering to the ground around them.

"As you warned, Wade was not very cooperative. I had to threaten to sue him to get the name of the rehab facility." Brian leans against the tree. "I spoke with the administrator, Edward Reardon, at length this morning. If he was irritated at me for interrupting his Sunday morning, he didn't show it. According to Reardon, Everett was a mess when he committed himself to the facility. But he's making excellent progress now."

"I'm so relieved." Presley sags against the tree beside Brian. "Can I talk to Everett?"

"Not yet. I told Reardon about the baby, and he promised to pass along the news to Everett. But he asked us to hold off a little while longer. He assured me that either he or Everett will be in touch soon."

Presley inhales a deep breath. "I can wait. As long as I know he's safe and getting the help he needs. Thank you, Brian." She stands on her tiptoes and kisses his cheek.

"You bet. I have a good feeling about this, Presley. I have faith that everything will work out for you and Everett."

They return to the porch where Stella and Rita are snickering about something. "What's so funny?"

"Lucy." Rita gestures at her sister, who is standing on the stone terrace, looking out at the mountains. "Look at her. She's a million miles away with that goofy expression on her face. She spent the weekend in Raleigh with Levi. I think she's in love."

"Good for her," Stella says. "She's been through so much. I'm glad to see her happy."

While Presley is happy for Lucy, she's worried Lucy isn't ready for a serious relationship. Especially with a man she spent the last thirty years despising.

Rita calls out to her sister, who waves and heads toward them.

"Let me hold my grandchild." Lucy takes the baby from Rita and sits down next to her.

"I hear you were in Raleigh again this weekend," Presley says in a nonchalant tone.

Lucy's eyes remain on the baby. "I came back this morning. Levi has to work this afternoon to prepare for a big case." She looks up at Presley. "He's coming to Hope Springs next weekend. He wants the three of us to have dinner together at Jameson's on Saturday night. Do you think you can get a sitter?"

"I'll check with my new nanny and let you know."

Lucy smiles. "I'll make the reservation for seven. Levi's really looking forward to getting to know you better."

"Me too." Flutters dance across Presley's chest at the idea of having dinner with her biological father and learning more about her three half siblings.

Presley's guests linger for most of the afternoon, soaking up the warm sunshine and cooing over the baby. Jazz and Angel are content to wallow in the leaves under the orange maple. It's nearly four o'clock when Jazz finally drags Stella away. "I have to do my homework."

Stella rises slowly from where she's been sitting on the edge of the porch. "I know, kiddo. And I need to run to the grocery. But I hate to see the weekend end."

Everyone departs at once and Presley's loneliness sets in again. After feeding and changing the baby, she straps her in the stroller and moseys down the hill toward the lake. She's nearing the wellness center when Kate comes flying out of the building. She's staring at the ground and swiping at her eyes. Kate doesn't see Presley until she almost runs into the stroller. "Watch out, Kate!"

Kate jumps back, startled. "I'm sorry. I didn't see you."

Kate appears shaken, and Presley takes hold of her arm to steady her. "Are you alright?"

"Not really. Not at all, actually. I can't do anything right," Kate cries.

"Do you want to talk about it? It might make you feel better."

"I guess," Kate says with trembling shoulders.

"Let's go out to the pier," Presley says. They pass the wellness center and stroll to the end of the pier, where they sit on the edge with their legs dangling over the side. "Tell me what happened."

Kate covers her face with her hands. "I have a bad habit of doing and saying things without thinking about them. And I'm always getting myself in trouble because of it."

"You mean, like an impulse control problem?" This makes sense to Presley, from the little she knows about Kate.

"Exactly!" Kate leans against a piling and tucks her legs under her chin. "I got fired from my last job for having an affair with a client's husband. My husband divorced me, but our marriage was doomed anyway. We got married way too young. Another example of my brilliant decision-making abilities. Anyway, I provided a fake reference on my resume, and Ollie found out about it."

Presley doesn't admit she already knows this. "What happened?"

"She was surprisingly cool about it. I told her the truth. I'm not a liar. I just really wanted this job, and I needed a solid reference. Ollie agreed to give me another chance, because I'm a good yoga instructor. But I'm sure I'll blow it."

"You can start by adjusting your attitude. Think positively."

"You don't understand, Presley. Even my father hates me."

Presley inches closer to her. "Oh, honey, I'm sure your father doesn't hate you."

Kate turns her head away and stares down at the water. "Maybe *hate* is not the right word. He loves me because I'm his daughter. But he's washed his hands of me. He's tired of bailing me out of my messes. He says I have to figure life out on my own. I might as well quit this job and move on. No one here likes me. Except maybe you. Do you like me, Presley?"

Presley brushes a lock of hair out of Kate's face. "Of course, I like you. If not for you, I would've been in big trouble the night Riley was born."

"So, you feel indebted to me. That doesn't mean you like me for me. No one here ever invites me to hang out. I can't really blame them. I dug my own grave with my big mouth. I know what the problem is. I just don't know how to fix it. I can't change how I'm wired."

Presley squeezes Kate's arm. "Maybe not. But you can get help to control it."

Kate grunts. "Help from whom?"

"I'm not sure. From a therapist, maybe. We'd have to do some research. I imagine this falls under the cognitive behavioral therapy umbrella."

Kate turns to face Presley. "You said *we*. Does this mean you're willing to help me?"

"Absolutely! I'd love to help you." Presley gives Kate's arm a squeeze before dropping her hand. "I hate to waste such a lovely evening. Why don't we grab an early dinner on the porch at Jameson's? We can talk more about your problem and come up with a plan of attack."

Kate eyes the stroller. "What about Riley?"

"I just fed her a few minutes ago. She had a lot of company this afternoon. She should sleep through dinner."

"Can I push the stroller?"

"Of course. Just watch where you're going this time," Presley says with a laugh.

They settle into a straightforward conversation about yoga on the way to the main building. Kate promises to help Presley lose her baby weight in exchange for Presley helping Kate find a therapist.

Both women order salmon Caesar salads, and while they eat, Kate confesses the disastrous impulsive decisions that have shaped her life. She's brutally honest, which Presley finds refreshing and comical. And more than once, she bursts into laughter.

When they've finished eating, while waiting for the check, Presley says, "You have a wonderful sense of humor, Kate. Stop trying so hard to get attention. Just be yourself and people will like you for you."

Kate smiles. "That's good advice. Thanks for the vote of confidence."

Presley is disappointed when they part in the lobby. Not only because she dreads returning to her lonely cottage. But because she felt a genuine connection with Kate.

30

CECILY

Lyle is gone for good. Yesterday morning, Cecily had parked a block away from his house, watching him drive away in a moving truck with his mom in the passenger seat beside him. She feels enormously relieved. She no longer has to look over her shoulder. The Lyle chapter of her life has ended.

Exhaustion prevented Cecily and Parker from being together last night when they got off work at almost one in the morning. Chemistry between them crackles. They both know what's on the horizon. As they hike down from the lookout on Sunday afternoon, Parker calls out to her from behind, "Wanna come over for dinner tonight? We can throw some meat on the grill and drink red wine by the fire."

"And see where the night takes us," Cecily tosses over her shoulder.

His laugh is deep and throaty. "We both know where the night will take us."

Cecily says goodbye to Parker on the inn's front lawn and returns to her apartment to get ready for her date. She takes extra care with her appearance, shaving all the important areas and blow-drying her honey blonde hair. She dresses in a low-cut black top with bell sleeves, tight faded jeans, and her cowboy boots.

She debates whether to drive to Parker's. If she spends the night, she'll have to make the walk of shame home in the morning. Then again, she can't resist the glorious autumn weather. Stuffing a spare toothbrush in her purse, she heads out on foot.

She's no sooner arrived at Parker's than Fiona calls. "Cecily! Get over here now. Norman Byrd, the critic from *Food and Travel* magazine is here."

"Wait. What? How do you know this?"

"I follow all the major food critics on social media. Don't you?"

"Um. No." Cecily looks over at Parker, who is watching her with a curious expression. This could spoil their evening, but what an opportunity. "On a Sunday night. That's pretty random."

"Maybe. But the restaurant is hopping. We have a lot of locals tonight. And the management team from the conference that's starting on Tuesday arrived early."

Cecily turns her back to Parker. "Who's serving him? Where's he seated? And what did he order?"

"Ron is the server. Byrd asked for the dining room, so we seated him at the table in the window alcove at the front. He ordered butternut squash soup, beet salad, and the lamb special. Byrd asked for a wine recommendation and Ron suggested the Barboursville Octagon."

"Best server, excellent choice of wine. I'm glad he recommended local." Cecily reaches for her purse. "I'm on my way. Be there in a second."

Cecily drops her phone in her bag. "I'm so sorry, Parker. I have to go to Jameson's. A renowned food critic is in the house."

"Cool! I'll drive you." He grabs his car keys, and they hurry out the front door.

On the way to the inn, Cecily says, "I don't want to ruin your evening. Why don't you drop me off, and I'll walk back to your house afterward?"

"I don't mind waiting. I can grab a drink in Billy's."

Cecily furrows her brow. "Are you sure? It might take a while."

He grins at her. "Then I'll grab two drinks, and you can drive home. Besides, the Cowboys are playing the Patriots."

Cecily rolls her eyes. "I see how it is. You're ditching me for football."

He turns on his blinker and whips into the employee parking lot. "Hardly. Waiting for you is my reassurance you won't stay all night."

Her lust for him burns deep inside of her. This is one night she won't put work ahead of her personal life. "I promise not to drag it out." She pecks his lips and hops out of the truck.

Racing to the kitchen, she finds Fiona pacing the floor and biting at her fingernails. "How's it going?" Cecily asks.

"I'm not sure. He's on the main course now, but he's not giving anything away."

Cecily follows Fiona across the kitchen, and they peek through the swinging doors. Byrd is a jolly-looking man with a rosy complexion and an ample girth earned from sampling rich cuisine. He carves off a bite of lamb and pops it into his mouth, closing his eyes while he chews. His expression is one of joy, clearly savoring the food. When he opens his eyes again, he looks idly around the dining room at the other guests.

When his gaze passes the kitchen doors, Cecily jumps back. "I hope he didn't see me." She turns away from the door. "I'll be in my office if you need me."

Cecily leaves her office door open and sits down at her desk. She goes over the lamb recipe in her head, wondering what she could've done to make it better.

Ron appears in the doorway a few minutes later. "Byrd is asking to see you."

Cecily shoots out of her chair. "Did he ask for me by name? Or did he ask to speak to the chef?"

"He asked to speak to Chef Cecily."

"Then I'd better go find out what he wants," she mumbles as she brushes past Ron.

Cecily approaches Byrd's table, and when he introduces himself, she fakes surprise. "Thank you for dining with us. We're honored to have you."

He eyes her attire. "Are you headed out somewhere?"

Cecily chuckles. "Tonight's my night off. I'm having dinner with a friend. I just stopped by to check on things."

"Do you have time to join me for coffee or a glass of wine?"

"I can spare a few minutes," Cecily says, easing into the chair.

"Will you help me finish this?" He lifts the Barboursville bottle. "Or would you prefer something else?"

"I'll have the wine." Cecily summons Ron for another glass. "The Barboursville is one of my favorites."

"It would not have been my first choice. But it pairs nicely with the lamb," he says, and lists the favorable characteristics of the wine.

When Ron arrives with her glass, Byrd takes it from him and fills it with wine, handing it to Cecily. "Margaret Walsh is a friend of mine."

The bottom falls out of Cecily's stomach. She remembers Lyle's mother's words. *You've ruined his career. And now I will ruin yours.* "How do you know Margaret?"

"We go way back," he says, but doesn't elaborate. "I owe her a favor. She asked me to write a negative review about Jameson's. I told her I would never jeopardize my career by doing something so underhanded. But I promised I would scrutinize the meal with my most finicky tastebuds."

Cecily's heart beats rapidly against her rib cage. A negative review could destroy Jameson's reputation. "And?" she says in a meek voice.

"Margaret will have to find another favor to ask of me. Because that was one of the most appetizing meals I've ever eaten. And I've eaten in a lot of restaurants, as evidenced by my gut." He chuckles as he rubs his belly. "Not only was the food delicioso, the service was impeccable."

Cecily lets out a steady breath. "I'll tell my staff you approve."

"I approve highly. And I aim to write about it in my review, which will appear in the December issue."

"I'll look forward to reading it," Cecily says, taking her first sip of wine.

"Out of curiosity, if you don't mind me asking, what did you do to make Margaret so angry?"

"I broke off my wedding engagement to her son." Byrd doesn't need to know the torture Lyle has put her through these past few weeks.

"That makes sense. Margaret always was a mama bear where Lyle is concerned."

This is dangerous territory. Cecily knows better than to discuss her almost mother-in-law with him. Besides, she's eager to get on with her evening with Parker. "Would you care for dessert?"

"I'm considering the bread pudding. But I don't want to hold you up. I know you have plans. I just wanted a chance to meet you."

"The pleasure was all mine." Cecily slips away from the table, taking her wine with her.

Instead of going to the kitchen, she walks in the opposite

direction to the lounge, where she finds Parker watching football with a group of regulars. He spins on his stool to face her. "How'd it go?"

"We got lucky. He's giving us a glowing review. You're not gonna believe why he's here."

"Tell me on the way home." Parker downs the rest of his beer and sets the empty bottle on the bar. Cecily follows suit with her wine.

They avoid the food critic by exiting the building through the main front door. On the way to the parking lot, she texts Fiona. *You nailed it. Great job! Stella will be pleased.*

During the return trip to Parker's house, Cecily tells him about her chat with Byrd. "Lyle's mother orchestrated the visit from the food critic. She tried to cash in on a favor Byrd owes her by having him write a negative review of Jameson's. But it backfired on her. I'm grateful he's publishing a favorable review in their December issue. But all restaurants have off nights, and his experience could easily have gone the other way."

"That's downright malicious, Cecily. Only an evil person would intentionally want to hurt someone their son cares about."

"Tell me about it. I'm furious at her." Then it dawns on Cecily. "Actually, I'm not mad. I'm numb. I'm tired of talking about Lyle. Tired of thinking about him. I'm so ready to put this whole thing behind me."

Parker glances over at her. "Are you sure?" The innuendo in his tone stirs feelings of lust deep within her. Not only is he asking if she's ready to put Lyle behind her. He's also asking if she's ready to move on with him.

She smiles at him. "Absolutely positive."

He parks his truck on the curb, and they hurry to his house. He pins her against the door, kissing her as he inserts his key in the lock.

The kiss ends. "What about dinner?" Cecily asks, her lips lingering on his.

"Dinner can wait. But I've waited long enough." He scoops her into his arms, and, pushing the door open with his foot, he carries her inside to his bed.

31

PRESLEY

Lucy and Levi stop by the cottage to pick Presley up and see the baby on their way to dinner at Jameson's on Saturday night. Presley introduces her new nanny, a woman in her sixties with a youthful spirit who has raised too many children to count. After exchanging pleasantries, Patty discreetly disappears into the kitchen while they visit.

Levi is enamored with the baby and surprisingly good with her. He knows just how to hold her and coos to her like a grandfather. *Grandfather.* Presley likes the sound of that.

She watches Levi and Lucy interact with one another. They sit close together on the sofa, their focus on the baby in Levi's arms. Their eyes are bright and cheeks rosy. They are comfortable with each other, intimate, like two people who belong together.

Presley thinks about all the years they've lost. What if Levi and Lucy had gotten married in college? They would be celebrating their thirty-first wedding anniversary this year. Their lives would've been so vastly different. Presley would've been raised in Raleigh. Chris would never have been born. Presley would never have met Everett. And she wouldn't have Riley. She can't change the past, but she can hope for a future where her biological parents are man and wife.

Lucy glances at her watch. "Our reservation is in five minutes. We should head over to the main building."

Presley takes the baby from Levi and walks her to the kitchen. "We'll be on the porch at Jameson's," she says as she places the baby in Patty's arms. "Call me if you need me."

Patty gazes adoringly at the baby. "We'll be fine. You run along and have a good time."

Presley is overjoyed at the prospect of adult companionship over dinner at a restaurant. She feels like her old self dressed in normal clothes—a new heather-colored cashmere sweater with her black leggings and knee-high boots. The evening is cool, with temperatures in the low fifties, and the vibe on the porch at Jameson's is festive.

She orders a glass of champagne, even though she's breast-feeding. "I can't think of a better reason to celebrate."

Levi's face lights up. "I agree. Make it a bottle," he says to the server.

The threesome settle into easy conversation as they sample cheeses and meats from the charcuterie board. Levi is an excellent storyteller, and he entertains them with tales of his mischievous sons—Douglas and Adam. Presley finds it odd he doesn't mention his daughter—the half sister she's eager to know more about. The champagne makes her giddy, and she's working up the courage to ask about her, when his gaze shifts and his eyes narrow at something over Presley's left shoulder.

"Is that . . . " Levi blinks hard and opens his eyes wider. "It can't be."

Presley turns her head to see the object of his attention is Kate, walking up the sidewalk toward the main building. "Do you know Kate?"

His jaw slackens. "So, it is Kate. She's my daughter." He stands abruptly and leaves the table.

Turning around in her chair, Presley watches Levi jogging across the lawn and calling out to Kate, who slows her pace as she approaches him. He holds her at arm's length, and they talk for a few minutes, but their expressions give little away. When Levi makes a sweeping gesture toward Jameson's, Kate gives a reluctant nod, and he hooks an arm around her waist as they walk to the porch.

Anger surges through Presley as reality sets in. This can't be a coincidence. Why would Kate keep something so important from Presley?

Kate avoids Presley's icy stare as she claims the empty chair next to her.

"I assume everyone's met," Levi says with an awkward chuckle.

"We've met," Presley says with a tight expression. "Although Kate neglected to tell me she's my half sister. Why is that, Kate?"

"I think you owe everyone an explanation," Levi says to Kate. "Including me. I've been so worried about you. What are you doing here?"

Kate stares down at the table. "You told me to figure out my life. So that's what I'm doing. I'm working here as a yoga instructor."

"You didn't land in Hope Springs by accident," Levi says. "You came here after I told you about Presley."

Presley's stomach does a somersault. *He told his daughter about me.*

Kate glares at her father. "You'd only met Presley for a few minutes, but you talked about her like she was the greatest thing in the world. Like you talk about Adam and Doug. Like you never talk about me."

The anguish on Kate's face makes Presley soften toward her.

When they were discussing Kate's impulse control problem, Presley remembers Kate saying her father hates her. How awful she must feel inside to think that. "Why didn't you tell me who you were?" she asks Kate.

"I came here on a mission. I wanted to see what was so great about you. I figured if I could be more like you, my father would be proud of me. But you've been so nice to me, and I've been trying to figure out a way to tell you the truth." Kate falls back in her chair. "At least now you know. Even if you hate me."

"I don't hate you, Kate. I understand your motivations." A smile spreads across Presley's face. "I was beginning to think of you as a friend. Even better that we're sisters."

Kate beams. "I think so too."

Levi summons the server for another champagne glass, and they place their orders for their entrees.

The foursome has much to talk about throughout dinner. Presley asks so many questions about her half brothers, Levi suggests they all have Thanksgiving together at the inn. "It'll provide the perfect opportunity for everyone to get to know one another better. I'll rent a couple of cottages for us on Cottage Row. I assume Jameson's will serve Thanksgiving dinner." Levi looks first at Presley and then Lucy.

"Why don't I have you all to my house?" Lucy suggests. "We'll be more relaxed. And Chris will be home. I want him to meet everyone."

A tipsy Kate claps her hands. "Let's do it. We'll all pitch in and help cook."

Levi smiles. "I'll check with the boys to see if they're available and make the reservations for two cottages."

After dinner, the four of them stroll through the lobby toward the main entrance. Levi has booked a room at the inn. If Lucy is staying with him, Presley doesn't want to know about it.

Levi offers to walk Kate home, but she refuses. "I'm fine. I only live a block away."

Levi smiles at her. "Then have breakfast with me in the morning. Just the two of us."

Kate's blue eyes twinkle. "I'd like that," she says, kissing his cheek before heading off down the long driveway.

Presley says goodnight to Lucy and Levi before returning to the cottage.

"She's an angel," Patty says, peering down at the baby sleeping soundly in her bassinet. "I fed her about an hour ago. She'll probably be out for a while."

"Thank you, Patty. I'm so grateful to have you," Presley says as she walks the nanny to the door. "If it works for you, I'd like to return to work part-time starting next week."

Patty holds her arms akimbo. "Fine by me. Just text me your schedule."

Presley locks up the cottage and carries her sleeping infant up the stairs. She's tucking Riley into her crib when she hears someone tapping lightly on the front door. Assuming Patty forgot something, she hurries on socked feet down the stairs and around the corner into the living room. She freezes at the sight of her husband peeking at her through the porch window. Her heart skips a beat. And then another. She still loves him, and it would be so easy to take him back, no questions asked. But he's put her through hell.

She swings the door open. "You have a lot of explaining to do."

"I'm aware." He steps toward her. "Motherhood agrees with you, Presley. You're positively radiant."

This would sound corny coming from anyone else. But her husband writes country music. His lyrics are full of corny sentiments. The tenderness in his tone and love in his eyes touch her heart, but is it real? She's eager to hear more.

"I wish I could say the same about you." His face is pale, and he's lost at least ten pounds. Weight he didn't need to lose.

Everett hangs his head. "You have no idea what I've been through. I feel like I'm returning home from war. I'm sorry I've been out of touch for so long."

"It's been months," Presley says in a matter-of-fact tone of voice.

"That long? I truly didn't realize that much time had passed. I've been so lost. And I was so ashamed. I let you down."

"We have a lot to talk about." Presley motions him to the sofa and takes a seat in the adjacent club chair. "Start at the beginning. And don't leave anything out."

Everett sits on the edge of the cushion, as though afraid of getting too comfortable. "Things went south quickly after you left the tour. We met Audrey Manning in Vegas. Wade went gaga over her. Audrey fit into my tour like a square peg in a round hole, but Wade refused to give up on her. He staged photo ops to make it look like Audrey and I were together. I swear I never touched her, Presley. I don't even like her. She's not a nice person. She and Wade deserve each other."

"Are you aware Audrey has taken over your tour?" Presley asks and watches closely for his reaction. He's been in rehab for weeks. Presumably, with no access to social media. This news is liable to hit him hard.

"Whatever. I don't really care. Wade and I are finished."

"What about your career? You could find a new manager."

Everett grunts. "My career as I know it is over."

Her heart goes out to him. Being a star was his dream come

true. Even if it had been his downfall and the source of problems in their marriage. "It doesn't have to be, Ev. You could find another manager."

"It's not about the manager. It's about the lifestyle. My doctors at rehab helped me realize I'm not fit to be a country music star. But I can still have a successful songwriting career. That's the part I love the most anyway."

"And what made your music so unique." Presley gets up and crosses the room to the window. "I guess this means you'll be moving back to Nashville."

Everett comes to stand beside her. "I have a lot of making up to do, Presley. And I promise I will in time. If you'll let me, I'd like to stay here in Hope Springs with you and Riley. We can make a comfortable life for ourselves. We can buy a little house and raise chickens."

She cast him a sideways glance. "Chickens?"

Everett throws his hands up. "Or horses or whatever you want."

Presley turns to face him. "Children. I want a bunch of children."

Everett's blue eyes are as electric as the night they met. "We can have as many as you want."

She palms his cheek. "You pushed me away, Everett. You broke our trust. You'll have to earn it back."

"I will. If it takes me the rest of our lives." He places his hands on her hips. "I'm a deeply flawed person, Presley. But, if you give me a chance, I can make you happy."

"I will give you a second chance, Everett. But not a third."

"I understand." He leans in and kisses her lightly on the lips. "Can I meet my daughter now?"

Presley kisses him again. "I thought you'd never ask." Taking him by the hand, she leads him up the stairs to the nursery.

Her friends may think her a fool for forgiving him so easily. But he's hurting, and he needs her. And truth be told, she needs him too. She doesn't want to raise their child alone. They are charting their courses. They made a slight detour and learned a lot about themselves and each other along the way. But now, they are on the road to a new beginning.

32

STELLA

A mass of second graders explodes through the barn's back door amongst squeals of laughter. They're dressed as firemen and skeletons, princesses and witches. They surround their teacher, begging to go through the haunted house again.

"Not today. Time for the hayride." Rebecca corrals them over to the trailer, which the grounds crew has outfitted for the event with bales of hay that line the sides for seating. Once everyone is loaded, Rebecca signals to Jack at the wheel of the old red tractor, and they head off for a slow cruise around the farm.

Cecily and Parker emerge from the barn, laughing as they tug off their monster masks.

"How'd it go?" I call out as I walk toward them.

"It was a blast!" Cecily says.

"Poor kids! Cecily scared the heck out of them." Parker draws Cecily in for a half hug and kisses her cheek. "If you decide to quit your day job, I hear Frankenstein is looking to hire."

Cecily shoves him away. "Ha ha."

Parker gestures at the refreshments table. "Anyone want a bottled water?"

Cecily raises her hand. "Me, please. I'm parched."

I shake my head. "No, thanks."

Cecily wears a dreamy expression as she watches him go.

I nudge her. "If you could see your face. You've got it bad. Things are obviously going well between y'all."

"Better than I ever thought possible." Cecily's smile fades. "He wants me to move in with him. But I know it's too soon."

"What's stopping you?"

She jerks her head toward me. "Are you joking? Aren't you the one who warned me to take it slow with Parker? Part of the problem with Lyle was that we moved things too fast."

"True. But you never looked at Lyle the way you look at Parker."

"I'm scared, Stella. I'm crazy about him." Cecily's starry eyes are on Parker as he chats with Ollie and Fiona at the food table. "But what if it doesn't work out? I don't want to get trapped in another dead-end relationship?"

"Why not leave your furniture in my garage apartment? That way, you'll have a place to go if necessary."

I can see the wheels in Cecily's brain spinning as she considers my suggestion. "I like that idea. We'd be living together on a trial basis. Are you sure you don't mind? Of course, I'd continue to pay you rent."

I cross my eyes at her. "No, you won't either. I'm not looking for another tenant anyway. At least not now. If I decide to hire a nanny, I'll offer it to her. But that's months away."

"You're the best, Stella." She throws her arms around me. "I can't wait to tell Parker."

Cecily takes off, running over to the table and pulling Parker away from Ollie and Fiona. I smile as I watch the scene unfold. When Cecily tells him the news, Parker picks her up and twirls her around. He puts her down and kisses her on the lips. My heart swells with happiness for Cecily. I've always thought Lyle's and Cecily's personalities clashed. Lyle is so laid-back and Cecily so driven. But her relationship with Parker feels right.

I mosey over to the stage where Presley is helping Everett test his equipment before his show. Nearby, Riley is sleeping peacefully in her stroller.

"Are you sure you're ready for a live performance?" I ask Everett.

Everett chuckles. "If I can't sing to a group of second graders, my problems are worse than I thought. Besides, I feel great. Being home with my family this past week and breathing this clean mountain air has worked wonders."

I study him more closely. "Now that you mention it, you look much healthier. Your cheeks have a rosy glow."

Everett winks at Presley. "My wife's fattening me up. Whatever weight she's losing, I'm gaining."

"If you can spare a minute, I have a proposition for you two."

Everett and Presley abandon the equipment and join me on the ground in front of the stage. "What's up?" Presley asks.

"Since you'll be busy in the coming months getting your party rental business up and running, Presley,"—I turn my attention to Everett—"I was wondering if you would consider being my assistant manager, Everett." I place my hand on my belly. "With the babies coming next spring, I need someone in place. You have plenty of knowledge of the inn from when you were a bartender. What you don't know, I can teach you. The position is part-time right now. Even though your responsibilities will increase when I go on maternity leave, you should still have plenty of time for songwriting."

Everett looks over at Presley, who nods.

"I realize you're looking for a house," I say. "But this would enable you to stay in the caretaker's cottage until you find exactly what you want."

A slow smile spreads across Everett's lips. "I'll take it! Songwriting may ultimately be a full-time gig for me, but I could use the diversion now. And this would enable Presley to launch her company right away."

Presley leans into Everett, resting her head on his chest.

"Then we have a deal." I wrap my arms around both of them, squeezing tight.

"Thank you," Presley whispers in my ear.

"You bet." I pull away as Jack returns with the hay wagon.

The kids spend the next hour grazing from the snack table and playing the games Kate and Amelia have organized on the lawn. I find my way to the food table for a slice of Fiona's haunted house cake. "What a shame to cut it." I fork off a bite of cake. "But I'm glad you did, Fiona. This is delicious. You should seriously consider starting your own cake business."

Fiona looks at Ollie, and they both burst out laughing. "Should we tell her?" Fiona asks with a mischievous grin.

Ollie shrugs. "Why not? Now's as good a time as any."

"Ollie has offered me the head chef job at her vineyard," Fiona says. "And I plan to venture into the cake making business on the side."

I fold my hands over my heart. "That's wonderful news. For you. Not for us. With your talents, I knew we wouldn't be able to hold on to you for long. But I'm grateful for the time I got to spend with you."

"You're not getting rid of me yet," Fiona says, "You're stuck with me through Christmas."

I smile. "Stay as long as you can." I notice Kate leading the children in a game of monster freeze dance. "The kids are really eating this up. I can see where Kate would be an excellent yoga instructor."

"The guests love her," Ollie says. "And she's mellowed the past couple of weeks. I still can't believe she turned out to be Presley's half sister."

I chuckle. "Nothing surprises me anymore. We're one big happy family around here."

"Speaking of which, the community table is all set for Jazz's adoption celebration tonight," Fiona says.

"Wonderful. Thank you," I say and wander off to find Jack.

It's almost five o'clock when Everett strums his guitar, and the kids gather near the stage. Many of the children have heard his music, and they go wild when he sings his two most popular songs.

They're chanting for more when he drags two stools over to the microphone. "I'd like to invite my talented young friend to join me onstage." He holds his hand out to Jazz in the audience.

Jazz, dressed in jeans and cowboy boots with one of Billy's Stetson hats on her head, looks the part of a country music singer as she makes her way onto the stage. She sits down on the stool next to Everett and adjusts the microphone toward her.

"You've probably never heard of my dad, Billy Jameson. But a long time ago, he was a rock star, a legend in Hope Springs."

Pairs of little eyes travel to the sign on the side of Jameson's porch.

She strums a few chords. "This is a song he wrote for my mom when she was a baby," Jazz says, locking eyes with me over the crowd.

Jack leans over and whispers in my ear. "She called you *mom*."

I nod, not trusting my voice to speak. Tears fill my eyes and stream down my cheeks at the sound of their angelic voices—Jazz's so pure and Everett's smooth like aged brandy—as they sing the ballad of a father's love for the baby girl he lost.

When the song ends, the children applaud loudly and swarm Jazz when she comes down off the stage.

Jack hands me his bandana, and I wipe my eyes as I eavesdrop on Jazz's conversations with her friends. "So, you own this place," says a blond boy I don't recognize.

"My mom and I own it together," Jazz says. "She's managing it until I'm old enough to help her."

"Cool. Which one's your mom?" the boy says, looking around.

"She's the one in the blue shirt with the baby bump." When Jazz points at me, I look away, pretending not to notice them staring at me.

"But she's white. And you're black. How can she be your mom?"

"Duh. Haven't you heard? Skin color no longer matters. We're all born equal in the eyes of God."

I clamp my hand over my mouth, and Jack says, "Where'd she hear that?"

Rebecca, who is standing beside me, raises her hand. "Guilty as charged."

Jazz goes on, "My teachers says God gave us the gift of life, and it's our responsibility to work hard, obey the law, and be kind to one another."

"I'm glad at least one of my students was listening," Rebecca says. "I'll probably get terminated for bringing religion back into the classroom. The children learned some valuable lessons this past month. It was a moment in time they won't soon forget, and I thought it important to put their experiences into perspective."

"Clearly, you made an impact on them." I turn to face her. "If you get terminated, we'll start our own school in the barn."

"I may have to take you up on that."

I embrace Rebecca. "Thank you. For caring. For not giving up. For loving the children."

"Thank *you* for trusting your child to me." Our eyes are wet as we pull away.

I think a lot about moments in time as we gather around the community table an hour later. My eyes tear up once again as I scan the faces of my new family and friends. Opal and Brian, Jazz and Jack have given new meaning to my life. They are my greatest joys.

Farther down the table, Cecily and Parker are lost in their own world, oblivious to others around them. I imagine a wedding on the horizon in the coming months. I'm happy for her. These past months haven't been easy. But she's matured, as have we all.

Presley and Everett are at the end, attempting to pacify their crying baby. They've suffered the most. But I sense their struggles have made their relationship stronger.

Next to Presley, Kate is chatting away at Ollie and Fiona, who look as though they want to strangle her. I chuckle to myself. She's a misfit. Then again, weren't we all when we first came to town?

We've learned so much from one another this past year. But our lives are changing. Some of us are expanding our families while others are moving on to the next phases in our professional lives. But tonight, we celebrate our love for one another. We'll remember these fleeting moments for the rest of our days wherever our journeys may take us.

This is the end of the road for our Hope Springs friends. Stay tuned for information regarding the Virginia Vineyards, a spinoff series featuring two of your favorite Hope Springs characters.

If you enjoyed Hope Springs, you might check out the Palmetto Island series for family drama and romantic suspense in the South Carolina Lowcountry.

And . . . to find out about my new and upcoming books, be sure to sign up for my newsletter:

Be sure to visit my website where you'll find a host of information regarding my inspiration for writing as well as book trailers, reviews, and Pinterest boards from my 20+ other books.

ALSO BY ASHLEY FARLEY

ACKNOWLEDGMENTS

I'm grateful for many people who helped make this novel possible. Foremost, to my editor, Patricia Peters, for her patience and advice and for making my work stronger without changing my voice. A great big heartfelt thank-you to my trusted beta readers—Alison Fauls, Anne Wolters, Laura Glenn, Jan Klein, Lisa Hudson, Lori Walton, Kathy Sinclair, and Jenelle Rodenbaugh. A special thank you to my behind-the-scenes, go-to girl, Kate Rock, for all the many things you do to manage my social media so effectively.

I am blessed to have many supportive people in my life who offer the encouragement I need to continue the pursuit of my writing career. I owe an enormous debt of gratitude to my advanced review team, the lovely ladies of Georgia's Porch, for their enthusiasm for and commitment to my work. To Leslie Rising at Levy's for being my local bookshop. Love and thanks to my family—my mother, Joanne; my husband, Ted; and my amazing kiddos, Cameron and Ned.

Most of all, I'm grateful to my wonderful readers for their love of women's fiction. I love hearing from you. Feel free to shoot me an email at ashleyhfarley@gmail.com or stop by my website at ashleyfarley.com for more information about my characters and upcoming releases. Don't forget to sign up for my newsletter. Your subscription will grant you exclusive content, sneak previews, and special giveaways.

ABOUT THE AUTHOR

Ashley Farley writes books about women for women. Her characters are mothers, daughters, sisters, and wives facing real-life issues. Her bestselling Sweeney Sisters series has touched the lives of many.

Ashley is a wife and mother of two young adult children. While she's lived in Richmond, Virginia for the past 21 years, a piece of her heart remains in the salty marshes of the South Carolina Lowcountry, where she still calls home. Through the eyes of her characters, she captures the moss-draped trees, delectable cuisine, and kindhearted folk with lazy drawls that make the area so unique.

Ashley loves to hear from her readers. Visit Ashley's Website @ashleyfarley.com

Get free exclusive content by signing up for her newsletter @ ashleyfarley.com/newsletter-signup/

facebook.com/ashleyhfarley

instagram.com/ashleyfarleyauthor

amazon.com/Ashley-Farley/e/B00BI8MKQA

bookbub.com/profile/ashley-farley